LIBRARIANS OF THE WEST

LIBRARIANS OF THE WEST

A QUARTET

---

by Award-Winning Authors

CANDACE SIMAR
MARK WARREN
CHARLOTTE HINGER
RANDI SAMUELSON-BROWN

EDITED BY HAZEL RUMNEY

With A Foreword By
Kellen Cutsforth

THORNDIKE PRESS
A part of Gale, a Cengage Company

GALE
A Cengage Company

LIBRARY OF CONGRESS CIP DATA ON FILE.
CATALOGUING IN PUBLICATION FOR THIS BOOK
IS AVAILABLE FROM THE LIBRARY OF CONGRESS.

ISBN-13: 978-1-4328-8106-1 (hardcover alk. paper)

Published in 2022 by arrangement with Five Star Publishing.

Printed in Mexico
Print Number: 01   Print Year: 2022

TABLE OF CONTENTS

FOREWORD

BY KELLEN CUTSFORTH

Around 1636, a Massachusetts clergyman named John Harvard donated four hundred books to one of the newly established universities in the American colonies. This college eventually adopted the clergyman's last name to honor him and became known as Harvard University. Soon after the opening of Harvard's University Library, free lending libraries were established all over the colonies.

Following the founding of Harvard's University Library, Benjamin Franklin in 1731 organized the Library Company of Philadelphia as a subscription library — wherein member dues paid for book purchases and borrowing privileges were free. Combined, these libraries are considered the earliest in the country. However, it was not until over a century later that libraries began to substantially emerge in the American West.

Sitting on the western side of the Mississippi River, the city of St. Louis, led by several concerned citizens, funded construction of the St. Louis Mercantile Library in 1846. Mercantile libraries operated similarly to Franklin's Philadelphia Company, on a membership basis. Started with $1,100 worth of books, the Mercantile Library was reputed to be a place where "young men could pass their evenings agreeable and profitably, and thus be protected from the temptation to folly that ever beset unguarded youth in large towns." Whether that was true or not is debatable, but following the organization of St. Louis's first library, several other mercantile libraries eventually opened in the city.

Along with St. Louis, mercantile libraries sprang up everywhere from Denver to San Francisco. However, later in the nineteenth century, free libraries found firm footing in the West, replacing the subscription model of the mercantile library. Beginning in 1883, Andrew Carnegie, the wealthy American steel magnate, started giving out a series of grants aimed at the construction of public libraries. Early in the process, Carnegie's philanthropy extended mainly to places he had a personal connection to. These were areas in and around Pittsburgh, where he built his fortune, and in his native country of Scotland.

In 1899, however, Carnegie expanded his vision for these libraries, handing out numerous construction grants. Women's clubs across the country organized local efforts to establish libraries and help with fundraising in multiple communities to support operations and collections. These groups were partially responsible for the establishment of what have become commonly known as Carnegie Libraries. All told, there were 1,681 libraries built in the United States and 2,509 constructed across the globe. The last grant for a library was given to Utah in 1919 and construction of the last library reached completion in 1929.

The Carnegie Libraries built throughout the region were not only instituted in the West's largest cities, but in the rural areas as well. Many of these buildings' architectural styles made accommodations for lecture rooms, research rooms, and areas for staff. With these new accommodations, cowboys and cowgirls of every stripe could tie their horses to a hitching post and walk into a library leaving with a book, free of charge. Books, and the knowledge they contained, were no longer just for the wealthy who could afford subscription prices, but for everyone. Libraries soon became the people's university and an essential part of everyday life for many on the frontier.

Not only did the books in libraries contain knowledge, but in the days before the wonders of radio, television, and the internet, they provided a source of entertainment. For the first time, a young child living on the plains of southwestern Kansas could pick up a library book and dare to dream. While reading by candlelight and peering up at the stars, these children could dream as big as Jules Verne or even dare to dream as big as the West.

Libraries were not only places where loanable items were checked out, but they became havens for those looking to reflect in quiet peaceful places. They became a place for people to study or to sit silently with their thoughts. These libraries transformed into institutions where more than just books were offered to the public as well. Eventually, some public institutions began collecting one-of-a-kind materials like manuscripts, maps, photographs, and, in some cases, rare artifacts.

By the early 1930s, many of the historical records and primary resources documenting the history of the American West were leaving the region and heading to eastern institutions. In response to this issue, organizations like the Western History Department at the Denver Public Library and various historical societies across the region mobilized, focusing their library's collecting practices on specific materials of historic significance. Through nearly a century of purchasing, collecting, and accepting donations, western libraries guaranteed these resources would remain in the West, where their rich and pioneering history was born.

As collecting practices enlarged to encompass more than books, so too, did the library buildings. By the 1950s, libraries graduated from the Carnegie style into larger and larger structures built to accommodate ever-growing collections and ever-growing populations. These buildings were designed to not only house but preserve their materials. With the instituting of environmental controls, these organizations helped to preserve their books, paper items, and photographs by reducing exposure to sunlight and other harmful elements sustaining those resources for future generations.

Though the buildings were changing, most architects designed the new structures with acknowledgement to the classic architecture of the West's first libraries and the Carnegie institutions of the past. Some of these libraries retained the large granite columns, endless staircases, and sturdy stone blocks most associated with libraries. However, these attributes were re-envisioned to make them more open and inviting. This reworked look now seemed to proclaim, "Knowledge is power . . . and it is for everyone!"

These new libraries also began incorporating artistic architectural implementations and permanent gallery instillations throughout their buildings, adding to their beautification. Many of these organizations are equal to, and in several cases, now surpass the eastern institutions that inspired them. Little libraries emerging in once "cow towns" like Denver and Kansas City have graduated into full-fledged institutions of higher learning respected the world over for their dedication to the preservation and sharing of western history and western literature.

Libraries are physical representations of progress and education in the West. The buildings are social institutions where all are welcome and have equal access to this education. The only requirement to leave with a book, or other loanable item, is the possession of a library card which, normally, is free of charge. These libraries now stand as testaments to the place where America became its most American, where the country proved its pioneering and enduring spirit, and that place is the West.

Kellen Cutsforth is the author of *Buffalo Bill, Boozers, Brothels and Bare Knuckle Brawlers: An Englishman's Journal of Adventure in America, Buffalo Bill's Wild West Coloring Book,* and the co-author of *Old West Showdown: Two Authors Wrangle over the Truth about the Mythic Old West.* He has also ghostwritten several bestselling books for multiple authors. Kellen has published over thirty articles featured in such publications as: *Wild West, True West,* Western Writers of America's (WWA) *Roundup Magazine,* and the Denver Posse of Westerners' *The Roundup* magazine. He writes a bimonthly column in WWA's *Roundup Magazine* under the title "Techno-Savvy." Kellen is also an active member of WWA and runs their Twitter account. Along with being an accomplished author and ghostwriter, Kellen is also a veteran speaker and presenter and has done multiple programs for numerous history groups, libraries, and genealogical organizations.

■ ■ ■ ■

Too Much Dancing Going On (The Making of a Montana Librarian)

RANDI SAMUELSON-BROWN

■ ■ ■ ■

Somewhere in the Montana Territory, 1882

Alone on a hired horse in the middle of next-to-nowhere, she was doing exactly what she wanted. Which isn't to say that the gunmetal blue of a rising storm didn't dwarf the prairie swells below. The eerie light cast down, painting the scrub and grass unnatural and vivid. The scene held such a peculiar quality that she expected to remember it forever, and it was cause for concern. The driving wind blew stark and unfettered in the force of the storm. Currents rippled through the horse's dark mane; he tossed his head and blew, catching the scent of approaching rain. Impatient, she held him still, pausing atop a hillock to consider the clouds as they gathered and formed.

The horse pawed the ground.

"Quit it." She struggled to hold him still. "Quit now, Declan. Whoa."

He was a large brute of a horse, and hard

17

to handle. The man at the livery opined, "He sure ain't no lady's horse." But she took him anyhow, surrendering to the familiar feeling of having something to prove. The main qualification for the job was the ability to ride. The women's society had told her that upfront. Well, she could ride and handle herself, but the horse made her fight for it every step of the way.

Judging by the rising clouds and the building wind, they needed shelter, and they needed it fast. But the landscape unfurled around them was wide open and empty.

Being caught out in a storm would be mighty cold and unpleasant.

A nudge started the horse downhill as lightning sparked, flashing in the clouds. White-hot bolts branched against the sky, reaching for the ground below.

Halfway down the rise, a god-almighty thunderclap and boom. The horse spooked. A violent sideways lurch. Almost unseated, she grabbed for the saddle horn just as the horse truly bolted. More thunderclaps far too low for comfort, deep and ominous.

For a very distinct moment everything slowed, her body rising off of the saddle. Poised to come unseated and fall.

Clinging to that saddle horn, she regained her seat and balance by the thread of chance. Heart racing and still struggling for control, the ground whirring below at a sickening speed. She yanked one side of the rein, turning the horse's head and forcing him to slow. The moment hung in the balance — if she pulled him around too hard, the two of them might very well go toppling over down the hill.

Riders and horses had been known to be killed like that.

Her neck broken or his, being left dead or horseless was no small matter.

Gradually, Declan came to a stop. And there they stood, each panting with hearts racing. It took a few moments to regain composure, for both of them. Yet the storm was still a-coming. More forks of lightning, even closer thunder.

Fortune, slim as it was, turned in her favor for the horse didn't spook a second time.

Together they loped over the expanse, Eliza desperately seeking out shelter of any sort. It wasn't so much the discomfort of wet clothes and a soggy bedroll that drove her, but the books carried in the large saddlebags were her charges.

It was those ten books she was hired to deliver safely, and the rain fringed from the clouds, driving toward them.

Something caught her eye. In the distance

19

was a dark spot between two hillocks. Pointing the horse in that direction, she rode as fast as she dared and a bit faster than comfortable. Prayers that he didn't step in a hole or buck her off in the flash of the lightning, another boom of thunder. The temperature dropped as the wind picked up stronger, gusts like an invisible wall as the prairie grasses flattened.

But there it was, a structure that resembled nothing so much as a railroad boxcar. No matter how humble it appeared, it was shelter. And shelter was desperately needed.

Wild wisps of hair danced about her face and got stuck in the corners of her mouth as she tore down, closer. Thudding toward the low structure and upon reaching the bald patch that served as the yard, she dismounted and approached the rough door. She didn't even have time to knock; the door opened a crack.

"Kind of rough weather to be out riding in," the man's voice said.

Virginia City, Montana, 1873
"I'm tired of reading the Bible."

That revelation meant nothing to the insects droning along in the blanketing heat. Summer was full on, and it hadn't seen fit to rain in weeks. The dirt billowed dust into the air, coating sagebrush and wildflowers that had the misfortune of growing too close to roads and footpaths. The mining industry clanked and thudded along in the distance, but for now at the cabin, the insects and the scrubbing of cloth against the washboard carried the morning hours.

Her mother paused, hands thin with taut skin over fine bones. "That's not exactly something to go spreadin' around, but I take your meaning. Some would say the Good Book is the only book worth reading, but I suppose modern stories can be nice, too. Now, go fetch me another pail of water."

Eliza lingered like the insects.

"Did you know that a dancer in France came to her ruin and had a baby that got sick, and instead of staying home to take care of it, she had to go to the theater to dance? What do you suppose they meant by 'came to her ruin'?"

Her mother blinked. "Where'd you hear such a thing?"

"I read it. It's on one of the newspapers on the wall."

"You don't say. I've been meaning to whitewash over all of that, and I haven't found the time. Where's that story?"

Suspicion came in a twinge, but she knew better than to lie. "In the corner behind the table. Guess they meant too much dancing. They dance in town, you know."

"And what would you know about that? At any rate, I'll have to take a look at that story for myself." The woman sat back for a moment.

The girl eyed her mother, hoping for a reprieve. None came. She grabbed up the bucket and crossed the dirt yard, dust settling on her boots. The story didn't make sense in some ways, she had to admit. And it didn't do much good to be the best reader in school if all she had to practice on was the Bible, plastered newspapers, and the occasional seed catalog thrown in for good measure.

There was nothing much to do, other than chores, anyhow. But the fate of the dancer was something else, something strange and tantalizing. Such a notion preoccupied her as she primed and the water gushed forth, like it always did. Predictable and boring. Just the way her mother liked it.

Every family she knew owned a Bible. Whether they read it or not was another matter. Eliza took a notice of such things as reading and books; and Bibles were all that most people had. Some lucky families even had two or three other books, but her mother made it clear that it wasn't polite to ask about them, unless for some reason, they brought it up first. Going so far as to ask to read them would certainly earn her a swat. Especially if the owners didn't offer on their own accord.

Lugging the bucket back to her mother, she chewed on a way to approach the subject of borrowing books. Should the opportunity ever arise, but especially at the Pomeroys. Rich as far as books were concerned, they had five tomes resting atop a lace doily placed on a small table. Without a doubt, it was the finest display she'd ever seen, but she'd never gotten closer than the doorway. From that distance she could only see their shapes and colors, and never the all-important titles.

Her mother grasped the handle, taking the pail from her. "You look mighty serious."

"I was just thinking about books, that's all."

A small, quiet laugh. "You sure do a lot of that. You know, you're growing up quickly. Before long, you'll be a young woman with a family of her own. Try to make something of yourself while you can."

Puzzled, Eliza tried to figure out what her mother was driving at. As it was, she already knew about families that came with boys. "If I have a family, I'd only want girls."

Another laugh, but something ran beneath the surface. "You don't get a choice in that. Why don't you go take care of Lucy, speaking of girls. She could use some attention while Stephen's away."

Poor Lucy. A boy actually *owned* her.

And her older brother made no secret that he didn't appreciate the fact that his horse was a mare.

"The fellows would laugh me out of town if they knew her name was Lucy. Shoot. I couldn't live it down. If Ma hadn't named her, I'd change it. Best to pretend she don't have a name at all and call her plain ol' Horse."

Eliza ran the curry brush over her withers, leaning into the horse's strength. "You're a good horse, and he knows it. But I sure wish he'd let me try riding you for a change. Nothing bad would happen. He just doesn't want to share with a *girl.*"

In fact, any time she attempted the subject, he cut her off short. "I don't want to be responsible when you fall off and break your neck."

The conversation always panned out the same way.

He didn't hold the same apprehension where Jake was concerned. He let his little brother get on and fall off just as many times as it took. She eyed the fence rails. Pretty soon she'd take matters into her own hands when no one was around. She could simply climb up on one of those rails and heft herself onto Lucy, one-two-three quick.

Every now and again she'd try at the dinner table. "I saw a girl about my size riding a horse . . ."

Stephen would normally just grunt something that meant he wasn't going to fall for it, while her father would usually argue the fine points of ownership.

"A man's horse is his own business, Lizzie." The tone he used didn't brook much further discussion. "Besides, even if he were to allow it, we don't have a woman's saddle."

"A girl might ride astride. Especially at her age." Her mother's voice held steady, with traces of flint.

Her parents' eyes met across the table.

"It's not like in the days when she might have to go riding for help or anything." He half-flinched as he tucked into his meal.

"You so sure about that?"

No answer came. Her mother dropped her eyes down to her plate, a nerve twitching at the corner of her mouth. Eliza knew that twitch and that expression. The matter of her riding wasn't over as far as her mother

25

was concerned, and that meant the matter wasn't over as far as her father was concerned, either.

But any further discussion would take place behind closed doors, in whispered voices that bore a strange resemblance to shouting. Her mother didn't hold with raised voices indoors, but that didn't mean arguments never happened.

Eliza figured she might just have to make herself content with reading the Bible and petting Lucy, although she wanted more. What that "more" consisted of, was hard to pinpoint with any certainty. Beyond the vague notion of discontent, something more fundamental lurked and lingered. She was pretty sure it all had to do with being a girl.

The matter of the ruined dancer didn't fall by the wayside, either. No matter how wronged she may have been in the matter of horses, her mother didn't show pity in a matter she deemed unsuitable. The next day her mother whitewashed the kitchen walls. Starting in the corner directly behind the table.

Pleading wouldn't have gotten her anywhere. The outcome would have been the same. The only interesting story she knew, painted over for good once and for all. But faint ghosts of the typeset words remained, and the mystery of the dancer's ruin held firm in her mind.

Whitewashed or not, the dancer's strange fate would remain in her mind for a mighty long time.

Virginia City was never known for its sense of propriety. Infamous throughout the territory, it sprouted from a shallow basin, surrounded by sloping rises whose trees had all been cut away for mining timbers and for town buildings. Some residents insisted those hills were actually mountains, a conversation lending itself to long, meandering debates used to fill the time as dullness set in. Boredom weighed heavily on the frontier, especially where men were concerned. True, there was no shortage of work, but the monotony perhaps arose from the silence of the vast spaces that swallowed settlers whole. That peculiarity sparked off quarrels, led to comment and hard feelings, and often resulted in increased whiskey consumption in any number of the saloons. Blowing off steam, they called it. And blowing off steam often led to problems. The town hadn't managed to shake off its early history entirely; for around its perimeters, in the margins and in the shadows, the legacy of vigilante violence remained. Whenever trouble arose over half-consumed bottles of rotgut, more than one old-timer muttered how they wished those old hanging days would return.

Some of them might have even meant it sober.

The evidence remained interred in Boot Hill; the notion of "resting in peace" for them in the afterlife was pretty much discarded. Violence begat violence, and those darker deeds were referred to in solemn and hushed voices. Unless alcohol entered the mix, and it usually did. Everyone knew that the vigilantes' and road agents' motives were suspect, their loyalties never quite clear. Whether they were on the side of the law or the outlaw often depended upon payment. By comparison, the matter of whether Virginia City was surrounded by hills or by mountains was a downright civilized debate, even if it occasionally ended in blows. And the year was 1873. Such dealings had presumably died out and ended back in the sixties, and there was no use lamenting deeds that had been done or wishing the past would somehow revive itself.

That didn't always stop some from trying.

In Alder Gulch, beyond the town, and eight miles back into the mountains that *really* were mountains, the genuine, serious mining took place. Things were done a bit differently back there. The miners were their own breed and come Saturday night they tumbled downhill into Virginia City seeking the dubiously termed "good time." But in those good times, arguments went off. Most of the trouble centered along lower Wallace Street with its mixture of grogshops, gambling hells, and women of ill-repute. Proper families moved into the loosely assembled city limits, but those desiring respectability, or at least an arm's length from notoriety, cut as wide a swath from the "district" as they could manage.

The grizzled miners and the fancy gambling men who plied their trade in the saloons found such concerns cause for derision. Comments were often made, well within hearing, of how decent woman "carried" an inbred abhorrence to violence. Especially when there were children to consider. And those children, unbeknownst to their parents, often lingered outside those very saloons to see whatever goings-on they could. Nothing got youthful excitement flowing like a good saloon brawl or inspired more laughter than a drunk falling down in the street.

Unfortunately, as far as the Gentry children were concerned, the placement of their home and makeshift small farm was on the outskirts, away from the excitements of town.

Her father believed in self-reliance. Her mother believed in opportunity . . . of a limited variety.

Eliza wanted to experience society as all young girls do. "Can't I go into town for you?"

Her mother would smile, and on occasion, give in.

The youngest of three children, Eliza was the only girl at that. At eleven years of age there was already a pronounced difference about her, a difference in outlook from her brothers' rough and tumble ways.

"Lizzie's always mooning about," they would chuckle, exasperated at the peculiarities of girls — or more specifically, their sister.

"Let her be," Margaret Gentry would chide. "Your sister's good at book learning, and that's nothing to be ashamed of. Maybe she'll even be a teacher one day."

The boys groaned but Eliza's ears perked up. That comment was the first inkling of a different path in life, even for her. Of course, there were certain unescapable facts. Girls grew up to be wives and mothers. She didn't have to look very far, for that was the fate of most of the women in town.

Women worn thin from rearing children and managing life in Montana.

The allure of town with its shops and activities proved almost irresistible. Like most girls, she dawdled in front of any and all shop windows.

Considering any and all goods displayed, she would memorize and rank them in order of desirability.

Killing time, the boys would call it; *passing time* their mother might correct them if she wasn't too weary to care.

Tack, saddles, millinery and canned goods, nothing fell beneath notice. At Rank's Mercantile, the colorful jars of candy tempted, and bolts of cloth sparked dreams of finery. In contrast, the shelves of glass chimney lamps and household items did not escape scrutiny. One day the time would come for her to choose her own household furnishings, and she would be ready.

"You lookin' for anything in particular?" Mr. Rank leaned on the counter, accustomed to the yearnings of young girls.

Trailing between the makeshift tables loaded with sundry items, all of which demanded at least some attention, she remembered her manners enough to formulate an answer. "Five pounds of flour today, please. But I was just looking to see what else you have."

Money was scarce in those days. Although looking was free, she'd been told not to tarry too long.

Still half-distracted, she sidled up to the counter to make the purchase, attention flitting from one object before alighting on the next.

In the process of handing over her three nickels, she spied an abandoned newspaper on the counter.

Mr. Rank noticed where her attention landed. "You can take that home if you want. Don't know who left it behind, but it's out of date. Course, if it was winter, that would be mighty valuable to the right customer. He might even pay twice the price." He winked at her. "Even old news is better than no news when the snow's piled high and people start getting cabin fever."

Considering the fate of the whitewashed newspaper, her mother almost certainly wouldn't approve. Thankfully, Mr. Rank didn't know anything about that.

What she had before her was a rare chance, and a gamble that demanded to be taken. She snatched up her prize.

"We don't get newspapers in the house,

usually."

"I guess I can tell by your reaction," the merchant grinned.

With great solemnity, she flattened out the pages with her hands, folded them with care along their creases, and tucked the treasured paper under her arm before heading out for home.

"Wait! You forgot the flour!" The merchant leaned over the counter looking after her, package in outstretched hand.

That would have led to trouble. Sheepish, she turned back and claimed it.

"Thank you," she replied.

He winked again with a smile and a nod.

Newsprint and newspapers made fine kindling if she wasn't careful.

As their house came into view, Lucy was in her corral, and her mother was moving about the yard feeding chickens. It was now or never. She could either be honest, or she could hide the evidence down the front of her dress.

Eliza waved, and kept walking.

"Here's the flour. And see here; someone left the newspaper behind. Mr. Rank said I could have it."

The unfortunate fate of the whitewashed dancer flashed between them.

33

"I was thinking of how I could read it to everyone after dinner . . . and . . . after I scrubbed the floor."

Her mother pursed her lips, masking a smile. The type of smile that said Eliza's ploy fooled no one, least of all her. "I see. The floor sure could use a good scrubbing. But I'll look over those articles before you get started reading. There're some things you're too young for, and there's no reason to go putting notions in the boys' heads that aren't already there in the first place."

But the boys were fourteen and sixteen, going on seventeen, respectively. They already knew plenty about the world, and they made it a special point to know about what went on in Virginia City. They were part of the saloon-door contingency that hung around for sport, and for a split second, she wondered if her parents knew.

But she had important matters of her own at hand.

"I'll read only what you want. Promise."

Her mother held out her hand for the newspaper. "You can go put the flour inside, and I'll take that paper for now."

And so, the matter was settled about as well as could be hoped.

That night, Eliza sat in the light of the kerosene lamp reading about happenings that her mother pointed out. She read about events in the territory and further afield, struggling with some of the words. Her mother helped her decipher the strange vocabulary, seated alongside darning socks. It was notable how her mother managed to keep an eye on both the work in her hands and on Eliza's progress with the newspaper. Just as her eyes caught a tantalizing glimpse of the word "murder," her mother guessed where she was headed. At that very same instant, Margaret Gentry set down the socks and took the newspaper away.

"That's enough for tonight now," she said. "We can let the rest of that news be."

Murder.

It was a not a word cast about lightly, at least not in Montana and especially not in Virginia City. It was said that road agents killed as many as one hundred men in the vicinity. She'd heard as much from her brothers.

One day, she'd come up upon them, their discussion more intent than usual.

"Why'd you stop talking?" she asked, a bit sensitive on the matter.

They rocked back on their heels, superior. "Because it's not for girls."

"What's not for girls?"

"Don't be so nosy. If we told you, you'd go running back to Ma."

"No, I wouldn't. I promise. Now tell me."

"We were talking about horse thieves. There were a lot of them around these parts, and I'll bet there still are. Lucy there would have been a fine target," Stephen said.

"Yup," Jake added. "Stolen for sure."

Not precious Lucy. Her eyes must have gotten big.

"You're not going to cry, are you?" Jake jeered, worried around the edges.

Stephen patted her on the top of the head, a gesture she hated.

"Don't worry. Horse thieves get hung, or at the very least have to stay in jail."

Either way, she had nightmares for a week.

"What's wrong with you?" Her mother asked on account of her overall skittishness.

"Nothing," she lied, and got a dose of cod-liver oil for her troubles.

Jake had overheard that brief conversation and saw the subsequent dosage. When their mother passed out of hearing range, he had the good graces to almost appear contrite.

"You're not still worried about them horse thieves, are you? Those were the days before they had the Law. They didn't have a school back then, neither."

Judging from his tone, the days before "the Law" were an altogether better proposition as far as he was concerned.

School. The five slim months of the school year in Virginia City coincided with the territorial government. On the fifth of March before spring had a chance to get going, both got started. The month was a drab, cold struggle for winter to release its hold, which it seldom did. Not until April, and sometimes not even until May or beyond. But to Eliza, the school session was more than welcome even if it involved fighting through drifts of snow.

Arithmetic and writing were all very fine, but it was the reading that held her. Real, proper reading, and the same old problem. Unless something changed, the books would be the same as they had the previous year: the Bible, a donated book of Common Prayer and a few tattered copies of *Webster's Blue Back Speller* for the smaller children.

And she could spell just fine, thank you very much.

As the first day of school neared, Jake started fretting, sulking and acting up. "I've had all the learning I need, and I'm fourteen years old. Why do I still have to go?"

The scene and the argument repeated multiple times, hardly varying one bit. Their parents would exchange glances, tiring of Jake's endless complaints. In fact, he eventually threw up such a fuss that their threadbare patience ripped in two.

"Durn it," their father snapped, "if you're going to be like this every time the subject comes up, then to hell with it. You've had plenty of schooling by now, and I'm not going to be the one to force you into it if you don't want it. But here's the thing. If you aren't going to school, you're going to have to work, and I mean more than just your chores around here."

Jake puffed up like a robin red breast. "Stephen started mining when he was fifteen, and he's had money ever since. It's about time that I have my own money, too, but I'm planning on staying above ground. At least for a while."

And Jake promptly found himself a paying job in one of the livery stables in town.

First day of school, Eliza was seated at the back with the larger children. One of the newcomers, a boy with a square jaw and a shock of unruly hair, ambled in late and wearing a holster and pistol. Sixteen and full of himself, he sat down beside her in

38

She all but forced him to accept her help with reading. And she listened and encouraged over their lunch pails as he sounded out words.

"They didn't have a school where we was, up near the Stinking Water. Now that we're here, Pa says I'm going to get some learning whether I like it or not. And I don't like it. Well, not much at least."

"Just keep trying." Eliza drummed up the courage to place her hand on his arm. "At least you're good with math."

And together they would sit on the low tree bough to the side of the school, working their way through *Webster's Blue Back Speller* yet one more time.

It became apparent that Percy'd never make much of a reader, but for some reason, that didn't matter all that much to her.

Soon, Eliza started displaying opinions and knowledge beyond that expected from an eleven-year-old girl. And this surprising font of knowledge was down to the fact that she had taken to frequenting Rank's mercantile with the sole purpose (other than browsing) of obtaining discarded newspapers.

"Too bad you ain't a boy," Mr. Rank exclaimed handing over a broadsheet saved just for her — the ever-present twinkle in his eye.

Eliza acted put out, but it was all just part of the game. "Because then my older brother would teach me to ride his horse?"

"No, but maybe that, too! It's because they have a lyceum started upstairs of the territorial legislature. But they say it's for civilized young men. Guess that leaves you out."

"A lyceum? What's that?" Wary, her eyes narrowed.

"It's like a reading room. With books and all."

That was the most startling news she had ever heard. "Can I go in?"

"No. It's for *civilized young men,* like I just told you. Not for schoolgirls in braids."

She didn't know how to respond.

"Aw, shoot. Don't take it so hard. They probably have to pay a subscription or something like it."

His wife came behind the counter, hands filled with button cards that she set down and started going through, barely sparing a glance for Eliza. "Couldn't one of those men with a subscription take a book out for her?"

Mr. Rank scratched along his collar. "Hadn't thought of that. But maybe they

He tugged her hair and took off, leaving Eliza to stand sentry until the weather turned and she got tired of standing anchored to one spot like a misplaced fence post.

As it was, one day Miss Robinson encountered her in her desperate obsession as autumn flashed in.

She quietly came up and stood by her side.

"There're books in there. A lyceum," Eliza offered, although no question had been asked.

A long-eyed stare. It just so happened a man approached the legislature door, and the teacher stepped from the boardwalk into the street. "Mr. Jessup!"

Eliza followed, dodging a wagon and ignoring a muffled curse cast in her direction.

The man turned, youngish and surprised. "Why, Miss Robinson. How nice to see you!" His gaze traveled to Eliza, puzzled.

"We were wondering if you were a member of the lyceum."

He swelled up a bit, running his thumb beneath his lapel. "Indeed."

"What books do they have? In fact, could we accompany you inside to see for ourselves?"

45

He deflated as a cagey expression stole over him. "I don't know about that . . ."

Miss Robinson waited him out, face pleasantly neutral and back ramrod straight.

"You see," he stuttered, "it's for *men.*"

"Of course. But wouldn't *civilized men* be willing to show a schoolgirl what books they had in their esteemed lyceum? That is, unless there is something she *shouldn't* see . . ."

The color rose to the roots of his hair. "I don't think there's anything like that. But rules are rules. I can't be the one to break them. Here's what I'll do. I'll ask. There. Good enough?"

"Are you going to ask now?"

Judging by his expression, he hadn't planned on it, but there was no polite way out. "I can try. But I don't know who will be in there at all."

He wanted her to say that it could wait. But Miss Robinson said no such thing. "We shall await your return. Right here."

The man had little choice as he entered the building.

Eliza got the distinct feeling Mr. Jessup was sweet on the teacher.

"Don't get your hopes up too high," Miss Robinson said softly.

They must have waited a full ten minutes before the man came out through the door, his demeanor something approximating contrite.

"They weren't in favor of it, I must say." He paused, gauging the woman's reaction closely. "The secretary said we would have to take it to a vote."

"I see," Miss Robinson replied. "That is unfortunate. We don't even have more than seven books for the entire school. Three of those are the same and two are Bibles."

He tore his eyes away from the teacher, deciding to take his chances with Eliza. "I'm real sorry, little lady. For what it's worth, I went over the books and I doubt you'd find them of interest anyhow. Maps, religious essays, and the classics like Homer and Swift are mostly what they've got. Some are even in Latin, which precious few can read. Does that help?"

It didn't.

Sweet on Miss Robinson or not, the lyceum never softened their stance about admittance. The members of the lyceum became the keepers of something she wanted, and something that she was denied on account of her sex. It just didn't sit right. In fact, it bothered her enough to talk to her mother about it.

"It doesn't seem fair," she complained.

Her timing was bad, for her mother seemed out of sorts.

"A lot of things in this life aren't," came the reply as she straightened from kneading dough, and ignoring the flour on her hands, pressed them against her lower back like it hurt.

For the first time, she noticed her mother's stomach was becoming more pronounced. Although she made no mention, Eliza had a feeling she knew what that meant.

On her twelfth birthday, a slim gift wrapped in folded butcher paper waited by her breakfast plate. Her heart hitched. It was the right size for a book.

She lunged.

Manners shot to pieces, her father laughed as she snatched up the gift.

She could tell by the weight of it, the solidity radiating through the wrapping. The first glimpse of greenish brown cover, the red slightly indented lettering was the most beautiful thing she had seen. Ever. *Evangeline: A Tale of Acadie* by Henry Wadsworth Longfellow.

Speechless, she handed the wrapping paper back to her mother but kept a firm grip on the precious book.

"If we'd known that a book would keep

you quiet, we might have bought you one before now." Stephen, eighteen and thinking himself a man, folded his arms in pronouncement.

Her mother refolded the paper for future use. "It's bound to be better than those cast-off newspapers."

An untold world in her hands and the expectant faces of her family couldn't entirely squash her loyalty to those tatty old sheets.

Her father grinned, unaware of her struggle. "That's from your mother and me. Now boys, what do you have for your sister?"

Stephen did his best to act pained, but Jake was ready to burst.

In fact, he did. "We're going to let you try Lucy and hope that you don't come off!"

Her mother, not entirely pleased with his choice of words, frowned. "You're going to help make *sure* that she doesn't come off, aren't you both?"

Either way, she'd take her chances. "Honest? You'll let me ride Lucy?"

"Honest," Jake replied, forgetting that the horse wasn't his. "We'll let you *try.*"

Stephen gave him a good-natured bump. "You're going to have to sit astride."

She flung her arms around Stephen's neck, who stammered and shuffled.

49

"Cut it out, will you?" Her brother grumbled, wiping his cheek where she managed to get him. "No need to go all mushy like that. It's just a horse."

A horse and book. And the heady inkling of freedom.

Soon she was tearing around the district on horseback.

"We can't have you growing up wild," her mother said, but it seemed too late for that. She was well on her way and couldn't have been happier.

In 1877 Eliza turned fifteen years old, and Virginia City was in the throes of dying. Two years earlier the territorial seat had been moved to Helena, and what had been a robust town whose citizens numbered in the thousands dwindled down into the hundreds as the mining gave out. Stephen struck out on his own for Colorado, taking Lucy with him.

"Heck, you'll probably miss this mare more than you do me," he teased at the time.

It was more than partially true. Ever since she had been allowed to ride, few days passed without her taking Lucy out, further and further away. Nothing suited her better than when she had the opportunity to carry messages out to Alder Gulch mines, although her mother didn't exactly approve.

"Mind yourself. Ruffians might still be out there, lying in wait for the unwary. In fact, I'm not sure I like this at all."

Which is how it came to pass that Eliza learned to handle a rifle. Jake took her out back, where they practiced shooting tin cans and bottles off of fence posts.

"Lizzie can handle herself," Jake crowed, probably prouder of himself than Eliza. "If I was a bandit, I wouldn't come within a mile of her!"

But ability to handle a gun wasn't really needed if there was no horse to ride. Unless there were intruders at the house, which struck her as plain unlikely. Jake must have gotten tired of watching her sulk around like her heart was broken, which indeed it was of a kind.

One week later, he came home from work leading a speckled horse.

"This is your birthday and Christmas present for the rest of your life," he swaggered. "Some fellow was leaving the district and needed traveling money. And this here is a pretty durn good horse for the money."

Eliza threw her arms around his neck and kissed him before hugging the horse. The horse seemed to like it, whereas Jake slapped

51

at the spot where she kissed him.

"I hate it when you do that."

But Eliza didn't care, and she had her own horse. "What's his name?"

"How should I know?"

She led the horse around so they could get used to each other. The horse nuzzled in close, and Eliza fell in love.

"Watch out that he doesn't spoon you," Jake called out, and got a whomp on the shoulder from their father.

"Spooner's the perfect name for him! That's it, I'll call him Spooner!"

And for the rest of that season Eliza carried on, riding up to Alder Gulch and through the hills and shooting targets with Jake, as the work dried up around them.

But as the mines of Virginia City declined, Butte, Montana, opened up, bold, brash and ready to make fortunes.

And the Gentrys, like many of their neighbors, had little choice but to follow the call.

Somewhere in the Montana Territory, 1882
The sky opened up before she had the chance to get any words out.

"Go ahead and put your horse in the barn and help yourself to what you find." His voice rose over the wind and the rain. Another fork of lightning, followed by the deep grumblings of thunder.

"Whoa, Declan. Settle down; it'll be OK." The horse tossed his head, the whites of his eyes telling.

Then man grabbed the other side of the halter. "He looks to be a lot of horse. You got him?"

"Yep. Close enough." Leading him up to the barn, she struggled with the door, but managed to get it open while holding on to him, good and firm.

Her shirt was sopping wet, and Declan was no better. There was something about the smell of a wet horse that tugged at her heart. She put him in an empty stall, pulled off the saddlebags, and set them on the floor, reluctantly. While dying to inspect the contents, she owed something to the horse, too.

"Good boy," she crooned, unfastening the girth and pulling off the saddle, followed by the saddle blankets. She hung them on the stall's wall to dry.

When the horse was good and settled, she checked the saddlebags and the burlap protection sacks. The sacks were dry, which meant the books were fine. Casting about the barn, she found a couple of discarded rags, which were pressed into use rubbing the horse down.

"Not sure if I'm supposed to go in the house or stay here," she said to herself as she pitched a couple forkfuls of hay into the stall.

Setting the saddlebags on a workbench, she returned out into the storm, running across the dirt yard. The door to the house was left ajar.

"Hello?"

The man came to the door. "Come on in, don't stand out in the rain. This is my wife, Emily. Emily, this is . . ."

"Eliza Gentry. I'm on my way back to Butte, riding books between towns."

The spark that lit the woman's eyes at that information was unmistakable, and did her heart good.

The Butte Years, 1878

Her father secured a position at the Anaconda Mine and was "damn glad of it," which meant the rest of them had better be pretty darn glad of it, too.

Most of the big furniture was stacked into the wagon on a first-run trip to Butte. "We'll get it set up for you, Ma," Jake promised, all earnest and excited.

For Eliza, it turned out a most peculiar sensation as her father and Jake drove off with the loaded wagon and most of their earthly possessions. The two women just stood in the road, unspeaking, until the clattering and clanging wagon passed from sight, her father waving a farewell with his hat.

"I've never been good in such events," her mother remarked, the light draining from her eyes.

Inside the cabin, memories crowded into the half-empty spaces. Eliza made a restrained effort to go about packing and preparing, but past history got in the way. Table gone, she found herself in the kitchen corner with the sole purpose of locating the story of the ruined dancer. Funny how she understood the meanings behind all of that now, the passage of time never so apparent. A spark of excitement buried inside of her flared and faded in turns, but her mother couldn't settle. Any task she started remained half-finished as she drifted from one undertaking to the next, from one window to the other, sighing aloud.

"What's troubling you, and please don't say it's nothing."

"The baby. I want to go visit the baby, one last time. It's all a pity, really. This cabin's had its share of good times and hard times, but just to turn our backs on it and leave. Somehow it doesn't seem right, no matter what anyone says."

That evening as the sun declined, opal hued with wide slashes of gunmetal gray, they passed through the town for the final time. Steps tapping out a staccato on the boardwalks, drawn to the cemetery with its tiny grave and its tiny wooden marker containing one of their own.

Baby Gentry. 1866

Not even a full name or date burned into the weathering wood marker. The sagebrush and scraggy prairie grasses rippled in the lonesome autumn wind.

"I hope you never lose a child," her mother said, ripping up intruding tall grasses fringing along the marker's base. "He only lived three days."

There was no adequate comment or response, so she said nothing. Every family lost loved ones along the way, but the loss of a child . . . It was true, some losses hurt far more than others.

The wind blew clean and clear while her mother fell silent, lost to memories Eliza could not reach. Hands on hips, Eliza gazed out at the land beyond, musing how events had come to such a pass of life and death and changes in fortune. A mumbled undercurrent that took her a moment to identify. Her mother spoke to herself, low and as if she were alone.

"Well . . . no sense in making this harder . . . the marker might last the winter . . . don't know."

The wind caught her mother's graying hair, strands tangling about her face, making her appear older and more tired than she already was. She must have forgotten that Eliza was along, for she started down the hill without another word.

Eliza jogged a few steps to catch up, bringing her mother back from wherever her mind had wandered.

The older woman seemed half-surprised. "Oh, I must have got carried away. You'll think I'm a silly old woman."

"No . . . maybe just sad. It's been a long, strange day."

"Promise me one thing, Lizzie. If you ever pass this way, that you'll stop and check on the baby. Maybe we can even get a stone marker put up if the mining pays out."

"I promise," she said and patted her mother's arm, the bone more pronounced than she could ever recall.

The men returned two days later, and their home, the only home Eliza had ever known, was poised to be abandoned. It was bound to fall prey to the shiftless, and that got her mother fretting. One final glance around the empty house, the few items that wouldn't fit in, or were of little use, abandoned inside. The Gentrys closed the door for the last time, shutting the memories inside that would one day be trampled under strange feet that knew nothing of them or their ways.

Her father helped her mother up onto the wagon seat, leaving Eliza to wedge herself in as best she could, preferring the comfort the closeness of her parents brought. Spooner, saddled and ready, was tied to the back of the wagon wondering why Eliza didn't want to ride. She patted the horse's nose, and looked into his trusting brown eyes, thankful. He'd have to be housed in a Butte livery, which was just another added expense, although no one said as much.

Jake blithely rode his horse alongside, no such misgivings bothered him. "You'll see! They've got different neighborhoods and everything. And better than that, the mines are right in the town. How about that?"

How about that indeed.

The town of Butte sprawled between dusty hills, without even cottonwoods for consolation. Her mother blanched when she saw it, before setting her expression into one of pure determination, a look that the family knew all too well. Headframes marking mines indeed sprung up within the town limits, and although the mercantiles and public buildings appeared prosperous enough, it was an industrial town, with industrial ways. The air vibrated and thrummed along with the stamp mill as it crushed and pulverized tons of ore.

"I guess we'll have to learn to live with it." Whether her mother meant the sound or something more remained unknown.

"That's the sound of industry and of money being made." Her father boasted, but after glancing over at his wife, he had the sense to keep his eyes trained on the road straight ahead.

Some of the differences between Butte and Virginia City were glaring. There were definite shades and variations of neighborhoods, and not everyone spoke like an American.

When the team pulled up in front of a tar-papered shack roughly the same size as the cabin left behind, their mother's face fell further.

"It's clean enough inside, Margaret. Before long, we'll be able to afford something better. Something real pretty."

Her mother gave a half smile as he helped her down from the wagon. Eliza stared at the exterior and wondered what on earth they were coming to.

It didn't help matters that her mother was ailing, although she never said as much. But her stomach was extended large and round, although she was past the age of childbearing.

The image of Baby Gentry's grave pricked along her spine.

Her mother's voice snapped that memory in two. "Ouch!" Clasping her side and face gone white, she acted somehow ashamed. "Don't mind me, I must be a bit stiff from the traveling."

Her father held his expression and said nothing.

After the moment passed, the worried note lingered as they crossed the threshold into the shotgun house. There was only one true bedroom, and a small, closet-like room that would be hers.

"Where's Jake going to sleep?"

"In the front room," her father replied, like it was the most natural thing in the world.

"Good thing we have a rug," her mother replied, trying to pretend she wasn't in pain.

Jake, in the obliviousness of young men, shrugged, uncaring. "Who knows? I might even move into a boardinghouse, or in with a group of bachelors."

"You'll do no such thing," their mother replied. "Not while I have a say about it."

At the age of eighteen, by all accounts he was a man. But at least he had the sense, in that moment, not to argue.

"You two, help me bring the things in," their father said, snapping back to the practical.

First off from the wagon was their mother's chair, which Jake carried overhead, and set into the sitting room with a flourish.

The walls were rough and unpapered.

Their father followed behind with one of the trunks. "Why don't you rest a bit, Mother. You can sit in your chair and tell us where you want things to go."

Her mother actually took the chair.

Outside at the wagon, he handed Eliza frying pans and the coffeepot.

"She's not well, is she?"

"Nope." He hefted another trunk out of

the wagon and set in on the ground. He sprang back into the wagon bed, rummaging.

"What about a doctor?" Eliza asked in a low voice. "They've got to have one here."

"We'll see." He avoided looking at her square. Instead he chewed the inside of his cheek, a habit that showed up in times of worry. He picked up the trunk and carried it inside, leaving Eliza to trail behind.

Her mother hadn't moved an inch despite the footsteps and the commotion. Eyes closed and resting, a strange smile played on her lips.

"Where do you want these?" Eliza asked, although most likely she should have left her mother undisturbed.

The older woman's eyes opened, focus as clear as a shot. "Why, back in the kitchen, of course. What a question. Where else would frying pans go."

Her mother recovered from the journey as her father went to the mines, taking Jake along with him. Eliza undertook most of the heavier work and kept a close eye on her mother.

"I wish you'd see a doctor."

"Don't pry; it's a women's complaint. Nothing for you to worry about."

To show just how fine she was, she bustled around doing nothing much of note before the wind seemed to die out of her and she tired. She lowered herself down in her chair, considering Eliza closer than comfortable.

"What is it?"

In all seriousness, she looked up at her daughter standing before her. "In life, there's only one thing that's certain. I'm right with my maker and that's the best I can do."

A stab in the stomach; her mother shimmering watery.

"No need for that now. How about you read me something out of the newspaper. This time I'll let you pick the stories, just as wild as you like."

"Please. Let me go for the doctor."

"No. Not today, maybe not tomorrow. If I want one, your father told me where one is. Now what about that reading?"

Trying to hide her panic, Eliza paged through *The Butte Miner,* hiding her face behind the newspaper as best she could. She started with the Eastern Wire and progressed to the next page.

"Oh dear. Listen to this. *'The need for a library was felt here last winter, when aside from dancing there was no amusement whatever to help pass the long, dreary evenings.*

Dancing, in moderation, will do very well, but it is generally allowed to have been somewhat overdone last winter. This library scheme will furnish a means of recreation that is more intellectual and more to be desired in every respect.' Huh. A man after my own heart."

Her mother opened her eyes, humor sparking. "Oh, I'd say there was more than dancing going on, wherever he was."

The desperate and failing attempt to find a neutral conversation. "I never did learn which books were in that lyceum. Not really. Maybe there is a chance that a real library will start up here. For both sexes."

"Maybe. You going to take the teacher's exam?"

Time was draining. "Once I know that you're better."

"You're not a child any longer, Eliza. I can't be with you forever. But I'm real proud of you. I want you to know that."

"Ma . . ."

"I mean it. Now, your father's not that strong about things like this. He's gruff, but you're going to have to help take care of him, come what may. And Jake, too. I don't like the notion of him going underground. Neither of them, for that matter, but your father's determined."

"Nothing's going to happen to you."

"No, of course not."

Both of them were lying to each other, if not themselves. And they knew it.

Margaret Gentry was buried on November 21, 1878, as the wind blew in cold from the north.

Snowdrifts revealed barren patches of the hardscrabble land underneath. The headstones blended into the color of melancholy, the barrenness of outlook. The three Gentrys dressed from head to toe in black stood out dark against the horizon, the only mourners in the cemetery. A solemn, lonely Thursday, the grave was an open mouth to receive the rough pine coffin.

"She was a good wife and mother," her father said, hat clutched to his heart.

"I wish Stephen could have been here," Eliza said, voice catching in the wind.

"He would have come if he were able," her father replied.

They had all read his words. A telegram explaining he couldn't be away from his work at the mine for the amount of time it would take to travel up and back.

The handful of dirt each tossed upon the coffin brought her life full circle. The shovelfuls of dirt landing on the coffin as they moved away caused the silence to fall between them like a shroud.

Back at the house, her father slumped in his chair and refused to make eye contact. Jake stared off at nothing in particular, while Eliza went through the motions of putting together a dinner. The dinner was nothing more than reheated soup, a panfried steak, and slices of day-old bread.

Nobody said much of anything as they struggled with the dinner no one wanted.

"That's it then," their father said when the clock struck eight o'clock in the evening. "I'll turn in now. Five o'clock in the morning comes pretty early."

Startled, Eliza stiffened. "You're not going to the mine tomorrow, are you?"

"Of course, I am. What else would I do?"

"Take your time to grieve."

He stuck his hands in his pants pockets and shrugged. "I'm going to work, Lizzie. We could use the money, and sitting around here won't bring her back. Jake, you don't have to go in tomorrow, unless you want to. I'll not force the issue."

Then in a softer voice. "She's never coming back."

Stunned by grief, the stamp mill reverberated in the distance, the same as if a life hadn't ended.

■ ■ ■ ■

She would honor her mother's wish and take the teacher's exam. But her heart wasn't in it. The undertaking took on gigantic proportions, all but insurmountable. Maybe it had to do with grieving. Maybe it had to do with something else.

Either way, the teacher's exam hung heavy, until the day she found herself standing outside of City Hall.

It didn't hurt to ask.

Still, she hesitated. Her reluctance spotted.

"You can come on in," a clerk prompted, breaking his stride.

She passed through the door, because it was easier than backsliding and being laughed at. "I was wondering about the teacher's exam."

"The Office of Education is down that hallway. Details are posted in the window if there's no one inside."

Down the tiled hallway, she found a placard posted in the window.

Teacher's exams are held in October and April. Notices are published in the newspapers and in this office. Experienced teachers are given preference, but all must have a Montana license. To obtain a Montana teacher's license, you must sit, and PASS, the exam.

She sucked in her breath. It would be another four months before she could try, and none of it was her fault. She turned to leave as the office door opened and a large man stepped out.

"Well, hello there, young lady!" He had red cheeks and a rounded belly. *Jolly* was the word that came to mind.

"Hello," she stammered.

"You look like you might be considering a teaching post. Am I right?" His voice boomed.

She wanted nothing more than to leave unnoticed. "I was considering it, but it seems I'll have to wait a while."

"You can sit the exam any time you've a mind to, but you'll have to pay five dollars for the expenses involved. I'm in charge of all of that. I'd be sitting with you while you took that exam. Harvey L. Thompson at your service." He touched his forehead as if he were doffing his hat.

It would have been rude to run. "Eliza Gentry. I'm uncertain what I want to do at the moment. I'll have to think about it."

"You always wanted to be a teacher, is that it? Good in school, were you?"

Rapid-fire questions. Too enthusiastic for comfort.

"Yes." It was the simplest answer, and at least true as far as the second clause was concerned.

"Don't suppose you're a good horse-woman, too, are you?" He eyed her up and down. "You've got the look about you."

"I know how to ride, if that's what you are asking. Astride. We've never had a woman's saddle."

His eyes sharpened, interested. "Do distances in open country bother you?"

"Should they? There used to be nothing I'd like better than to deliver messages from Virginia City up to Alder Gulch. That was eight miles one way." And a lifetime ago.

"But that wasn't overnight — was it?"

She considered the man more closely, wondering at his probing questions. Her mother had warned her about giving out too much information to strangers — especially men. "No. I guess if the weather'd turned, it would have turned out that way. Why?"

He laughed and patted his belly. He didn't look much like one for riding. "Sorry for all the questions; I get enthusiastic. You see, a

69

women's society is opening up a book co-operative of a sorts. They'll need someone to deliver and exchange books between Butte and Bannack, or that's the plan they told me."

"The position is for a teacher to ride between the two? Anyhow, I don't know distances here yet."

"No, actually the post is for a librarian of sorts. The distance between Butte and Bannack is about eighty-five miles, depending on how you go. But I'd stick to the main road. There're a few ranches to stop at along the way, but sleeping out rough is a likelihood, I'd say."

A librarian on horseback. For the first time since her mother's death, her heart lightened a measure. "I know how to shoot, too."

He stepped a half-foot closer. "Say, that's not a bad thing, either. May I take it you are interested?"

"Yes, sir." She blinked, astounded at the opportunity.

"The idea is to keep the books circulating, and to keep track of what you left off where. The women's societies will take care of your pay — and they're good for the money. It pays four dollars and fifty cents a circuit. Interested?"

"I am. Truly."

"Splendid. But it won't start up until spring. No sense taking needless risks with the weather. I'd guess April, but I'm not sure."

"And if it's a dry winter?"

His eyes were sharp. "I suppose they're game if you are. Reading materials get mighty scarce in the winter. You'd better talk to your parents, assuming you still live at home."

A stab. "I'm still at home. I'll speak to my father." A quiver she couldn't quite extinguish. "My mother passed last month."

A flicker of understanding. "I'm sorry. Handle it all as you see fit, but you might want to wait a while. No need to cause your father extra worry, not while you all are still grieving."

She needn't have worried about causing her father extra worry at all. It was more the other way around. Two months later, her father started keeping company with a younger widow going by the name of Lola. Her mother was barely cold in the grave, and he was out walking with another woman, wearing fancy-smelling shaving lotion and pomading his hair.

Civility wore mighty thin.

Her father *seemed* not to notice her

71

distress, although it probably was an act on his part. There was no denying the spring in his step that had been missing for quite some time.

"*He* seems to have recovered from the loss just fine," Eliza remarked to Jake.

"Women are in short supply, and I oughta know. Funny how an old badger found someone already." His eyes sharpened. "Say, isn't it about time you found yourself a fellow?"

The memory of Percy Smith and that brief season in Virginia City flashed. "I'm sixteen."

"I know how old you are. Sixteen going on seventeen more like twenty. But a new broom sweeps clean, and all of that. There's got to be some miner that would take you on," Jake grinned. "That way you'd have a house you could boss over all by yourself."

She threw her cleaning rag at him, aware of the looks young men cast in her direction. "You don't think they'll marry, do you?"

"Hard to say," Jake replied, "but he's acting mighty happy for a grieving man."

The uncomfortable silence of an important question. "Jake, am I pretty?"

He looked about ready to say something like "pretty ugly" but changed his mind when he caught her expression.

" 'Course you are. Didn't Ma ever tell you that?"

Tears stuck in the back of her throat, a nuisance. Her mother had always been far more interested in "content," as she called it.

"What's all this about?" he asked, voice soft and measured.

"Too many hard changes, I guess."

He sat still, listening.

"I went to see about getting a teacher's license."

Relief as the conversation steered toward safer territory. "They tell you that you were too young?"

"No one even asked. But the exams are only free two times a year. Next opportunity is in April, unless I want to pay five dollars."

"Is that all that's bothering you, the money? Hell, we can scrape that together."

Everything felt so uncertain, yet there was that glimmer. "I got offered a different position. Something better, but in a way, harder at the same time."

"Oh?"

"It's kind of a book-lady position. I would ride books between Butte and Bannack and back again. The superintendent said I had to ask Pa for permission."

He rubbed his head, leaving tufts of hair sticking up, which she had half a mind to smooth back down, but didn't.

"I'd say so. And I'd say he's not going to allow it. Besides, that's a lot of riding. A real lot of riding. You sure you're up for it?"

"Of course, I am. Are you saying that you don't think I can do it?"

"Now don't go getting riled up. You used to ride to Alder Gulch and back; sixteen miles in all, and you'd get a rest halfway. Plus, there were plenty of people about. How far do you think you and old Spooner can go in a day?"

"As far as we have to. I thought you'd understand."

"I do. I'm just asking you to be practical."

"I am being practical. I want out of the house, and this involves riding and books. The two things that I love most in the world. What could be better?"

"For you? Probably nothing. But there's a lot that could go wrong."

"Just like here," she replied.

Determined to create her own life on something approximating her own terms, February had other ideas. It proved a snow-filled month, and March looked set for more of the same. Counting her days until the weather cleared and stayed that way, her father's courtship progressed heedless of any of her feelings on the matter. Of course, grown children weren't consulted in such matters, for a child was still a child. And that's how she was considered, and a *female* one at that.

Unfair or not, her father, as far as all of that was concerned, didn't care for her opinion. Not where his private life was concerned. Well, two could play at that game.

As a result, her plans never came up in conversation.

"The widow and I have come to an understanding," he told her in that slow way of his, one night over supper.

Eliza's spoon stopped midair. Jake continued to eat, lowering his head and eyes fixated on his plate.

"She's agreed to become my wife. In a way, she'll be your new mother." He looked at Eliza as he added that last part.

She took a deep breath. "I'm partial to the one I had."

"Now don't be like that, Eliza. No one can replace your mother; it's true. And not for any of us. But the widow and I have agreed to combine forces, as it were. I'm asking you to give her a fair chance. You know what? She likes book learning. You two might just find that you have something in common after all."

With a name like Lola. A sharp criticism followed by the pang of unfairness. *Book learning* notwithstanding.

In the widow came, regardless of her feelings on the matter. And the weather held bitter with snow. The wedding took place at City Hall on a Friday afternoon late in the depths of March, with only Eliza and Jake acting as witnesses. The widow wore a durable black dress to the wedding — hardly anything odd in that — but it sure had a saucy flounce. Her father wore his only suit jacket; in fact, she had pressed it for him that morning. Not to mention he also sported a new necktie to mark the occasion.

"I pronounce Robert Gentry and Lola Hamilton as man and wife."

The bride and groom kissed with a bit more enthusiasm than Eliza would have liked.

Eliza felt like sobbing, and she'd be damned if she was going to look happy about the nuptials taking place.

And there her father stood, beaming at his

new bride while her mother laid cold in the grave. Only four months old.

And after the brief ceremony and after they all signed their names to the Certificate of Marriage, they adjourned to a nearby hotel's dining room for the wedding dinner. Eliza had little to say, but for once, her father truly didn't notice.

But his new wife certainly did and tried her best to pretend she wasn't bothered.

After the strained meal they adjourned home, Jake fortunate enough to make a getaway to the late shift in the mine. Eliza, being a girl, had no other place to go. As soon as polite, she slipped into her small closet of a bedroom.

She spent the night with the pillow clamped over her ear to block out the sounds coming through the wall, praying for morning's swift arrival. And she prayed for herself to be somewhere else, anywhere else than where she was located, stuck in a home that no longer felt familiar.

Any lingering doubts about the advisability of riding a circuit faded in light of her circumstances. The desire to make herself scarce quashed misgivings, with the possible exception of bears. In her worse moments, she thought even facing down a grizzly might be preferable to the ignominy of being a third wheel. Although they never said as much, their giggling and secret laughter rendered her presence unwanted. Jake found a place in a boardinghouse for much the same reason.

But he was free, and she was left to fend for herself — a nearly grown-up daughter lingering around in a fresh new marriage.

"You remember that conversation we had about brooms, don't you?" Jake asked, hefting his belongings over his shoulder as he was on his way out to set himself up in his new lodgings.

It was never that far from her mind.

She picked up any work that came her way, anything to get her out of the house and out of their way. Although the widow had a morning job at one of the big houses, she was around during the rest of the day and anxious to put her mark on the house. The two women, uncomfortable in each other's presence, tried to divide the living quarters into unspoken territories, but it never truly worked.

The widow, however, at least read newspapers and would share them.

"The women are opening up a reading room," she commented, showing Eliza the advertisement.

She was pretty sure those were the same women for whom she'd be riding the circuit. Located on Park Avenue, it was close by.

"I heard something like that might be going in," she remarked, but said nothing further.

Eliza found the address without a problem — a small placard placed in the lower right-hand side of a shop window:

Butte Reading Room — All Welcome

Probably an improvement over that old lyceum.

A bell above the door rang as she entered, interrupting a woman intent upon the contents of a box.

"Good afternoon." Graying hair and a half smile, it was the woman's blue eyes that caught her.

"Are you in charge here?"

"Yes. My name is Mrs. Elizabeth Jenkins. What can I do for you?"

"My name is Eliza Gentry, and I'm going to be delivering books for you to Bannack and back. This place is marvelous."

The woman appeared concerned . . . and wary. "We're just in the beginning phases. Perhaps you've seen our appeal for reading materials — specifically books — in the newspapers. We've had the hardest time getting people to part with their reading materials."

Eliza drifted over to the single bookcase — five shelves high that held a smattering of books.

"There's twenty books set out, and we have about twenty more in the back. Duplicates, would you believe it?"

Eliza ran her fingertips over the tops of the books, considering the titles. Shakespeare, *Geography of the World*, *The Sentimental Song Book*, *The Adventure of Tom Sawyer*, and a *Rose in Bloom* along with a dash of mining, religious, and farming tracts.

"My. It's really happening."

"Slowly. So much depends on how well all of this catches on. Volunteers will staff the room as available — we're aiming to be open on Saturdays and Sunday afternoons, as well as weekday afternoons and evenings. Maybe three in the afternoon to seven at night . . . I can't say that we expected a girl courier, however."

"The weather seems good enough these days to ride."

Mrs. Jenkins's eyes darted. "Now, I don't know. Snowstorms can still blow up, can't they? Are you sure about this?"

"I'm a good distance rider, and I know how to shoot. So, if you're worried on either of those counts, you needn't be."

The woman eyed her, guarded. "If you were my daughter, I'd tell you 'no.' "

But she wasn't this woman's daughter, and her temper flared.

"I'll tell you the truth. All my life, I wanted nothing more than to read. There was a lyceum in Virginia City at the time. One for 'civilized men.' Of course, I tried to enter, but of course I wasn't allowed. For the simple fact that I was *female.* If I can prevent that from happening to one other young girl who wants nothing more than to read, well then, I've done my job. I'd hate to think that *women* would be unwilling to give me a chance at something I know I can do."

Eliza's argument struck the desired chord. Mrs. Jenkins held up her hand in surrender. "Would you consider yourself an *expert* horsewoman?"

That might have been stretching things a bit far, but she was good.

"I have my own horse who is as reliable as they come. I've always been around horses, handling them on the ground when I was young and riding them later. I've fallen off,

81

slipped off, and a couple of times got bucked off. I always get back on."

"Suppose you're a crack shot, too."

"Had to be. My brothers made sure of it. Besides, at $4.50 a circuit, I'm not too sure many reliable men would sign up."

The woman's expression held a different type of consideration, and something altogether more grown-up. "You've got a valid point."

Eliza waited her out; Mrs. Jenkins still not entirely decided. "May. If the weather allows. That gives us additional time to collect donations, although what it will get us, I surely don't know. As it stands, we are prepared to allow for the cost of a hired horse, along with the payment for the rider. You don't get that money if you use your own horse. Our intent was to guarantee a sound creature."

"My horse is sound." Of course, Spooner was getting older. But she trusted him, and that counted for a lot.

"Make sure. Remember, a slow horse means sleeping in the rough. One prone to lameness could pose a real problem."

"Well, we can worry about that later when the time comes."

Her eyes traveled to the bookcase. "If you could use another volunteer in the meanwhile, I'd be happy to pitch in. I'd have to fit it around my restaurant job, but other than that . . ."

A spark entered Mrs. Jenkins's eyes. "Well, speaking of donations. There's a man who lives two miles out of town on the road to Deer Lodge. If the tales are true, he lives in a cabin surrounded by books. How about you go on out there and see if you can get him to part with some?"

"Does this man have a name?"

"Mr. P.R. Wilkins. He's one of the mine supervisors, so he shouldn't be too hard to find. Now, I don't know that he'll give you a thing or not, but it would be a nice walk or ride if the weather's fair. It's about two miles out."

"How about this Sunday?"

"Excellent. Don't know if Mr. Wilkins is a churchgoing man, but a Sunday afternoon usually finds a body at home."

Or, in a saloon, Eliza thought — but she kept that notion to herself.

The next Sunday broke fine and fair. The wind was out of the south, lending to the general sense of an approaching thaw. Spooner had thrown a shoe the day before, but Eliza figured the walk wouldn't do her any harm. Pulling on her coat and selecting a covered basket on her way out the door, she considered her rifle hanging on the wall. It wouldn't seem all that friendly to ask for donations, armed and ready. Still . . .

Her father and his wife returned to the house as she was about to leave; they met in the doorway as she dithered.

"Good morning." Her father eyed her uncertainly. His wife eyed her with the cautious suspicion of a woman who had never had children of her own.

She aimed her explanation at her father. "I'm going out on the road to Deer Lodge for book contributions for the reading room and circulating library, for lack of a better term. I'm going to walk; it seems a fine enough day for it."

"Take the rifle. You never know what might come up."

His wife latched onto all of that pretty firm. "You aren't just going about asking strangers, are you?"

"No. I'm going to see Mr. P.R. Wilkins, a mine superintendent and reader. He's about two miles out of town on the Deer Lodge road."

His wife was torn between her notions of propriety and the promise of new reading material. "Tracking down strange men all for the sake of books . . . couldn't you just write him a letter?"

"I could, but it's harder to say 'no' to someone in person."

Her father glanced from one woman to the other. "Especially if that person is a pretty young woman. I suppose even if there's method to your madness, *take the rifle.*"

The widow Hamilton, for that is how Eliza continued to think of her, sniffed. "I'm not sure we should let her go traipsing around soliciting for donations, heaven help us all."

Her father appeared about ready to concede to his wife's wishes, so Eliza grabbed up the rifle and angled her way past them and out the door.

"I'll be back within a couple of hours. Bye!"

As she walked off, she could feel her father's gaze aimed right between her shoulder blades. Worried.

Skirting the main streets of Butte, sure enough, she looked like she was going hunting.

Hunting for books, she thought with a grin.

Armed, she passed by a group of young men, standing on a corner.

"If you're going berry hunting, you might want to wait until June when they've had a chance to at least bloom," one wit offered, while the others laughed.

Her cheeks stung from more than the wind. It was a stupid comment all the same.

The road to Deer Lodge stretched long and plain. It took roughly 2,000 steps to cover a mile, and she didn't feel like counting. It'd be easier just to ask as she went along.

After walking what she judged to be about far enough, she stopped at the first cabin located near mine tailings.

Her knock was answered by a woman in a faded blue dress.

"Do you know Mr. P.R Wilkins, one of the mine superintendents?"

"Sure," the woman eyed her and the rifle. "That for him?"

"Oh, no!" A self-conscious chuckle. "My father made me take it. Could you point me in the right direction?"

"Up a bit further. You'll see a fork in the road, so stay to the right. You'll come on to a cabin in about a third of a mile, maybe less, and that'll be his. He's a queer duck, although the men say he's a good boss."

"Do you know if he has any books?"

A suspicious shrug. "I don't know about that, but I've seen him reading."

■ ■ ■ ■

True enough, after the fork in the road she found a cabin, and hoped it was his. The dull thud of wood chopping carried from somewhere behind the house. Drawn by the sound, she found a youngish man poised to arc the axe.

"Hello," she said soft and slow. "Are you Mr. Wilkins?"

His eyes sparked when he saw her. "Can I help you?" He set the axe back down, resting on the ground.

"I hope so. My name is Eliza Gentry, and I've come from Butte to see if you would consider making a donation to the Butte Reading Society room."

Incredulous, he scratched his neck. "You came all the way from Butte for a dollar?"

Eliza felt a telltale flush rising on her neck. "It's said that you have a fine collection of books in your cabin. I've been sent to ask if you could part with a few of them."

No response.

"For the common good," she added.

A slow, lopsided grin. "Oh, I don't know about that. I'm mighty partial to my books."

She couldn't blame him. "We're setting up a reading room where everyone is welcome, and books are in short supply. Are you certain you can't be persuaded to part with one or two?"

He sighed, pulling his suspenders up over his shoulders. Low clouds mounted in the distance, the wind pressing down, insistent. He eyed her rifle.

"Expecting trouble?"

"Maybe," she laughed.

He gestured for her to join him in going around to the cabin's front. Inside, Eliza paused, and suppressed a delighted laugh. One entire wall was filled with shelves, and on at least five of those shelves were nothing but books.

Forgetting any semblance of manners, she propped her rifle against a wall and went straight to the collection. "Oh, look at all of these!"

He leaned against the doorframe, watching her. "I've always had books, and truthfully wish I had more. You see, what you're asking for is something I would consider quite a sacrifice." A deep inhalation. "So, they sent you out here to see if you could melt my cold heart, is that it?"

"It wasn't phrased that way." Not sure whether he was teasing, she observed him from beneath her lashes and thought not.

He looked at her square. "Did Mrs. Jenkins tell you that I've already turned down her request?"

A flush shot up, before draining back down. "No. She didn't."

He seemed kind of tense as he shut the door. "Of course not. Then you wouldn't have come."

Dividing her attention between the man and his books, she was torn as to whether to look at him, or to study the bindings. Truth be told, she wasn't sure which she was more interested in.

"Well, then," he said in a soft voice. "It seems you made the long walk out here for nothing."

"Oh, I wouldn't say it was for nothing," she replied, tracing her finger over the bindings. "Are you *certain* you couldn't spare just one or two? You could put your name in the cover, and if you missed them too badly, you could just ask for them back."

"Mrs. Jenkins doesn't look like she'd take kindly to a change of heart."

She grinned. "No, she doesn't, does she?"

"And, they might get stolen. Depending upon the high moral standards of my fellow Montanans might be a bit of a risk, wouldn't you say? Especially where valuable reading material is concerned."

A brief laugh, although it was the truth.

Another nice smile that said he found her pretty. "Well, since you've come all the way out here, I guess it would be poor manners on my part to let you leave empty-handed."

He looked at his collection, poised to select one, finger hovering in the air. He paused before he chose a different one. Then he selected another . . . and one more. "For the Butte Reading Room and its lovely messenger, with my compliments."

Their hands briefly touched as she accepted the volumes; their eyes searched as words ran out.

Heart surging, her mind drew a blank. It was foolish to just stand there staring at him like some great, gawky girl. "I'd best get going. The weather's turning."

"Will you come again — if I tempt you with books, that is? Or perhaps I might call on you when I'm down in Butte." A long pause with a deep current. "How old are you?"

A stab. "Eighteen," she lied.

"I'm twenty-four. Is that too old for you?"

Her father would certainly think it was. "Probably not, if you mind your manners."

Placing the books in the basket, she picked up her rifle and stepped toward the door. He pressed on the latch.

"Well, Miss Eliza Gentry, it smells like

snow's coming. Perhaps you'd best stay here until it blows over."

A moment of indecision. "I can't. My father will have my head. Butte's only two miles away. I'll make it if I hurry. But I must leave, and I'd better leave right now."

"I can hitch up my team and drive you."

"So, then you and your horses will be caught out in the storm instead."

"Something like that," he replied.

She darted out at a half run. Everyone knew that storms could turn fierce, even in the spring. And she left behind one Mr. P.R. Wilkins, considering her retreating form.

The snow thickened as the wind picked up and caught in the trees. A full-on blizzard threatened. She trudged forward with her precious cargo, ever so careful not to miss the fork in the road. More than one person had been found half-frozen in the thaw, proving spring storms were no laughing matter.

What could P.R. stand for, she wondered, despite the driving snow. But to really consider that, she'd have to wait until later, once she'd gotten herself to safety and shelter. Fortunately, the faint outline of the woman's cabin was visible in the driving snow. Clambering up to the door, her knocking came close to pounding.

The woman didn't seem all that surprised when she answered. "Well, come on in. I don't know about all of this traipsing around you're doing."

Eliza crossed the threshold. "Oh, thank goodness. And I'm sorry to be a bother, truly I am. Do you mind if I set these on the table?"

"Not at all. I take it you got something out of him. Well, well, well."

She set the books on the table. *Brewer's Dictionary of Phrase and Fables, The Lives of Irish Saints and Martyrs* and *Essays in Criticism.*

The woman pressed in closer. "How's this all supposed to work?"

"It's a reading room, and these here are donations. You can go there, too; it's on Park Avenue. A book exchange is going to be established between Butte and Bannack, maybe some other locations, but I don't have any better details. However, I'm going to be their courier."

The woman eyed her sharply. "You just got caught out in the storm today. Doesn't that set you to thinking, and maybe have you just a bit worried?"

A pang of truth. She *had* misjudged the weather. "The riding part won't start until the weather clears. Besides, there's places to stop along the way, or so I've been told."

"You take coffee? So, are the people in these towns supposed to pay?"

"Not that I've heard."

She was itching to open up one of the new books, and the woman caught it.

"My husband won't be home for a few hours yet, and if the storm doesn't lift, he may just stay where he is. Why don't you read to me as I get the dinner ready and we can hear what those books have to say."

The storm broke an hour and a half later, setting Eliza on the course toward home.

Her father glared when she entered but didn't bother to get out of his chair. "I've got a good notion to bend you over my knee!"

"I'm sixteen, Papa. I stopped at a cabin to wait out the storm, and read to the woman while she fixed supper, so all is well."

"Hmph. Did you eat with them?"

"No, the storm broke and I figured you might be worried, so I came straight back."

"Well, that's something at least. Mrs. Gentry put some dinner aside for you, didn't you, dear?"

The woman looked relieved to see her. "Did you get any books?"

Proud, Eliza smiled and revealed the contents of the basket.

"Oh, *Irish Saints and Martyrs.* May I?"

"Please do. But I'll have to take them in tomorrow."

"That gives me tonight," the widow Hamilton said, book raised in triumph.

"And the reading room later." Eliza added, heading toward the kitchen. "You can always read it there later."

Undaunted by the weather and anxious to leave the old newlyweds behind, Eliza was eager to ride come May. The days on the calendar slipped away, and it was closer to June when she finally got the go-ahead.

Mrs. Jenkins supervised the preparations, far less enthusiastic than Eliza. In fact, Mrs. Jenkins kept eyeing her up and down as if weighing her chances.

Nevertheless, twenty books were counted and placed in the large canvas saddlebags. Her bedroll tied secure behind her saddle, another saddlebag added, loaded with food for the trip. Three canteens hung from the saddle horn, just in case. One loaded-down Spooner, but he didn't mind, sensing the greater occasion. Mrs. Jenkins and other ladies of the literary societies were on hand for the inaugural event, and Mr. Thompson handed her a hand-drawn map marking out the mileages and ranches where she could stay. The widow Hamilton stood off at a distance, lingering at the edges of the commotion, arms wrapped around her middle. When she met her stepdaughter's eyes, she offered a tentative half wave, before lowering her hand.

Eliza figured to go say something to her, something that would make her feel better. She made it halfway over to her, when Mrs. Jenkins cut her off.

"To be clear," Mrs. Jenkins said in a low voice, back turned so no one would see or hear, "You understand that if something goes wrong, you are reliant upon sheer luck of the draw for help to come by. The roads aren't empty, but you never know the characters you might encounter."

Her rifle was secure and ready in its scabbard. "I'm fine. I can walk twenty miles, or more, if need be."

A sharp look.

"And carry the books," she hastened to add.

"Not with a broken leg," Mrs. Jenkins replied, ending the conversation on a rather unpleasant note.

With a hearty wave and what she hoped was a reassuring grin to the widow, Eliza mounted up and took to the saddle as the assembled group twittered and fluttered like meadowlarks.

"I have prepared a short speech," Mrs. Jenkins announced to the crowd with the complete expectation that the crowd would settle. "This is an important event in the history of Butte and the Territory of Montana. Let it be recognized that this endeavor is made in the name of spreading civilization to the remote and furthering the aim of literacy and education. Without reading materials, the exchange of ideas is severely curtailed. Without reading, ignorance continues unabated. Without books, base urges for entertainment win out over that which is productive to society. We wish our young courier well, and Godspeed."

With a cheer and clapping, Eliza and Spooner took off at a good, confident clip.

Which she slowed, once they passed from view.

One hour in with the weather fine, she wondered what all the fuss had been about. The road to Bannack was traveled enough, with little chance of getting lost. Two hours in, everything still struck her as fine; the road remained level and in decent repair, the horse content and agreeable. With plenty of rivulets and water trickles from which to choose, Spooner seemed to recall the old days up to Alder Gulch and back. However, three hours in, Eliza started getting a bit sore, and shifted in the saddle trying different poses to the point that the horse came to a standstill, wondering what her problem was.

Nothing like the slightly quizzical expression from a horse to bring the rider to the conclusion that a brief rest might be in order. Choosing an area with a slope and a boulder to aid in remounting, she got off Spooner and stretched out.

Perhaps a trifle overly cautious, she remembered the adage to "never ride away until after the person shutting the gate remounts."

One hard-boiled egg and a drink of water later, it wasn't a Sunday picnic, so she got on with it. About another hour in, that trotting didn't feel so great in her joints. For variety she loped for a while, slowing when Spooner's neck showed sweat. She let him rest a bit, and they walked a ways, slow and steady. Hips and thighs sore enough, she reminded herself that it took a while to become conditioned.

Judging from the sun's position in the sky, she had three more hours of daylight left.

Doubt nibbled around the edges. Another mile in, the doubt took bigger bites of her confidence. Two more miles and that doubt moved into her gut as a damn near certainty.

All of which was before she got a cramp in her hip joint. Thirty miles in one day was further than she'd ever tried before. Again dismounting, preferring to walk off the cramp and leaving the saddle. There was no firm requirement that she cover thirty miles a day, but Bannack would have been telegraphed. The last thing she wanted was a search party sent out because she was just too dang slow.

As twilight started falling, blue and chill, she saw a light up ahead. If it wasn't the Johnson Ranch marked out on her map, that was just too darn bad. She'd stop there anyhow, unless they ran her off.

She remounted with difficulty, all for the sole purpose of making a better impression upon her arrival.

She rode into the yard as a man emerged from the barn, no doubt having heard the horse.

"Are you Mr. Johnson?"

"Maybe. Who wants to know?"

"My name is Eliza Gentry. I'm delivering books to Bannack. The school superintendent, Mr. Thompson, said I could spend the night here."

"Did he now? That's a mighty peculiar thing to go promising, ain't it?"

She shifted. Pain. "Can I get off my horse?"

"Sure. No one's stopping you."

She landed with a thud on the ground, and almost fell over as her knees buckled. "Well, are you Mr. Johnson, and can I stay here for the night?"

He stuck his thumbs under his armpits, screwed up his face, and appraised her with shifty blue eyes.

"I'm Johnson, but I don't have a wife. How do you think it'd look, a young girl like yourself staying unchaperoned in a bachelor's house like this? No siree. That kind of trouble, I sure don't need."

Half-hanging from the saddle horn from pure exhaustion, all she could do was stare at his long gray beard with tobacco stains running down from the corners of his mouth.

"I can't ride any further."

"No one said ya had to. I figure you and your horse there can sleep in the barn. You'll have each other for company, and should someone come by, it won't get anyone to talking. Of course, it'll be cold in there, and you can't go lighting any fires. What d'ya say?"

"Sounds fine," she replied, although it didn't. Not really. Still, cover of any sort was preferable than sleeping in the rough.

And Mr. Johnson wasn't done with his instructions.

"Well, get him unsaddled, and he can have some of the hay in there. Then you can come on in and share some supper. Don't let it be said that Erwin Johnson turned away anyone who was askin' for help. It's just that I have a reputation to maintain. There's a ditch behind the barn if you want to wash up."

She wasn't *asking for help* dang it; she was *providing a service.*

She bit back telling him as much. Maybe shelter and help amounted to the same thing in Mr. Johnson's eccentric mind, and a hot meal sounded mighty tempting. So she held her tongue, led Spooner to the stable, and washed up in the freezing creek that was nothing more than snow runoff.

Cold and sore, she hobbled her way into the house, so tired she barely made it through dinner.

"I can't say you're much for conversation," the old fellow grumbled, as she struggled to keep her eyes open.

100

She returned into the cold dark barn without even so much as a lantern. She untied her bedroll, wrapped the blanket around her, and using Spooner's saddle blanket for a pillow she fell asleep in a pile of hay.

And the funny part was, she was just too damn tired to even care.

The next day, the sound of Spooner pawing, stomping, and peeing brought her around. Sore and stiff. She half-sat, thigh muscles protesting, and for the wildest of moments wondered why in heaven's name she was in a strange barn. The sounds of a man's heavy gait clomped up to the outside and yelled, "Are ya decent in there?"

Mr. Johnson. If one overlooked the straw she found clinging in her hair, she was.

"Yes," she answered, but her voice came out kind of rough.

That one word barely uttered, before the door swung open and light streamed in.

"Chores. I gotta muck out them stalls." He stuck his hayfork into where she'd just been lying a moment earlier and pitched it over into one of the stalls.

"You've got a nice barn," she commented, for lack of anything better to say.

"It works. There's cowboy coffee in the

house, if you want it."

Stiffly walking across the yard and into the house, the interior come across as worse in the light of day. Dust and tattered, everything scattered about. She found an old, battered tin mug and poured herself a cup of the bitter coffee.

This was another first she thought, sipping at the bitter brew. Her first night on the circuit had come and gone. She was still standing, and her horse wasn't lame.

Saddling up Spooner was easy, being happy about getting back in the saddle wasn't. Tightening the cinch, putting on his bridle, lifting up the heavy saddlebags filled with books, and hefting herself on, she was starting out on day two, and another thirty miles to ride. The first couple of miles hurt as her body re-accustomed itself to the hardness and contour of the saddle. By what she figured the fifth mile, her muscles relaxing into the saddle, the ride was looking up.

The countryside, populated with swells and hillocks, was gentle enough and nothing much at all transpired. Just riding, just transporting books. Anticipating the excitement of Bannack's residents caused a smile. Pride would keep her from failing.

The second night she even got a bed, and

was grateful for the more conventional surroundings, especially the kind woman of the house.

"What about us ranch people?" The question was posed in the wistful tone that Eliza knew all so well.

"Maybe the ladies will add more stops," was all she could offer. "Don't suppose you could go into Bannack, could you?"

A disappointed flick of the wrist. "I guess I could if I have to. Normally we only go there for supplies."

Eliza pulled the slimmest volume from her bag. "If I do the washing up, maybe you'd have enough time to read this tonight. That is, if you want to."

The woman took the volume and pressed it between her palms. "I'd sure like to give it a try."

Eliza smiled as she fetched water for the washing, as the woman sat down at the table in the light of the kerosene lamp to read.

On the third day, she rode into Bannack, right down the center of the main street. Half-expecting some fanfare like the send-off she received, there was nothing like that awaiting her. Instead she found a dying town, much like Virginia City had been, right about the time they left. There were people moving about, a hotel, and a few stores still in business, but it was nothing like Butte. She located the Express Office and figured it as good a place to start as any. She lifted off the saddlebags with the books, lugging them inside the office with her.

A grizzled old-timer sat behind a desk. "Hello there! Can I help you?"

"I hope so. I'm bringing books from Butte, but I'm not exactly sure who I should bring them to. Do you handle the telegraph?"

"I do. And it seems to me something came through about you a couple of days ago. But I guess that's unprofessional. Name please."

"Eliza Gentry."

"Well then, now that's settled, yes, we are expecting you. I'd go over to the mercantile next door, which serves as the post office. It's a gathering place of sorts, not counting the church or the saloons. And I even expect the lady who runs it, Mrs. Anderson, will have something for you in return."

Tired and dusty, she entered the mercantile, and had to stand there waiting as an old prospector settled up his bill. The woman behind the counter gave her an apologetic glance as the man fumbled around.

"I'll be right with you," she said.

The man turned to consider who was standing behind him. "Good heavens! You look like you've been on the trail a while."

"Now, is that a nice thing to say?" Eliza snapped.

"Beggin' your pardon, miss," he mumbled.

She set the saddlebags down on the floor. The man gathered his coins, tipped his hat in her general direction, and with no further eye contact, left.

"My name's Eliza, and I'm delivering books from Butte."

"You're the girl! Well, that's just wonderful. I have some for you here." The woman hurried from around the counter. "Let me take those from you. And I'm sorry about Earl. Manners can get kind of rough when they're not used that often."

"It's fine. I'm just tired, that's all. I shouldn't have snapped like that. It's been a couple of days of hard riding."

"I'll bet it has. Say, if you don't have any other plans, why don't we set you up at my house for the night. You can get a bath at the hotel. You'll feel better then. That, and after you've had some food. Then I guess you head back to Butte tomorrow, if you're ready. Is that how it goes?"

"As far as I know. And I thank you for putting me up."

"Of course, dear. It's a treat for me too, having some civilized company."

And the next day, she was back on the road to Butte.

Eliza rode back, much the same as the trip out, but only in reverse order. She even stopped back at Johnson's ranch for lack of a better alternative. This time, she tried to be a bit better of a conversationalist. As a reward, Mr. Johnson offered her the loan of a pillow, a loan which she respectfully declined.

Her body was hardening to the rigors of the road, but she was certainly relieved when Butte came into sight. She went straight to the reading room to deliver the Bannack exchange.

"Why, you've made it!" the volunteer exclaimed, a woman Eliza could not recall ever having seen before.

Eliza half-laughed. "I did. And I've brought what Bannack sent." The saddlebags thudded down to the floor.

"Let me get Mrs. Jenkins out of the back. She'll want to know that you're here. Say, a young man stopped by for you while you were gone. A Mr. Wilkins. Do you know him?"

Her eyes must have given her away, considering the woman's expression. "Did he?"

The woman leaned in, confidential. "Is he your beau? He must be worried half-sick about you riding up and down the roads."

"He's someone I met, that's all." She could feel the flush starting.

"Well, he seemed rather taken with you, I must say." She lowered her voice. "And I wanted to be the one to tell you. Mrs. Jenkins can be, well . . . a bit hard. She was here when he came, and doesn't exactly condone romances that might get in the way of her plans. Now, I'd best go get her. It wouldn't do to have her catch us here talking."

"Surely she's not that bad," Eliza replied with a bit of a laugh.

But the woman inclined her head in disagreement, as she passed to the back room.

"Mrs. Jenkins, Eliza Gentry's back and she's in one piece . . ."

"Thank heavens for that. I didn't want to go deliver to her father any bad news." She bustled out from the back room.

"How was it?"

"Fine, but a bit harder than I thought."

Mrs. Jenkins's eyes lit with a triumphant spark. "You made it through, at least. Well done. Now, do you think that's a circuit you could manage, say . . . once a month?"

Although tired, she tried to appear enthusiastic. "Yes. That's manageable."

"What about Deer Lodge?" The question came out measured.

Eliza blinked. "Are there enough books for all of that?"

"Reform movements back East will supply them on account of the prison. Any objections? It's actually of less distance than Bannack. Thirty-five miles or so, as the crow flies."

"No. I suppose I can do that. But not this week. That was a lot of distance for my horse." Not to mention herself.

"Of course not. I understand. I'll see if I can arrange it for next week. Now. A slight matter has been brought to my attention."

The other volunteer's eyebrows lifted, right before she turned away with the pretense of arranging and tidying the books.

"That mining superintendent, Mr. Wilkins, came by asking for you. Some nonsense about how he could have his books back if he wanted them."

"He did?"

Her startled expression satisfied Mrs.

108

Jenkins. "I feared it was all a ruse," she exhaled. "*That* was the excuse that I got."

Relief. "Oh, I see. He didn't actually want to take his books back, did he?"

"Well, I'm not sure that you *do* see, to be frank. I believe he's entertaining an interest in you. And you're far too young for that type of thing."

"I'm almost seventeen," Eliza countered.

"And I'd say he's twenty-five. Now if your father has no objections, it's not my place to interfere. But if you were my daughter . . ."

"You'd tell me 'no,' " Eliza finished.

"It's for your own good. I understand your mother is deceased. I'm only trying to give you good advice."

A stinging reminder. "For right now, I'm very tired, and I'm going to take Spooner to the livery and go home. I guess I can worry about anything else a bit later."

"Spooner? What kind of name is that?"

"An accurate one. He's very affectionate," Eliza called over her shoulder, just in time to see the friendly volunteer smother a smile.

That Sunday, it stood a foregone conclusion that she'd take a walk out along the road to Deer Lodge. A known destination by this point, she wouldn't stop at the woman's cabin unless she saw her. And then, it would just be for a few shared words and a short visit. Luck was with her, and no one delayed her progress. With the slight pang of guilt, Eliza continued along, careful to keep right at the fork in the road. When Mr. Wilkins's cabin came into view, she let go of the breath she'd been holding.

Smoke coming from the chimney, she smiled to herself and took a few more steps in that direction. She stopped, realizing that she had no good idea what she would say. It was a very forward thing that she was doing, knocking on a man's door with no purpose at all — other than she heard he'd been asking for her.

As she hesitated, the cabin door opened, and he stepped outside. He stopped when he saw her.

"Why, Eliza! Is that you?"

She took a few tentative steps forward. "I heard that you wanted your books back. Is that true?"

He had the good graces to look sheepish. "Ah, that was just an excuse. But let me tell you, I don't think I'd manage to get those books back even if I were serious!"

His smile beamed.

"So, I can't persuade you to make another

contribution to the reading room?"

His eyes went a bit wild, although her tone was teasing. "Hel . . . I mean no. I don't think so."

She laughed, and he joined in a half-beat later. "It's nice of you to come out this way. Could I give you a cup of coffee?"

"Of course," she replied. "After you tell me your first name. All I know is P.R."

"Paul Rogers Wilkins at your service."

She half-twirled her skirt. "Pleased to meet you, Paul Rogers Wilkins."

"Likewise, Miss Eliza Gentry."

And so a courtship started, over cups of coffee. Laughter and discussions of literature.

"You can borrow a book to take home with you, if you like," he offered, although he sounded a bit pained.

She wanted to tell him her real age, but she didn't. "*Hamlet,*" she replied. "I believe I would like to borrow *Hamlet.*"

He smiled and pulled it from the shelf. Their fingers touching in the process.

"I'll be gone next week, riding. Deer Lodge this time," she said. "It should be a bit easier than Bannack. And I won't take the book with me, so you needn't fear that it will come to harm."

A trifle wounded, he inhaled. "I was actually thinking more about you."

"Never you fear. I'm fine. I like riding . . . within reason."

He offered a slight bow. "In that case, I won't expect this back next Sunday, nor will I go asking for you in the reading room. In any case, I got the feeling that Mrs. Jenkins didn't approve."

Eliza offered a gentle smile. "In her own way, I believe she's trying to help, but she's a bit . . . commanding. She thinks I'm too young."

"That? If you want my opinion, I believe it's more that she doesn't want to lose her courier."

That caught her short.

"Why would she lose me? Our keeping company is nothing to prevent me from riding."

He seemed to flinch in disagreement, and colored. There was something he wanted to say but thought better of it. "Just promise that you'll be careful."

"I promise," she said. "It's not like I want to go out and get hurt or am looking for trouble to get involved in."

"Glad to hear it," he replied.

She laughed. He didn't.

The following Wednesday, Eliza clipped

down the Deer Lodge road, this time on a hired horse. Keeping her eyes peeled for a glimpse of Paul while she and the new horse became accustomed to each other. Spooner was left behind this time, but she'd take him out again. Riding an unknown horse added a bit more worry about the journey, but time would tell. As they passed through the mining camp, Paul was hidden away and busy at work in one of the buildings, but she kept a sharp lookout, just in case.

Soon the familiar landscape slipped away and turned wide open, empty. As the distance stretched on, the hills changed, faceted small cliffs overlooking the waves of grass green and stands of cottonwood trees along the banks of Clark's river. A bending, meandering river had dense brush for long stretches at a time, a growth which would provide perfect cover for moose and bear, and Eliza had no intention of stopping for the horse to drink until it opened up.

No use taking unnecessary risks.

Still, having a nearby river was a source of comfort. Regardless, those faceted hills caught her imagination, bringing to mind mine-cut diamonds and notions of engagement rings.

"I'm getting ahead of myself, Red," she

said aloud, and nudged him into a faster pace.

That night, however, she had to sleep in the rough. Thirty-five miles was just a bit more territory than she could cover in one day. She chose a place near enough to the river, and back away from where she thought wild animals might water. When she led Red to the river to drink, she kept a lookout for tracks and found enough for her to move with Red away into the distance.

She picketed the horse, and gathered enough wood to make a fire once the darkness set in. She hadn't slept out in the rough before, but she made herself as comfortable as she could, and ate the sandwich she packed while the horse pulled up the long grasses to feed. As the sun dipped down, and darkness drew near, the stars shone ever so bright. She rested back against her saddle, and watched the night sky, admiring the stars as they glittered.

"More diamonds," she murmured.

And so the trip to Deer Lodge passed without incident; there were no bears lurching from the brush, or moose crossing their path. She rode into the town and past the prison with its high walls. Across the street was her delivery point, and she got a fine selection of books in return for the books she dropped off.

"You're a brave one," the woman behind the desk said.

Eliza smiled. "I don't know about that. I guess being so close to the prison would give me more cause for worry."

"Well," the woman replied, "I'd rather have them all behind bars and walls rather than roaming loose, wouldn't you?"

"Do these books go into the prison?"

The woman shook her head. "Not unless you've brought us a load of Bibles. These are for the people of town — the ones that work at the prison, or on the ranches nearby."

"No Bibles," Eliza replied.

A smile. "Are you spending the night here?"

She thought about it, figuring she might be able to catch Paul the following day. Three hours back in the direction of Butte, another night out under the stars, and then maybe . . . if she timed it right. "No, I'll head back. After I get something warm to eat."

So she went to a café, had some pancakes and coffee, and turned around to head back to Butte with the new selection of books. The day was pleasant and bright, and they took off at a fine clip. About three miles from Deer Lodge, Red threw a shoe. She didn't hear it come off, but felt it in the way he stepped, all of a sudden kind of squishy.

"Whoa." She pulled him to a stop, got off, and lifted his rear left leg.

Sure enough, the shoe was missing.

"Darn." Still crouched in beside him, it was better to walk him back to Deer Lodge and get him re-shod. It was either that, or risk him going lame. She pulled the reins over his head and led him back to the town. She'd lose a couple of hours in the doing, but it didn't matter that much. She found a farrier without problem, and he took care of the horse then and there.

"That's a dollar," he said, considering her again. "You're riding all by your lonesome?"

Eliza nodded as she fished in her saddle-bag for the meager money she kept for such emergencies. "It's not so bad. Gives a person time to think."

"Wouldn't like one of my girls or my wife tearing all over the countryside, but you seem to have a good head on your shoulders. Many a fool would have just kept on going. At least you know how to care for your animal."

Eliza resumed riding toward Butte, passing along the same way as before. She rode a couple of extra hours, and spent the night under the stars, thinking more about her life than just the shooting stars above.

The following morning, she took her time about hitting the trail again, but her timing wasn't right when she passed by the mine. And so she headed on home on a hired horse, to return to the house that she so desperately wanted to leave.

And so, Eliza rode circuits that entire first season, until the snows fell in October.

Every Sunday she was in Butte even before it snowed, Paul would come into town or she might ride up to his cabin. It was a courtship that progressed nice and steady. But the lie about her age nagged at her. Somewhere in the depths of that first winter, she came clean.

"Paul, I have something to tell you."

He heard the change in her tone, the seriousness behind her words. He turned in her direction and waited.

"I'm listening."

"I lied to you about my age. There's no easy way around it. I was sixteen when I first met you. I'm seventeen now."

His eyebrows shot up. "Well! No wonder Mrs. Jenkins wasn't any too pleased. She obviously had a better idea of some details than I did!"

Then he laughed. "I guess it doesn't really matter much. But I'd have to say that I'm definitely too old for you."

"How do you figure? I was always going to be seventeen at some point, and you haven't had a birthday yet. A six- or a seven-year difference doesn't sound that radically different to me!"

He smiled at her. "I was just seeing if you could do math as well."

Ready to throw the book in her hand at him, she didn't want to hurt the book or its pages.

"I can do math," she laughed. "I can do math."

Somewhere in the Montana Territory, 1882
Eliza slept under the table after having spent a pleasant night with people she now knew to be Emily and Roy Christiansen. They made her as comfortable as they could. Under that table she was warm and dry, and that was saying something. They all rose at first morning light.

"Well," Emily said, "it's sure been nice having you. Sometimes it gets a bit lonely out here. You think you'll be passing this way again?"

Eliza shook her head. "This is supposed to be my last circuit. I'm getting married next month. Then my name will be Eliza Wilkins. My husband-to-be is a superintendent at one of the mines on the road between Butte and Deer Lodge. If you come that way, please ask for us. We'd be mighty happy to see you."

"Think you'll miss riding on the range?" Roy asked.

"Probably. There's something about the wind in my hair and the openness. Of course, I've learned along the way that it is certainly a chancy prospect that can go either way."

And they all laughed in agreement, knowing the Montana wind and weather could turn harsh and cutting, in no time flat.

EPILOGUE

Eliza went on to become Mrs. Wilkins, a wife who no longer rode any of the circuits, although secretly she missed it. Her husband didn't forbid her from making the journeys, nor did he discourage her pursuits. It was just that she found she didn't like to leave her own home, and the company of her husband.

There was, she figured, a time and place for everything.

And in 1890, Butte was in the exalted process of opening its first public library. Although the Wilkinses didn't exactly need the income, when the position of librarian was offered to Eliza, she leapt at the chance.

"Normally it's a man who holds that position," Mr. Thompson told her at the time, "but by all accounts, you've earned the right."

And so, she had.

She thought about it all the same and

came up with only one conclusion. It never did anyone any good to play it shy, not where opportunity or books were concerned.

ABOUT THE AUTHOR

Randi Samuelson-Brown is originally from Golden, Colorado, but now lives in Denver. She is the author of *The Beaten Territory* and *The Bad Old Days of Colorado: Untold Stories of the Wild West* and is a contributor to *The Spoilt Quilt Anthology.*

■ ■ ■ ■

The Cowboy, the Librarian, and the Broomsman

MARK WARREN

■ ■ ■ ■

Lyle Hardiman can be forgiven his first veer into the new community library at Burnt Creek. It was a simple mistake. But I will wager his grand entrance into that humble facility will not likely be forgotten by those who witnessed it. The one-room book depository had been tacked on to the back of the schoolhouse, which made sense, but *what* — everyone in the room wanted to know — had possessed Lyle to meander off course into that out-of-the-way place and, with spurs ringing, actually push through the door and enter . . . with his horse?

Being in search of a book on wildflowers of the Montana prairie, I was among those present on that summer's day to experience the event. We all knew Lyle from his occasional visits into town to buy supplies, which is why all of us in the library wore the same expression of surprise. It was a well-known fact that Lyle Hardiman could not read a lick. The same should be assumed for his horse, I supposed, even though it was an intelligent looking animal.

Like Lyle, most cowhands of that time were illiterate, and few aspired to the rarefied status of deciphering the written word. There are a couple of plausible arguments for that. Listening to a story around a campfire or over a cigar in the bunkhouse seemed a lot easier than struggling through all those scratchy markings on a stack of papers. Plus, absorbing a tale by ear carried the advantage of the storyteller's carefully applied dramatics: like those whispery moments of suspense that seductively draw the listener in . . . or surprise gunshots rendered by explosive sounds from the mouth . . . or poignant pauses that allow the time to digest what had just transpired in the story or what might happen next.

What a lot of literate folks don't understand is that words have a "look" about them. For example, most of the unschooled range hands I'd met were readily able to recognize the word "saloon." As Lyle would explain to me later, it was those double "o's" in the name. He said they were like a pair of eyeballs gawking at a passerby, convincing him to stroll inside from the heat or the cold for a look-see. And to the left of those "o's" was that tall "l" extending upward like a schoolboy's raised hand, getting a man's attention. That word "saloon" fairly called out: *Hey! Look over here!* Pair those identifying points with the fact that the sign was hanging on the false front of a noisy building with a pair of swinging batwing doors, and it was a sure thing.

"Doctor" is another revealing word, Lyle would further educate me. Inside that word you've got the double "o's" again — those same eyeballs — but this time they are separated by a horseshoe shape and a small cross. That would, of course, refer to the "c" and the "t." All of which bring to mind a man kicked between the eyes by a shod mule, the injury so rattling that he's already considering a modest crucifix for his grave marker. Such a man would have urgent need of a doctor and would be able to find one by a shingle so-named.

The "look of a word" might seem a trivial thing to a school-educated man who can read and write, but, to men like Lyle, learning the internal geography of a printed word was often a necessity. From what Lyle would tell me, such a crude technique of reading was probably a natural step for men who were fluent in the symbolic brands burned into the rumps of cattle. There were, at least, similarities in the two methods of communication.

You might see where I'm headed with all this. Take a close look at "library" and consider how the word bears a strong resemblance to "livery." Both begin with that "l" standing tall. For "livery," that raised arm represents a bronc-buster's free limb flailing high in the air as he hangs on for dear life. At the back end of the word, the "y" hangs down like the tangle-free tail of a freshly combed quarter horse. In both words the jumble of letters in between first and last is fairly unremarkable, just taking up space.

So, there Lyle stood just inside the library door, his eyes shaded by his broad-brimmed hat, his Colt pistol strapped to his hip, his plaid shirt patched with three different colors of material, his denim trousers worn down to the softness of chamois, and his dusty boots looking like they had walked down to Mexico and back. With one hand on the cheek strap of his buckskin mare's bridle, Lyle stared at all of us, probably wondering why a group of Burnt Creek citizens had decided to read together inside some horse stalls made up of bookshelves. Under the circumstances, he acquitted himself well, never betraying any confusion

or embarrassment. It was generally understood that cowboys were adept at wearing
stoic masks in almost any situation that
arose, and sitting in the library that day I
saw proof of that. Lyle's eyes scanned the
room as if he were idly checking the horizon
for incoming weather out on the prairie.

My first guess was this: Lyle was following through on some bet he had lost across
the street at the North Star Saloon. But
after standing in the threshold half a minute,
he still had not cracked a grin. I started to
rise from my chair to let him know, privately,
that animals were not allowed in the library.
Not that I had any problem with his handsome mare. I only wanted to spare the
cowboy any humiliation or ordinance fine.
No sooner had I pushed back my chair than
I was saved the trouble when the new librarian intervened. That was when my second
guess about Lyle's unexpected arrival occurred to me. This could be about the librarian.

Rebecca Spark was something to behold.
Her hair was yellow as a field of buttercups
and her eyes like slate full moons that shone
softly from an inner light. This fetching
countenance was the kind that pulled a man
from across the street for a better look. But
to hear her talk, that same man might cross

the Montana Territory just to partake of the melody in her sweet voice. She was shy to the extreme and inclined to speak in a librarian's whisper, even out on the street. When you asked her a question, it seemed she could shed light on any topic under the Montana sky. Typically, she shrugged off such compliments with a charming modesty and simply attributed her range of knowledge to reading books.

"I *am* a librarian, after all," she would say ever so quietly and with a cute little twist of a smile. "A cook samples her recipes and a milliner tries on the hats she makes, so —" She liked to leave her sentences unfinished like that. It made the other person in the conversation feel important and intelligent, as if the unspoken conclusion was a secret kept by both parties.

As this erudite lady of letters stepped before Lyle, the cowboy dutifully removed his hat and swept it out to his side in much the way I imagined General Lee bowed to Grant at Appomattox. With Lyle standing so close to Miss Spark, I noticed for the first time the chiseled good looks in his face. This was strange, as I had known Lyle for over three years. Now that I studied him, his alert eyes and weathered skin suggested a man truly engaged with the world, especially when compared to someone like me, a bald-headed broomsman who swept the floors of a lawyer's office, a bakery, two saloons, the marshal's cellblock, and a millinery. All I did, it seems, was to transfer dust from one place to another. Lyle had probably risen before dawn and done more sensible work out on the range than all of us in the library combined.

On that morning it was all males spread out among the reading tables. At Lyle's entrance, the room had gone quiet as a tomb. There was not even the sound of a page turning. I leaned forward, trying to hear the words spoken between the two at the door.

"Pleased to have you visit," the librarian said, her voice soft as an evening breeze stirring the leaves of a summer cottonwood. "I am Miss Rebecca Spark."

I immediately racked my brain, trying to remember if she had afforded *me* such an intimate welcome upon my first visit.

"Lyle Hardiman, ma'am," said Lyle, concentrating on the toes of his boots. He poked a thumb over one shoulder. "We work over at the Rocking J Ranch coupla miles up the river."

"We?" Miss Spark asked.

He poked the thumb again, this time at

the horse. "Me and Shep." When he brought up his eyes, he offered a shy smile of apology. "Guess we didn' realize 'xactly where we was. Don't look like any kind o' place for a horse, do it?"

"Well," Rebecca Spark said, waving away any misunderstanding, "you are both most welcome." As if expecting formal introductions, she turned to the buckskin with an attentive smile.

You would have thought the animal had nudged him the way Lyle looked back quickly at the mare. "This here's Shep," he offered. "We been partnered up a long time."

"Well," said Rebecca, "you two will be happy to know I have received seven new hitching rings the blacksmith made for the front of the building. Perhaps Shep would be proud to be our first customer, so to speak." At this pronouncement, Miss Spark produced a winsome smile, the kind that could have launched a thousand Sheps from the livery. She swept a hand toward us readers. "I was going to ask some of the patrons to install a few."

Without knowing I would do it, I shot my hand toward the ceiling like a bolt of lightning in reverse. I looked around at the others. Their arms were vertical, too. We

134

looked like the fence posts of a poorly designed paddock before the rails are nailed on. I racked my brain again but could remember no mention of hitching rings from Rebecca Spark.

Lyle pursed his lips and slowly began to nod. "I reckon I could attach one for you. I'll just need a few tools." He nodded toward the grove of vertical arms standing tall around the tables. "Looks like these fine boys might wanna contribute some, too."

That right there was Lyle Hardiman down to the bone. Even if I had not already liked the man, I would have followed him into battle for this grand gesture of generosity.

"Very kind of you," Miss Spark said. "I can bring out a bowl of water for Shep. And I should have a carrot packed in my lunch." She flattened her palms together under her chin and performed a silent clapping motion, her hands fluttering like a dainty butterfly. Her smile went off the charts. "It will be like a grand opening for our equine visitors." Again, she gestured toward the room. "And when you are ready to browse the shelves, I'll be happy to help you find something you might enjoy."

"Yes, ma'am," Lyle said, gracious as ever but clearly not grasping her meaning.

By this point in my eavesdropping, I was

surprised to feel a little flame of envy crackling at the center of my chest. A bowl of water? A carrot? Nowhere in my brief conversations with the new librarian had such complimentary refreshments been proffered.

I tried to get a hold of myself. Lyle Hardiman and Rebecca Spark were just talking, for heaven's sake, but the two of them standing there together in the doorway made quite a picture. Instinctively, I looked around to see if anyone had noticed my juvenile reaction. Every man there sat mouth agape, eyes wistful and vulnerable, one ear cocked forward to listen, and one arm still raised stiffly in the air. It seemed to me an epidemic of jealously had spread through the reading room.

When Lyle backed his horse out the door, he did his best to minimize the ringing of his spurs and the clopping of hooves on wood, but, compared to the customary quiet of the library, it was like the sound of a pots and pans peddler overturning his wagon. Miss Spark appeared not to notice as she retreated behind her checkout counter and began rummaging through her lunch basket. Because I was already standing, I felt compelled to go somewhere, so I ambled out the door to find Lyle parking his mare on the honor system in the alleyway. When he had finished up ordering the mare to stay put, he took off his gun belt, buckled it into a loop, and hung it from the pommel of his saddle. This he topped off with his wide-brimmed hat, exposing the thick curly locks of his ink-black hair. When he saw me he smiled.

"Guess I'm a little addle-headed today, Walter," he laughed. "I thought maybe Cal Grissom had moved his livery up here." He squinted at the sign above the door. "What is this, a bookstore?"

"It's a library," I said and shrugged at the foibles that all men are destined to endure. "They loan a man a book so he can read it. Then when he finishes, he brings it back so somebody else can have a go at it."

Lyle pursed his lips and looked out over the scrub brush rolling away from the edge of town. The Bitterroots in the distance seemed to hold some special interest for him. Finally, he nodded.

"Lie-bury, you say," he remarked and then shifted his gaze to me. "I heard tell o' one o' them in Missoula, but I figured it to be connected to a graveyard." He shrugged with a cant of his head. "You know . . . you *lie* down . . . they *bury* you. *Lie-bury.*" He laughed this off with a shake of his head and then made a thorough inspection of me from boots to bald head. "So, how's the sweepin' bus'ness, Walter? You got the mornin' off?"

"I finished up early at the law office," I explained. "I came by here to find a book about wildflowers. I've been thinking about expanding my occupational range to include tour guiding. I could offer it to the stage-coach passengers when they have to lay over here for a few hours."

From behind his stoic mask, Lyle studied me as if I had told him I was going to run off to live with a family of antelope. I felt bad about lying to him. I had no intention of being a tour guide. I wanted to learn the names of flowers simply because Rebecca Spark always kept a fresh batch of local blooms in a vase of water on her desk. I wanted mightily to impress her with my knowledge of the colors that popped out on the prairie. It would give us something to talk about.

"Say," Lyle said, snapping me out of my botanical reverie, "do you reckon we could borrow a drill and a turnscrew from the far-rier?"

Before I could answer, the door opened and Rebecca Spark emerged from the build-ing carrying a blue porcelain bowl of water in both hands. Behind her came two men toting a wooden crate, which they set down on a few tufts of grass as if the box were a newborn baby. Lyle leaned over the contents and then nodded his approval.

"Looks like you're runnin' ahead o' the pack, ma'am. This's ever'thin' we'll need. Walter and I can mount a ring for you in no time."

Happy to be included in this impromptu team of hitching ring specialists, I knelt to inspect the crate. The bottom was filled with hefty iron rings attached on a swivel to their mounting plates. Lying on top were a crank-drill, various metal bits and screws loose in a jar, and a turnscrew with a walnut handle. When I looked up I discovered that a dozen more volunteers had joined us from the reading room.

"You're all so kind," Rebecca Spark whispered in her unassuming way.

Walking as quietly as a cat, she carried the bowl across the alley and set it before Lyle's horse. She might have been Perceval delivering the Holy Grail to Arthur. Then, slipping a slender carrot from a fold in her dress, she offered the treat to the mare, who lipped it from her hand and began a rhythmic dedication of hollow crunches. For a full minute she watched as the animal chewed, both she and the mare in obvious delight.

Demurely lowering her eyelids, Miss Spark turned and went back inside to oversee her realm of literature, but not before pausing to smile back at me. In that moment, the blood in my veins turned airy and light, like the foamy head on a freshly tapped beer. She seemed to be smiling at my bald head, of all things, until I realized that Lyle, who stood a good four inches taller than I, was positioned right behind me.

Lyle and I attached the first ring in under three minutes and passed on the tools to the other boys awaiting their turn at hitching ring immortality. Lyle gave me a pat on the back and walked to his horse, who was lapping water from the librarian's bowl.

"Where are you off to?" I said.

Lyle took up the reins of the buckskin and began walking her out the alley. "To the livery." He patted the mare's neck much the way he had done to me. "This ol' girl is due some sweet grain and seasoned hay, and I got some bus'ness to tend to in town."

"You're not even going to tie your horse to the ring we put up? It was supposed to be a grand opening, remember?"

Lyle stopped, turned, tilted his head to one side, and gave me an amused look.

"Walter, you know I can't read the first word in a book." He nodded toward the building. "A man like me's got no bus'ness in there." He lifted his hat from the pommel, pushed it onto his head in a practiced motion, and stroked the long muscles of his mare's neck. "And as for Shep, I don't reckon it matters much to a horse where it gets tied up. Ask me, a horse would rather be known for its speed than for its hitchin' knot."

I probably should have employed the cowboy's poker face for the occasion, but I frowned at him. I couldn't help myself. I had seen the way Rebecca Spark had smiled at him. And, besides, I was not a cowboy. A broomsman doesn't have a need for such stoicism.

"Lyle," I said in my most earnest and personable manner, "I think you have arrived at a crossroads in your life. As I see it, a crucial path has opened up for you."

Lyle smiled and narrowed his eyes. "You're not turnin' preacher on me, are you, Walter?" He pointed with his chin toward the front of the building. "Say, would you do me the favor o' returnin' that water bowl to the lie-bury lady?"

I turned to see the bowl being passed around the crowd at the hitching rings.

Each man sipped from it, nodded once, and then reverentially passed it to a neighbor. It was like a communion of lost souls, each trying to align itself somehow with the pristine spirit of Rebecca Spark.

"Lyle," I said, leaning in closer to drive home my point, "you need to take this moment seriously. Life does not often provide a little *spark* for a man to fan into flames. You should —"

"Hold on there, Walter," he interrupted in his friendly way. He flattened a palm and eased it toward my chest without actually touching me. "I gotta sense o' where you're headin' with all this. Seems to me there's a *spark* right here that's aw-ready broke out into quite a few flames. I'd just as soon not get too close to this fire, if you catch my meanin'."

I watched him lead his horse down the street toward Grissom's Livery, Lyle walking like a man without a care in the world. He seemed to have no idea that he had piqued the interest of the most sought-after single woman in the village. I suppose it was this innocence of Lyle's that endeared him so to me. You had to admire a man who could so fluidly decide which issues should involve him and which not.

I looked back down the alley, past the

cluster of men spit-polishing the ring plates with the cuffs of their shirtsleeves, beyond the flat prairie to the palisade of mountains that had captivated Lyle for a few precious heartbeats. Like every other Montanan I knew, I had committed my share of selfish deeds and petty offenses toward my fellow man. But peering out at the Bitterroots, I felt a warm glow of goodness swell inside my chest and begin to radiate from me. It was like heat lifting off my skin. I actually got a little chilled, and here it was the first day of July.

That was the moment I — the brooms-man of Burnt Creek — decided to dedicate myself to Lyle Hardiman's romance with Rebecca Spark. I was convinced it was meant to be. This mission was the most uplifting experience of my life, so far.

"Doing for others, does for you in the eyes of God," I said aloud to the far horizon, reciting my late mother's favorite adage.

Deep down, I knew that my *doing* for Lyle would *do* nothing for me and my ambitions with Rebecca Spark. But that seemed to matter no more. This was a higher calling. I was about to embark on a task that was more important than Walter Wren. I stepped before the new glass panes of the library window and checked my reflection, half-expecting to see some kind of aura or halo hovering around me. The only illumination visible was the July sun shining off the top of my bald head.

When I stepped back into the shade of the library's reading room, every man at the tables had fixed his worried eyes on the front desk, where Miss Spark flipped through the pages of a large reference book. She appeared a little flustered, which was something new to us boys. Her usual angelic presence was what anchored us to a small claim on stability and serenity and even hope, but her present state suggested that all was not right with the world. I dared to tiptoe over to the counter.

"Here's your bowl, Miss Spark," I said, placing the ceramic piece carefully on the polished wood. "Can I be of any help?"

Exhaling a long, whispery sigh, she placed her hands flat on the open tome as if checking the book for a pulse. She graced me with the kind of beatific smile that could inspire a man to climb to the highest peak of the Bitterroots in his bare feet. Tilting her head to one side, she managed a grateful smile.

"Thank you, Mr. Sparrow, but —"

"It's 'Wren,' ma'am. 'Walter Wren.' "

A blush of red darkened her face. Closing

her eyes, Rebecca Spark performed an endearing little shake of the head.

"Of course, I'm sorry, Mr. Wren."

"You may as well call me 'Walter,' ma'am. Everybody else does."

She nodded, took in a deep breath, and let go with another sibilant sigh as she returned her gaze to the book. "I want to dress up the library a little," she explained. "Because the stagecoach passengers often visit here during their layover, I had an idea to hang up some pictures of Burnt Creek to chronicle its history. I thought a plaque would be nice. Something that told the story of our community." She opened her delicate hand toward the book. "But this *History of the Montana Territory* barely mentions our town. There's really nothing in the text but a reference to a fight between soldiers and the Indians who had once occupied the flatlands inside the bend of the creek." When she looked up at me, her silver-gray eyes were like two freshly minted coins held up before a candle flame. "I don't even know how Burnt Creek got its name. Do you?"

I'd never even considered that. It *was* an odd name, now that I thought about it. I mean, how do you burn a creek?

Miss Spark leaned a little closer and

145

lowered her already whispery voice. "It seems to be an oxymoron," she confided.

I chewed on my lip for a moment, trying to think of an intelligent reply. Oxymorons had always fascinated me. Why had this one never occurred to me? I racked my brain for any myth or legend I might have heard and forgotten about the naming of Burnt Creek, but nothing came to mind. I turned to face the men behind me, all of whom seemed to be waiting for my question.

"Any of you boys know how Burnt Creek got its name?"

Every face compressed into a frown. Then, in unison, they shook their heads as if they had practiced the maneuver for weeks with a coach. When I turned back to Rebecca Spark, I smiled my own apology. I had no answer. But I had an idea.

I caught up with Lyle again in the afternoon, just as I finished whisking out the dust from the North Star. He was leaning both elbows on the bar and idly staring down into a mug of beer. After putting away my broom, I eased up next to him and ordered a cold one, positioning myself strategically for the plan I'd been conjuring up all through my work.

"Well, howdy again, Walter," he said in his

friendly way. "Did those boys manage to mount those rings in a straight line?"

I offered my doubtful face. "No, but they justified it by saying the varied heights could accommodate all manner of animals: from big Percherons and Morgans down to mustangs and the occasional Shetland pony. Miss Spark thought it improved the building. She claimed it added 'some character.' "

Lyle made a dry laugh through his nose and sipped his beer. "Well, I reckon that fits purty tight with a *lie-bury.* Ain't most o' them books about 'some char'cter'?"

I laughed outright. "That's a good one, Lyle."

When Arthur Smoot, the bartender, brought my beer, I raised it as a toast to Lyle. "I needed that laugh, old buddy. This has been a hard day, everybody complaining about all the dust of midsummer." I took a sip and set aside the mug. Belatedly, Lyle completed his half of the toast and drank to the expungement of my troubles.

Like an actor on a stage, I very casually slipped a folded paper from my trouser pocket and began flattening it out on the countertop. It was nothing more than a list of my sweeping jobs for the next week, but Lyle could not know that. Seemingly engrossed in the handwriting scrawled across the page, I said nothing for a full minute. As I folded the paper and stored it away, I tried for a subtle laugh deep in my chest.

"Lord, but that's the best medicine a man could ever ask for. Every time I read it, it's like a cool mountain spring rising up inside me, refreshing me from my shiny pate down to my toes."

Lyle faced me and leaned on just one elbow now. "Well, read it to me, and let's see if it has the same effect on me."

I gave Lyle the most pained expression I could muster. "Well, see, that's the thing," I explained. "I can't say the words out loud. Nobody can. That was the terms I agreed to."

" 'Agreed to' with who?" he asked.

I settled in for the whopper I had polished up over the last few hours. "Was a Blackfeet medicine woman who'd set up shop outside Fort Peck a few summers ago. It was the year my dear mama died." I averted my eyes slightly when I felt tears starting to cloud my vision. I had not counted on this, but I welcomed such a convincing stage prop for my performance. I shook my head at the wondrous memory I was fabricating. "That old Blackfeet woman couldn't even say the words herself, which is why she wrote them down for me. She said any man who formed

148

the words on his lips would anger the spirits of the Thunder Gods and the result of that would be to bring some kind of calamity down upon the speaker."

Lyle leaned back to gulp the rest of his beer. By the look of his eyes over the mug, I could see that I had piqued his interest.

"Long as I read the words quiet to myself," I continued, "it works just fine. The incantation just turns my heart into an eagle who's soaring high over the mountains. There's nothing like it, Lyle. Whenever I read it, my troubles just slide off my back like water off a duck's feathers."

Lyle set down his beer mug without so much as a sound. Pursing his lips, he stared out the door in the direction of the Bitterroots.

"Soarin' eagles and drippin' ducks. Sounds like some special words you got there, Walter." He intoned the comment as though this might be his parting line on the subject, and so I scrambled for another prompt to goad him on. While I was straining for a solution, he added these magic words. "Sure wish I could partake of 'em. Ever' man has a need to get shed of his troubles now and then."

"Well, what about this, Lyle? What if you learned how to read?"

Lyle smiled and looked down into his empty mug as he rotated it by increments with his thumb and forefinger. "I don' reckon I could sit in a schoolroom with a bunch o' kids, Walter. I'm just too old for that."

"You could take private lessons," I suggested. "It would be just you and a teacher."

He looked at me with one eye squinted. "Well, who would that be? I hope you ain't thinkin' about Miss Addie 'the Peacock' Lipstock. Some o' the schoolboys tell me she's gotta be kin to the Devil."

To allay his fears, I raised both my hands, palms outward. "Heavens no! I wouldn't wish that fuss-bucket schoolmarm on my worst enemy. But I could ask around and maybe find you a proper educator. What would you say to that?"

Lyle kept up turning that mug like clockwork. A half minute went by, then the mug went still and a concerned look stiffened his face.

"Well, how much do you figure it would cost me?" he asked.

I pretended to think about it as I watched two men at a back table engage in a game of cards. It looked like stud poker they were playing, but I was betting there was more guile and maneuvering going on at the bar

150

than any of the gambling tables in the establishment.

"Maybe I can arrange a barter," I suggested. "You could give something back for the lessons."

Lyle lifted his arms from his sides and looked down at himself from boots to belt buckle. "What would I have to trade?" he said, his eyes beseeching me for an answer.

This was just the kind of response that made me admire Lyle Hardiman. Here was a man who could maneuver a horse through a thick grove of yucca without so much as a scratch to chaps or horseflesh. He could tie more kinds of knots than a spider. Using only his pocketknife, he had converted small chunks of juniper into animal carvings that could have sold in the gift shop at the stage depot. I'd seen them: buffalo, mustang, beaver, eagle. Lyle knew the names of trees, shrubs, vines, and weeds . . . and how to use them the way the Indians did. I had no doubt Lyle could have expounded at length on every blossom in Rebecca Spark's flower vase.

"Lyle," I said, leaning in close and lowering my voice, "I believe your tangible assets are too numerous to list. In addition to those, you have some intangibles that might be invaluable."

He gave me the one-eyed squint, this time with the other eye. "What's that mean?"

"It means you know a lot about this territory that others don't. You are the only native Montanan I've met in this town. The way I heard it, most of the people of Burnt Creek were drawn here by the gold discovered over at Deer Lodge. Of course, the ones who struck it rich took their fortunes and headed off to places where they could spend it — San Francisco, Denver, or Salt Lake. The ones who went bust just stayed on and tried to get absorbed into some kind of life that didn't involve mining."

Lyle laughed. "Well, that's true. I was born right down there by the creek on a small potato farm." He raised an arm and pointed southwest through the building. I had no doubt that his aim was as true as a surveyor's line. "You know," he continued, "Burnt Creek was settled long b'fore all that gold business. But it took that strike and that flood of dream-broke miners who shuffled in here with their tails b'tween their legs to earn us a dot on the map."

Listening to Lyle reminisce over the early days of Burnt Creek pumped me up with hope for my plan. "So, you know how our town got its name?"

"Sure," he answered, as if I had asked him

at which end of a steer the horns are mounted. "You see there was —"

"Lyle," I interrupted as politely as I could. Arthur Smoot, polishing the countertop with a rag, was sidling toward us, as if he might edge in on our conversation. Wanting Lyle to be the only person in town to hold the secret of Burnt Creek's naming, I quickly changed the subject. "How in the world did you become a cowboy, Lyle?"

The bartender yawned and went back to his work with the rag. He'd probably heard a hundred versions of how-I-got-to-be-a-cowboy stories.

"Well," Lyle began pleasantly, always adaptable about changing directions in a conversation. "When the cattle ind'stry found good grass here, I was about twelve or thirteen. I'd already forged a strong relationship with horses. I'd corralled a few wild mustangs and trained 'em by my own methods. Purty soon, before I knew it, I earned my way to foreman at the Circle Q. Worked for the Q about four years."

When he ordered another beer and appeared absorbed by the card games in progress in the room, I had to prod him on to continue. "Then what?" I said.

Lyle just shrugged.

"He disappeared . . . that's what," the

bartender butted in, gloating as if he had solved the ancient riddle of the Sphinx.

I turned to Lyle for confirmation. He only shrugged again.

"Where did you go?" I asked.

Lyle performed a third shrug, which I knew to be a cowboy's limit. I would ask no more.

I'd heard the rumors that he had scouted for the army under Mackenzie in Texas and then later for Carrington in Wyoming. Apparently, he had amassed quite a reputation. When he returned to Burnt Creek seven years later, he'd joined the Rocking J Ranch up on the Clark Fork. One of the hands who worked there once told me you could drop a burlap sack over Lyle's head, sequester him in a dark cave, spin him around a few times, and he could still point out true north by the casual lift of a finger. I had overheard Mr. Judd Jackson, owner of the Rocking J, tell the lawyer I swept for about how Lyle had located a new well site by using a Y-shaped willow wand. The well paid out in full and remains the primary water source for the ranch to this day.

"How'd we get on this subject, anyway?" Lyle chuckled. "I thought we were tryin' to figure out what I had to barter with for my readin' lessons."

I gave Lyle my most confident smile. "Why don't you let me figure that out once I secure a teacher who might be interested."

He leaned in closer and studied my face. "How'd you learn your letters, Walter? Maybe you oughta be the one to teach me."

This caught me by surprise, and I must say I was flattered. After scrambling to think up a reason why I would not be a good candidate, I shook my head ruefully.

"I ought not be the one to teach you, Lyle. I've been diagnosed with a condition called 'reader's block.' They say it's contagious."

"Well, dang!" Lyle said. "That don't sound good. What's it like?"

I thought for a moment, trying to put my fabrication into terms that might be familiar to him. "Imagine you're galloping along out on the range . . . just doing your job and rounding up livestock . . . and suddenly this big lasso comes whipping down out of the sky and the loop falls over both you and your horse. Then . . . wham!" I smacked my fist into the open palm of my other hand. "You and your horse are frozen in time . . . sitting stock-still like a tintype of yourself on horseback. Meanwhile the world keeps going on around you . . . cattle moving on . . . the wind blowing in the trees . . . the river gurgling . . . and your crew riding on ahead with the herd."

I watched him try to process this information. The frown he wore cut three deep creases into his forehead.

"That's the way it happens," I said. "I'll just be reading along and then — wham!" I punched my fist into my hand again. "I'll get stuck in the middle of a sentence and that's it for the rest of the day." Gravely, I shook my head. "I'd hate to pass that on to you, Lyle. It would sure put a sag in your spirits, far as reading goes." I tried for a well-meaning smile. "But look . . . enough about my problems. Let me think a while about a good teacher. How long will you be in town?"

"Got today and tomorrow off," he said. "Thought I'd shoot the moon and pony up for a bath and a hotel bed tonight. It's been a while for both."

"So, I can find you at the Montanan?"

He nodded and winked. "Already paid the bill."

The plan that hatched in my head kept me busy for the next hour. The maid who swept out the hotel owed me a favor, as I had filled in for her a couple of weeks when her husband had come down with a bad case of Rocky Mountain Hives. On the sly she was able to slip me a sheet of hotel stationery. Upon this I wrote a beautifully penned invitation to Rebecca Spark and had the telegraph boy deliver it to the library on one of his runs.

Meanwhile, at the back door of the hotel restaurant, I parleyed with the head cook. This was the place where all the stray dogs in the village gathered to check out the garbage bins every night. Food scraps from the restaurant were, of course, a delicacy to the loose curs of Burnt Creek. This was a growing problem for the staff, who had to clean up a royal mess each morning. Flaunting my reputation as the town's leading authority on cleanup, I offered my services to solve his problem in exchange for a table reservation for three that night. Using the money I had been saving for a Montgomery Ward #10 Deluxe Stiff-Bristle Broom, I prepaid for the best meal on the menu and gave strict instructions for a candlelight dinner at their most private table.

With everything set into motion, I ran back to the North Star just in time to see Lyle making his exit from a poker game with three other cowboys. I was nearly breathless from my dash up the street, and I used this condition to good effect for my announcement to Lyle.

"Did you hear the good news?" I said, gasping for air.

Lyle slanted his eyebrows with a question. "Somebody found a cure for reader's block?"

I took three big breaths to recover, and then I put on a celebratory smile. "You won the Librarian's Lottery! They're throwing a special dinner banquet for you at the hotel! Free of charge!"

Lyle frowned and laughed at the same time. "Well, that don't hardly seem right. I didn' throw in my name for any lottery."

"It's automatic," I explained. "Anybody who walks through the library door gets his name put in the hat. Danged if you didn't win it!"

He slapped his hat onto his head and seesawed the brim up and down a few times as he took in this news. "A banquet, by golly. Are you goin'?"

"Of course, I'm going! I wouldn't miss it!"

Lyle looked thoughtful. "So, what do I gotta do?"

"Go take that bath, put on some clean clothes, and show up at the restaurant at seven sharp."

"And that's it?" he said.

"That's it," I affirmed.

158

We walked out of the saloon together, and once again I watched Lyle Hardiman traipse off down the street in his insouciant way. It was as if he knew better than to hurry. Mama had always taught me that hurrying is when you start missing the little things in your day. Lyle was not going to be denied one moment in enjoying his life. I admired him even more for so effortlessly embracing that ethic, and that seemed like a validation for all that I was doing for him. He deserved a woman as wonderful as Rebecca Spark.

At ten minutes to seven I parked myself in a chair next to the hotel desk and watched customers clop down the stairs, cross the carpeted lobby, and pass through the entrance to the dining room. A few of the more well-to-do townsfolk came in from the street and did the same, several asking me if I was now sweeping the hotel.

"No," I replied, a little giddy and unable to restrain myself. "Mostly I'm helping sweep people off their feet now." I got some strange looks over that comment. The mayor even picked up one foot and inspected the bottom of his shoe.

At five till the hour Lyle — hatless and spurless and whistling a lively tune — came down the stairs in his supple gait. He appeared more curious than excited as he approached me.

"Well, how do I look? Never dressed for a lottery banquet b'fore."

I stood and looked him over. "You look splendid," I said.

And he did. He had dampened his dark hair and combed it with a part as straight as an irrigation ditch. His shirt was solid blue — like a cloudless Montana sky — without any patches and buttoned up all the way to the lump in his muscular throat. The denim trousers he had changed into appeared to have endured less mileage in the saddle than his other pair. The boots were the same he always wore, but it was evident he had applied saddle soap, for the old leather boots shone as if they'd been left outside on a winter night to be covered by a rime of ice. A faint scent of pine sap soap lifted off his body like a message of good intentions. In short, Lyle looked at his best.

Together we entered the restaurant, where I spotted an empty back table glowing with candlelight and adorned by a bowl of assorted prairie flowers. That lone table sat waiting like an illuminated island beckoning from a dark sea. The hostess approached us with a smile.

"Good evening, gentlemen. Two?"

Lyle stood like a fence post as he looked around at the crowd. He was, no doubt, impressed that the mayor had turned out for his award banquet.

"That's our special table right there," I told the woman as I pointed.

"Oh, you're Mr. Eagle?"

"It's 'Wren,' " I corrected.

She covered her mouth with a fist and giggled. "I'm so sorry, Mr. Wren," she said. "I got mixed up." She was smiling at my bald head, and I knew exactly how that "eagle" slipup had occurred. After leading the way to the beautifully set table bordered by three chairs, she pointed to a wall on which the day's menu was posted. "May I recommend the sage hen tonight, gentlemen?"

"I've already preordered and prepaid," I explained. "The cook knows what to do."

"Very good, sir," she said and took her departure when another customer appeared at the entrance. I swept my hand toward the middle chair that faced the room.

"This is the seat of honor, Lyle. It's for you."

As Lyle settled in, I saw the hostess greet Rebecca Spark across the room. It looked like fate was working overtime tonight, because Rebecca wore a sky blue dress that was a near-perfect match to Lyle's shirt. She had produced a paper, which she unfolded and held before her for the receptionist to read. Raising my hand high, I got the librarian's attention and she began weaving through the tables toward us. I sidestepped to position myself right in front of Lyle.

"What a splendid turnout," Miss Spark said, smiling at the crowded room and then bringing around that smile to bear upon me. "I had no idea so many people would be interested."

When I stepped aside to pull out a chair for her, Rebecca Spark's smile transformed into a complicated mix of surprise, delight, and reticence. She and Lyle stared at one another with a powerful connection. I imagined a telegraph wire stretched taut between their heads, and I wondered what silent message was being tapped out in the noisy room.

Thankfully, Lyle's natural instincts of chivalry kicked in. Standing, he made a motion to take off his hat, which segued into a deft stroke across his hair when he realized his mistake.

"Good evening, Mr. Hardiman," Rebecca Spark said demurely. When she sat, I snugged her chair closer to the table and took the seat across from her. She stared down at her hands on the white tablecloth. Lyle sat down and stared at her.

I felt pretty proud about what I had accomplished. Seeing the two of them wearing blue and sitting together in candlelight brought a lump to my throat. This evening surely marked a high point for me. There was no doubt I was *doing* for others, and it affected me just the way Mama said it would.

"So you're interested in history, too?" Rebecca Spark said to Lyle, no doubt trying to fire up a little conversation.

Before Lyle could answer, I leaned forward with my fingertips pressed into the tabletop. "You'll be excited to learn, Miss Spark, that Lyle was born in Burnt Creek. With the last generation gone, he goes back farther than anyone else living in these parts." I pointed out the side window. "He was born right down at the creek on a small farm." Lyle nodded toward the corner of the room, correcting the aim of my finger. I adjusted accordingly.

Rebecca Spark appeared to light up at this news. Her eyes rivaled the candle at the center of the table. She pressed her hands together under her chin.

"And," I continued, "you'll be happy to

know that Lyle holds the secret to our town's unusual name."

Lyle, a little embarrassed, occupied himself by tucking a corner of his napkin into the front of his collar.

Just as they had in the library, Miss Spark's dainty hands performed a mute and fluttery butterfly-applause beneath her glorious smile. Lyle seemed to loosen up a little. It would be hard for any man not to wax whimsical in the presence of Rebecca Spark's displays of joy. With everyone a little more relaxed, it seemed like an opportune time for Burnt Creek's sweeping man to come clean.

"I have a confession," I began. I reached across the table and picked up the piece of stationery folded next to Miss Spark's silverware. The paper crackled as I opened it, making me think of a jury foreman about to read off a verdict while the people in the courtroom sat on the edge of their seats. Turning the notice around, I held it up for both to see. "I wrote this," I blurted out, trying for a tone of dignity in my admission.

She frowned at my apologetic face. Lyle frowned at the paper.

"Well, what is it?" he said.

Turning the sheet around with a solemnity

that matched the occasion, I began to read aloud. *"'Miss Spark, you are cordially invited to the first assembly of the Burnt Creek Historical Society. We shall discuss the town's inception, its naming, and the exciting chapters of community development that followed. A first-class supper will be included at no cost to those bearing a written invitation. Meet at seven p.m. in the dining room of the Montanan.'"*

Rebecca Spark turned three shades of red. Breaking all gentlemanly protocol, Lyle leaned both elbows on the table and arched one eyebrow at me.

"You're tellin' me you tricked 'er?" he said and hitched his head toward the librarian.

I raised my hand to the height of the candle flame and positioned my thumb and forefinger to show the tiniest gap possible between them. "Maybe just by a broomstraw."

Our female guest seemed to shrink in her chair. "So, there is no Burnt Creek Historical Society?" she inquired.

"Well," I hedged, "not exactly . . . not by that name, anyway." I made a little *voilà* swoop of my hands toward Lyle. "What we do have is Lyle Hardiman."

I remained in that pose as they both stared at me. The sounds of conversations around us made our table seem like a graveyard situated at the edge of a chicken coop.

"And I guess there ain't no lie-bury lottery neither," Lyle mumbled. "Did you pull one on me, too?"

I held up my measuring hand again, this time making the gap two broom-straws. "But when you think about it, Lyle," I argued, "your entrance into the library *was* like a winning ticket for Miss Spark. She needs to know about Burnt Creek's past, and you're just the man to tell her." I gestured toward her. "And you want to learn how to read! With her being an expert on reading and being so patient and kind like she is, she's *your* winning ticket, don't you see? You each need something the other has got. I'm just trying to be the mediator in this horse swap." I looked from one to the other to determine if I was going to walk out of this room in a dignified fashion or if my tail would be curled up under me like a scolded dog.

Rebecca Spark's candlelit eyes turned on Lyle with surprising tenderness. "You really want to learn how to read, Mr. Hardiman?"

Lyle nodded with the certainty of a man who has a firm grip on his ambitions. "Yes, ma'am, I do. Seems to be a lotta books I gotta catch up on." He glanced at me long enough to pass on a furtive wink. "Not to mention some old Blackfeet words I come across." Leaning on his forearms, he cupped each hand around the opposing elbow and canted his head to study Rebecca Spark. "And you really wanna know 'bout Burnt Creek?"

She made that cute little twist of a smile that had brought so much male clientele into the new library. "I do," she said quietly. As those tiny words hung in the air, I could not help but imagine her repeating them at an altar one day. It just warmed my heart for Lyle Hardiman's future. And hers, too.

A waitress brought out two plates, one in each hand. As she hesitated, I pointed at the place settings of my two companions and watched her present two big T-bone steaks, stewed corn, fried potatoes, and cooked greens. Another waitress tilted a coffeepot over the two cups set out.

"Nothing for you?" the first waitress asked me. Lyle and Miss Spark turned, attentive to my answer.

This was my cue. I was no longer needed here. With my Cupid's mission having gotten off to a satisfactory start, I would now let nature take its course. I had one more sweeping job waiting for me at the millinery before I could retire for the night. Pushing back my chair, I started to rise . . . but hesitated.

"Before I take my leave," I said, "I'm wondering if I might hear about the origin of the Burnt Creek name. I've been contemplating on it most of the day, and it's got me curious. Is it an oxymoron, or is there more to it?"

Lyle frowned at me for several seconds before his face relaxed with a revelation. "Ohhh, you must mean Buck Bagwell, who wandered into town by accident back in fifty-eight."

"Who?" Rebecca said, whipping out a notebook and pencil from her carrying purse.

Lyle scrunched up his face and shook his head. "Naw, he didn' have nothin' to do with the naming. Buck was just a big ox of a man who hunted meat for the railroad survey crew."

"How does a man come into town by accident," I asked.

Lyle cut into his steak, forked it up, and spoke around his chewing. "Well, in Buck's case, he was a wide man of narrow intelligence. Not much of a hunter either. He'd struck the trail of something big . . . and heavy . . . something with hooves. He wasn't sure if it was moose or elk or buffalo. They

168

say he followed it for six weeks and some-how the animal kept attracting similar beasts one at a time. The new tracks just seemed to materialize out of nowhere. So he just kept on tracking, planning to bring back even more meat than he had at first estimated. After those six weeks of trailing his quarry, he discovered he'd been travel-ing a big thirty-mile-radius circle and fol-lowing his own tracks, which naturally had multiplied with each circumnavigation. He just slid off his horse here and took on a job as night watchman at the cemetery. That way he didn' have to talk to people, who were always wantin' to hear the story of his huntin' travesty."

Miss Spark scribbled industriously in her book. I marveled at her speed. As Lyle scooped up a forkful of corn, I felt my forehead wrinkle like a plowed field.

"What has this Buck Bagwell story got to do with Burnt Creek?" I asked.

Lyle stopped chewing, surprised. "Like I said . . . nothin'!" He finished demolishing that mouthful, swallowed, and waved his fork in a circle through the air. "He's just the closest thing we've had to a oxy moron around here."

I looked at our note-taking librarian, expecting her to rip the page from her notebook and start over. But that didn't happen. Miss Spark's moon-tinted eyes brightened as if a skein of clouds had cleared from the night sky.

"This is wonderful material!" she exclaimed. "It's just what the tourists and other sojourners will want to learn."

"What about the name of Burnt Creek?" I reminded.

Lyle gave me an amused grin. "Hold your horses, Walter, I'm gettin' there." He shot me a paternal wink. "You're the one who asked about Buck, you know." Turning to our enthusiastic note-taker, Lyle quieted his voice to a solicitous query. "What about your supper, Miss Spark? We could send it back to the kitchen to have it warmed up."

She smiled and shook her head. "I'm too excited to eat. I would love to hear more stories. Especially about how the community earned its contradictory name." With pencil hovering over paper, she waited, her untouched meal at her elbow. Even though that plate of victuals represented almost half the price of the #10 Deluxe Stiff-Bristle Broom I had sacrificed in the name of love, I harbored no regrets.

Lyle seemed to take it all in stride. He shrugged, sawed another chunk from his steak, and commenced to chewing. I'd never seen a man enjoy his meal as my cowboy friend savored this one. The hotel restaurant enjoyed a good reputation, but I knew Lyle's bliss had less to do with recipes than his slow approach to living and the gift of appreciating every moment. I was inspired just watching the man eat.

Washing down another mouthful of food with a slurp of coffee, Lyle settled in for the telling. He pointed toward the corner of the room again in the direction of the former Hardiman potato farm.

"The creek was known to be the best drinkin' stream in these parts. Used to be called by the Blackfeet name for 'Sweetwater.' B'fore the white man come and ruint ever'thin', it was common for hunting parties from other tribes to go a hundred miles out o' their way just to sip the natural nectars of Sweetwater Creek. These're things I know from conversin' with some o' the Blackfeet elders who stayed on in the area. As a boy I knew several ol' medicine men as well as some regular ol' men. And their wives. If I weren't workin' the potato field or doin' some chore for my ma or pa, I could usually be found with these old-timer Injuns soakin' up whatever they had to teach me."

"What about the language barrier?" Miss

Spark asked, pausing in her furious scribbling.

Lyle frowned and pursed his lips. "Never saw one. All the trails were purty clear. We just faced each other and let go with a sentence the usual way — one talkin' and the other'n listenin'."

The librarian put down her pencil. "Do you mean you could understand Blackfeet?"

Lyle waved that off. "Sure . . . understand it, speak it, think it, dream in it . . . I've even been known to hiccup in Blackfeet. I picked it up early, you see." He bounced once with a quiet, self-deprecatory laugh. "Can't read word number one in a book o' English, but I always had a purty good ear for pickin' up the different ways o' talkin'."

Rebecca Spark studied Lyle's face the way I imagined an artist took in the features of a grand vista before attempting to paint it. Her food was getting colder by the moment.

With a dreamy look on her face, she let go a long sigh. "Do you suppose you could say something to us now? In Blackfeet, I mean?"

Lyle narrowed his eyes as he surveyed the remains of his meal. After a time he brought up his head and leveled his gaze squarely into Rebecca Spark's moonstruck eyes. What followed next was close to a spiritual event. Lyle started throwing out this long chain of choppy sounds that seemed to be bound together by a smooth and fluid undercurrent of breath. When he closed his mouth, ours fell open. Each of Miss Spark's cheeks showed a quicksilver trail left by a tear.

I was afraid she was about to burst out sobbing and create an unwanted scene in the dining room. But, despite her moist eyes, she flashed a stunning smile and again performed the little butterfly clapping with her hands beneath her chin.

"That's just wonderful, Lyle," said our librarian. "What does it mean?"

Without even moving, Lyle appeared to strike a pose for the recitation. "Once, the buff'lo of the plains were thick as the hairs on a mange-less dog," he translated. "No one went hungry. The Great Spirit provided the People with all that they needed. The world was a good place, and every man, woman, and child knew what part to play in it."

Lyle paused, keeping his eyes on the tablecloth to give Miss Spark time to compose herself. With her napkin she patted her cheeks and eyes dry.

"O' course, that was all to change," Lyle continued. "As usual, the white man would come in like a plague and spoil just about

173

ever'thin' he touched."

" 'Paradise Lost,' " said Rebecca, putting a literary moniker on it.

Lyle finished his coffee and shrugged. "Don' know about 'lost.' More like 'ruint.' "

He picked up a biscuit and slathered it with butter with careful strokes of his knife. Then we watched him smear one half with chokecherry jam. Upon the other half he dribbled a spiral of honey. He ate them in alternating fashion, a bite from one, then a bite from the other. Talk about living in the moment! When he was finished, he cleaned his hands with the white linen napkin hanging from his collar, twisting one finger at a time inside the pristine cloth.

"Like I said, we were potato farmers," Lyle began anew, "just scrapin' by. We ate a lotta taters, but you know the old sayin' . . . 'man don't live on taters alone.' So we depended on tradin' out taters for meat and greens and such. When the Irish potato famine peaked out, our neighbors just flat out refused to trade for taters. They was Irish, theirselves, and they felt it was a sin to enjoy taters over here while their families in the old country were tater-less."

He shook his head at the memory. I could see it still weighed on him. Miss Spark's faucets were opened up again, and she held the napkin across the lower half of her face to soak up the jeweled beads that made their way down her alabaster cheeks. But at least she was functioning, writing it all down at a determined pace.

"My pa had to figure somethin' out quick, so he went into business with a fast-talkin' feller from back East who had more ideas about how to make money than a porcupine has quills. He convinced my pa that our taters needed a new gimmick . . . a new taste. Bakin', boilin', steamin', and mashin' was *out*!" Lyle pointed at his plate. "Deep-fryin' was *in*!"

Miss Spark's face opened in awe. "Your family introduced deep-frying?"

Lyle shrugged. "Well, o' course plenty o' taters got skillet-fried over time, but this deep-fry was somethin' else. Our taters were already special. They had a sweet taste that people said was on account of us irrigatin' the field from Sweetwater Creek. But deep-fryin' brought out the best in a Sweetwater tater. It went over big, 'specially with preachers and philosophers, lawyers, politicians, and such as that. People who put a high premium on anythin' deep: like deep thinkin', deep devotion, deep pockets, and such. You know . . . people who wanted to be known for being deep." He waved away such shallow deepness. "Anyway, this business feller footed the bill for a big cookin' vat. My pa filled it with rendered fat from the buff'lo killin' fields, fired it up over a big pit fire, and the business was off and runnin'.

"Pressured by his partner, Pa changed the name of the farm from Hardiman's to 'F Ranch.' That 'F' was the first letter I was ever introduced to, and I was told it stood for 'fried.' We even branded our taters with the symbol." He reached for Rebecca's notebook. "Can I show you?"

When she surrendered her notebook, Lyle, with a slow meandering journey of the pencil, carefully rendered his family brand on the paper. It read: *FRANCH.*

I leaned forward and pointed to the front end of the word. "Why no space between the 'F' and the 'R'?"

Lyle shrugged. "Weren't room on the tater. That's what got the name of 'Franch fried taters' goin'." He sat back and laced his fingers together over his belly. "It could'a gone purty smooth and it did for a while, until the deep-thinkin' business partner decided we should expand our marketing to the neighboring territories and up into Canada. He had plans to form a complicated delivery service modeled on the Pony

Express. Wanted to call it 'Hot Potato on the Hoof.' "

A little nostalgia had worked its way into Lyle's handsome face, but now a shadow of resentment flared. "Mr. Deep-Fried Deep-Thinker drew up plans for a giant cookin' vat . . . about four times the size of the hotel bathtub. Well, let me tell you, that vat required one danged big fire to get the grease a-boilin'. With just my pa workin' it — you see, Mr. Deep never seemed to soil his hands on anythin' — the fire got away from 'im and burned up ever'thin: the vat supports, the house, the barn, the potato field, and about seventeen miles of forest all the way up the creek to the headwaters in the hills. It was a scorcher! That fire just left this whole area black and gray. Charcoal and ash ever'where."

As his eyes glazed over with the memory, Lyle seemed to leave us for a while. The image of that fire must have burned a permanent scar into his mind. He seemed to snap back to the present, and he looked from me, to Miss Spark, and then back to me.

"When the deep-fry supports collapsed," he said solemnly, "the oil spilt into the creek, catchin' fire along the way. It was the strangest thing a little boy on a potato farm could likely ever see. That burning oil just floated down the creek, the flames a-leapin' about six foot or so. It was like a magical ship made o' fire settin' off on its fairy tale journey. After it rounded the bend, I never saw it again."

So absorbed in the story was I . . . and with my mind flooded with the image of the conflagration Lyle had described . . . I didn't connect the dots right away. Then I sat forward quickly and snapped the finger and thumb of my right hand.

"So that's how it got named 'Burnt Creek'!"

Lyle shared none of my excitement. He only shook his head.

"Nope. That came later." He nodded toward the back wall. "All that forest timber was burnt to a crisp. Over the years the blackened trees continued to fall into the water, givin' it a burnt taste. Nobody wanted to drink from it anymore. It still carries that burnt flavor today." He picked up his fork and stabbed it into the greens, which he had not eaten. "You can taste it in these garden greens."

Lyle set down the fork and saw that Rebecca was waiting for more. "The few Blackfeet who were left in the area," he continued, "they revoked the original name and changed it from 'Sweetwater' to 'Stink

Water.' The white folks just called it 'Burnt Creek.' " He turned to me, ballooned his cheeks with air, widened his eyes, and exhaled. "That's it," he said.

When Miss Spark had scribbled the last of her notes, I stood and lifted her untouched plate. "I'm going to ask the kitchen to warm this up for you."

I'm not sure she heard me, so busy was she directing all her admiration Lyle's way. The librarian seemed not to be needing the sustenance of a professionally cooked meal. She was finding all her nourishment in this knight of the plains — a simple Montana cowboy with a rich pioneer history.

"Have a good evening," I said and delayed just long enough to catch a friendly wink from Lyle. As I headed for the kitchen with her plate, I heard her ask Lyle to speak her name in Blackfeet. Two minutes later, as I headed into the hotel lobby, he was still explaining to her that American names could not be so easily translated unless the name meant something.

On the following day I made brisk work of my sweeping jobs at the Pearl of the Prairie Saloon and at the marshal's office. By the noon hour I had ensconced myself inside the shade of the library reading room on the pretense of finding a book on sweeping techniques from around the world. I had found only one publication by an author from Arabia, but the book was about janitorial work in general, with sweeping rating only a brief mention. This particular section of the Arabian Desert was too dry for corn, sorghum, or even grasses to grow — all the typical construction sources for brooms. According to the book, the tool utilized by Arabian broomsmen was a camel's tail. The text did not expand on this. I hoped this did not mean they lopped off the tail of some poor beast, but it was difficult to picture a housemaid lifting a thousand-pound, humpbacked animal and going through the gyrations of my trade.

At twelve-thirty on the dot, Lyle Hardiman came through the door . . . without his horse. Tiptoeing carefully so as not to jangle his spurs, he approached the counter where Miss Spark was busy sorting through a stack of returned books. When she looked up and saw him, you would have thought the sun had just risen behind her comely face. They spoke so quietly I could not make out the words, but soon enough she presented Lyle with a brand-new notebook and a lead pencil and together they retired to the empty table nearest the front window.

I snuck a peek at my fellow readers — an all-male group again — and saw that every eye was fixed on the couple silhouetted by the bright glass panes. Burying my nose in my Arabian book again, I felt a big smile stretch across my face. I had nothing to learn from this camel-abusing author, it seemed, but I had plenty to celebrate. It looked as though my plan to get the boulder at the top of Romance Mountain rolling downhill was a success.

They worked as teacher and student for a solid half-hour, Miss Spark carefully enunciating the letters she printed on a page, and Lyle struggling to echo her pronunciations and then render the letters by his own hand. In the half hour that followed, Lyle leaned in and mumbled through a long monotone of a story as Miss Spark took notes. Sometimes Lyle drummed out a galloping rhythm on the tabletop with his hands . . . or held out a pointed forefinger like a pistol and produced make-believe gunshots with his mouth. Once he stacked a few books together to make what appeared to be a model of a box canyon, and he used the improvised construction to illustrate some point as one of his hands trotted into the defile on nimble fingers. I assumed the hand represented a horse. But it might have been a sprightly, stray cow.

At one-thirty sharp, Lyle quietly took his leave. He was back by two-thirty, and the same agenda followed for another hour. When Lyle returned again at four-thirty, I knew that my rolling-stone romance had escalated to an avalanche.

On the way to the boardinghouse from my last sweep at the lawyer's office, I detoured behind the schoolhouse when I noticed a light shining in the window of the library. My first thought was of a break-in. There shouldn't be much cash in a library, I deducted — not with overdue book penalties being a matter of pennies — but there *were* a lot of books in there. I didn't know if book bandits existed in Montana, but I put nothing past the criminal element.

I'd read about a desperado in Billings who broke into a boot and shoe shop, where hundreds of pairs of footwear lined the walls on six-tier shelving. The boots were left alone, but the laces of all the shoes were taken. Just the laces.

You never know, do you? When the shoestring thief was finally caught, the deputies found in his home a sixty-foot length of laces tied from end to end by fisherman knots to make one long, lumpy cord. They also discovered dozens of empty laudanum bottles under the man's bed. When asked why he stole the laces, he admitted he was simply strung out. This is no joke. It was in the newspaper.

I was not an officer of the law. I was a broomsman. So I decided to go back to the marshal's office to seek professional help. As I turned to leave, a soprano warbling of light laughter floated through the window. The delightful melody made me think of a butterfly flitting from flower to flower in a peaceful meadow of colorful blossoms out on the prairie. I would have known this voice anywhere. It was Miss Rebecca Spark.

Creeping closer to the window, I saw a two-inch opening at the bottom. When a breeze stirred at my back, the curtains inside the room gently billowed and rippled, parting in the process and allowing me a brief glimpse of Lyle slumped over a notebook with pencil in hand. His face hovered only inches above the paper as he moved his pencil across the sheet in a swirling motion. He wore a big smile as his tongue curled upward to touch his top lip. One eye was squinted, as if Lyle were sighting down the long barrel of a rifle. He was concentrating, it was plain to see, but having the time of his life in the bargain.

"It's true," Rebecca Spark said, her laughter trailing off. "A lower case 'b' does look like a 'p' that's standing on its head. And a 'c' — whether upper- or lowercase — certainly resembles a horseshoe. It's like a code, Lyle. It's fascinating and ingenious."

"Naw," Lyle said with a modest growl. "It's just a way to get by. Cowboys had to figure out some way o' recognizin' what all the signs are sayin'."

"Now, what about a capital 'G,' Lyle? What does it stand for in this cowboy language?"

"Bent horseshoe with a loose nail," he answered without hesitation.

"And a capital 'Q'?"

"Feller smokin' a cigar," he replied. Lyle sounded like a star student during an oral exam.

"Capital 'E'?" she quizzed.

Lyle chimed in immediately. "Sleepin' pitchfork with a broke-off handle."

"Why sleeping?" she asked.

" 'Cause we got three other pitchforks. 'M' is a stuck-down pitchfork, and 'W' is stuck-up. All with broke handles. Then 'F' has got a broke handle and a broke tine."

"That's brilliant, Lyle!"

As I began to feel like a window-peeper horning in on a conversation not meant for my ears, I quietly backed away and stared at the uneven line of hitching rings attached to the front of the building. This is where it had started — Lyle attaching that first plate, as if he had been staking his claim on the right to court the librarian. Then that slew of also-rans came pouring out of the building hoping to throw their names into the pot. It was pathetic. Not one of them had mounted a ring to match Lyle's. I was convinced more than ever that Lyle and the lovely Miss Spark were meant to be.

On the next morning, my newly acquired sweeping job at the tonsorial parlor was delayed due to high winds. The barber informed me that more haircuts are performed on windy days than any other, and there would be no room for me to work with so many customers packed inside the room. When I asked him why high winds inspired so many haircuts, I learned something about the price of getting married. It's a pretty simple equation: High winds are prone to make hats fly. Without his hat, a man's hair is at the mercy of the forces of nature. He can look pretty far-fetched. About that time comes a comment from the wife, and the next thing you know he's headed for the barber.

Having some free time on my hands, I

ambled down to the creek. I was curious to see if Lyle's story would hold up to a taste test. At the water's edge I knelt and dipped a cupped hand into the steady current. Sipping the cool water I closed my eyes and focused on my taste buds.

"Smoky," I said aloud in a gurgling voice and spat out what remained in my mouth. Burnt Creek was still living up to its name. Even though it was early yet, this seemed like a perfect rationale for visiting the North Star to wash away the burnt taste of my impromptu investigation.

Pushing through the doors of the saloon, I stepped out of the wind and was surprised to see the room nearly full. All but one of the tables hosted card games in progress. The men clustered around these games were the same who had regularly shared the library reading room with me. On my way to the bar, I stopped at Mose Broussard's table and watched the four-way game of Kansas Two-Spot until Mose folded and looked up at me. I knew him from the days when he was a deputy marshal here in town. Though retired now, Mose had been a good officer, once helping me out as a character witness when a traveling salesman had rooked me with a Chinese-made broom whose bristles broke apart on the occasion of its first use.

"You boys are throwing your money away early today, Mose," I said. "How come you're not at your regular roost in the library?"

Mose gave me a hard look. "Looks like the prodigal rooster has come home to roost for good. Us other cluckers ain't gotta chance."

I felt my forehead tighten and lower over my eyes. "You mean Lyle Hardiman is over there?"

Mose worked up a scowl. "As we speak."

"He was supposed to report back to the Rocking J this morning," I said.

"Well, he's sittin' in that library right now, readin' out loud from Sir Walter Scott, if you can believe that." Mose shook his head. "And she lets 'im jabber away without so much as a 'shhh' or a 'quiet please, sir.' She just sits there a-smilin' and a-flappin' her hands together before her neck." He nodded toward the others in the room. "Couldn' none o' us concentrate on our own readin' and didn' none o' us wanna listen to Lyle read *Rob Roy,* as we've all read it ourselves. Plus, Lyle reads too fast. My ears can't hardly keep up with his mouth."

" 'Too fast'?" I said.

Mose shook his head once, as if a fly were

worrying his ear. "That cowboy has picked up the art o' readin' somethin' fierce." Mose's body bounced once in a private laugh, but the grunt he emitted carried no humor. "When us boys read, we're like a old single-shot musket, takin' on each word one at a time, tryin' to remember the last word in the chain so we can hook it up to the next one once we figure it out. But Lyle, he's a Gatlin' gun firin' off rounds so fast it's all a blur." Mose's eyebrows floated upward as he let go a sigh. "I have to say, he is a danged marvel to listen to."

I strode out the back of the saloon as if bound for the privy, but as soon as my feet hit the ground I headed northwest for the library. It was still windy, and as I passed the tonsorial parlor I noted a line of customers waiting on the boardwalk — two dozen men with their hands pushed into their pockets, all in deep conversation. Through the window I could see that the room was packed. I could imagine all the loose locks I would be sweeping up when the wind abated.

I knew I was going to have to devise some new technique for debris disposal with my new barbershop job. I couldn't just sweep hair out onto the boardwalk and then out onto the street like I did with the dust from my other jobs. It would look unseemly, and there was a city ordinance about it because of the lice epidemic of '71. I was considering bundling it all together into a giant hairball, taking it to the leeward side of town, where I would let the wind take it out onto the prairie like one more tumbleweed.

When I reached the library, I heard Lyle's voice carrying on as if he were in a tussle with somebody in the reading room. Rushing in to give him assistance, I found him standing in a semi-crouch, one hand holding an open book, the other hand fisted and outstretched as if holding on to the end of a rope attached to a stubborn mule. Miss Spark sat at a reading table, her eyes sparkling with excitement and fixed on Lyle's performance. As soon as he saw me, Lyle straightened and lowered his arms, an embarrassed smile playing at his lips.

"Good morning, Walter. You have caught me in the throes of a sword fight with the Duke of Montrose's men." I must have looked shocked, because Lyle walked over to me and placed a hand on my shoulder. "It's just a little theatrics . . . a way to bring the book alive."

Awestruck, I looked him in the eye. "You're reading as fast as a college professor, Lyle!"

Miss Spark was quick to comment. "He's the most apt pupil I've ever had the pleasure to teach. Such an ear for pronunciations! And he picks it up so quickly." As she praised him, her eyes softened to the silvery sheen of a serene lake on a cloudy day. Then she seemed to snap out of her state of adoration, and she flashed a smile my way. "And I'm learnin' so much about our community. I'm goin' to petition the mayor's office to establish a new position in our city government: town historian. Lyle will be a shoo-in."

I looked at Lyle to see how he was taking this flash flood of compliments from Rebecca Spark, but his head was lowered into the book, his concentration on the printed pages complete. I had to clear my throat three times to get his attention.

"I thought you had to report back to the Rocking J for work today," I whispered, not wanting to embarrass him, lest he had forgotten his work schedule.

Showing no surprise at my mention of his obligations, he pursed his lips and shook his head. "No, I quit. I sent word to the ranch by way of Charley Coltrane, who came in for supplies yesterday."

I couldn't believe my ears. The best damned cowboy in the territory just up and quit on the biggest spread in the Bitterroot Valley. The word around town was that the Rocking J paid top wages according to a man's abilities. The better a cowboy's skills, the higher the pay. Lyle's salary had to be considerable.

"Well, how do you plan to bring in some money?" I asked.

Lyle's friendly grin stretched into a wide slice of a smile that showed a lot of teeth. "I have a new job right here," he said and pointed a finger at the floor. I looked down, expecting to see some floorboards that needed replacing . . . or perhaps a few nails that had pried loose. It was well-known around town that Lyle was an excellent carpenter. When I saw no structural defects and remembered that the library was brand-new, I looked to Lyle for an explanation.

"You are standing before the new assistant of the library," Lyle announced, now apparently elevated from his former use of the word "lie-bury." He had been wearing a light coat draped over his shoulders, letting the garment serve as a cape, I suppose, for his reading performance. Now he removed it, and right there on his vest was a new name tag pinned to his left breast. It read: *Lyle Hardiman, Assistant Librarian.*

Rebecca Spark stood and performed that

fluttery, silent applause under her chin. The little wind currents she produced with her hands stirred the loose strands of pale hair that twined down at her temples. In her newfound happiness over the doubling of her staff, she appeared more beautiful than ever.

"Lyle has already developed an innovative code system for catalogin' all our books," Miss Spark announced. "And he's implemented a more efficient way of coordinatin' book checkouts and returns. Not to mention how overdue book fines are processed." Miss Spark's reticent ways seemed to yield to the excitement of acquiring such a stellar employee. "Oh!" she added, turning to Lyle, "and let's not forget your idea on indelibly markin' the books as library property."

"That ought not be credited to me," he protested, pushing at the air with his hand. "Cattlemen have been branding their livestock since the time of the ancient Egyptians. That trick is old as the pyramids."

Such a modest reply only served to multiply the constellations in the slate sky of Rebecca Spark's fawning eyes. "Lyle was born for this kind of work," she said with admiration. When she stepped beside him, Miss Spark actually placed a hand on Lyle's shoulder. Smiling at her new assistant, she spoke with an intimacy that seemed both natural and proper. "Since you two are good friends, would you like to be the one to share the announcement, Lyle?"

I tried to swallow, but my throat was so dry I couldn't. Involuntarily, my eyes checked Miss Spark's fingers for any sign of intended betrothal. There was none. Yet the glow lifting off her fair face promised some kind of special news.

Lyle closed his book and walked it to the front desk, where he picked up a sheet of paper. Looking over the document as if he were a copy editor at the newspaper, he finally nodded his approval and approached me with his old crooked grin back in place.

"What do you think?" he asked, holding out the paper for me to read.

Attention citizens, the paper read in a neat cursive handwriting, *merchants, ranchers, farmers, traveling businessmen, tourists, and cowboys! This invitation goes out to all ages, both genders, and people of every ilk who are curious about the beginnings of our community. The first assembly of the Burnt Creek Historical Society will convene tomorrow on the Fourth of July at 9 A.M. as part of the town's holiday festivities. Meet at the new library behind the old schoolhouse. A short lecture and refreshments will be followed by a*

193

field trip to the site of the first potato farm in the valley. This educational event will be led by Lyle Hardiman, native son of Burnt Creek.

When I looked up at Lyle and Miss Spark, they seemed to be awaiting my reaction with strong expectations, especially Rebecca, who appeared about to burst with excitement. "We used your idea about a historical society, Walter," she admitted in a grateful tone.

This was the first time she had called me by my given name. A tingling sensation stirred my blood, originating in my toes and rising up through my chest to my head. I felt like a just-opened bottle of champagne.

"Don't you think it's perfect?" Miss Sharp continued. "Lyle wrote up the entire text. We're havin' posters printed up. We'll place 'em all over town this afternoon. After tomorrow's program we hope to sign up dozens of new members for the Historical Society, and then we'll be off and runnin'."

"To where?" I asked, looking from one to the other.

"It's a metaphor," Lyle said in his friendly and edifying way. "It means we're aspiring to a strong tourist trade here, which will bolster the economy of the town. We believe people will come from all over the country . . . maybe the world . . . to enjoy a little hometown nostalgia and learn about our roots."

While I tried to parse this idea for its practical merits, Lyle stepped next to me and threw an arm over my shoulders. You might as well have crowned me King of the Montana Territory and draped a royal cape down my back.

"By the way, Walter," he said in his personable way, "when can I have a look at your Blackfeet medicine woman's secret prayer? I think I'm ready for it."

Patting my pockets, I pretended to be crestfallen. "I don't have it on me at the moment. I loaned it out to a man who had fallen into a deep depression."

Lyle leaned back to better see my face. "Well, let us go extract him from it posthaste. I will retrieve my horse and rope from the livery."

"It's not that kind of depression, Lyle. It's a state of mind."

Lyle nodded and gave me an understanding smile. "Well, when he has reaped the benefits from the magic words, perhaps I can make a copy for myself . . . now that I know how. Would that be breaking any Blackfeet rules, do you suppose?"

"I think that would be fine, Lyle." I cocked my head and stared at him, trying to put my finger on something about him that had changed in the last twenty-four hours. "There's something different about the way you're talking," I said, wagging a finger at him.

"Oh, that," Rebecca said with a demure chuckle. "It's all the cowboy contractions and elisions. He doesn't use 'em anymore." She made an elegant shrug and spread her hands at shoulder level as if checking for rain inside the building. "Lyle's three 'r's' used to be 'ruint,' 'ridin',' and 'readin'.' Now it's 'ruined,' 'riding,' and 'reading.' "

Lyle's shrug was quicker and to the point. "Now that I've seen all the letters that belong in a word, I feel rather obligated to let each one receive its due. Unless, of course, it's a silent 'g' as in 'rough' or 'laugh' or something like that. To do otherwise would be like ignoring one of your cousins at a family reunion. It's just would not be fair, do you agree, Walter?"

Bowing to Lyle's new dedication to the alphabet, I felt compelled to support him, so I nodded. To have debated the point, I realized, would have been like a slap in the face to him, now that he was a man of letters. Lyle had been a man worthy of respect even before he was educated on the fast track by Miss Spark. There was every reason

196

to believe that he would command even more esteem among the people of Burnt Creek, now that he was so careful with his words.

"Let me know when you get this printed up," I said, gesturing toward the mock-up announcement. "I can help distribute them in the establishments where I sweep."

Rebecca Spark treated us to a dazzling smile and one of her soundless clappy-hands-under-the-chin celebrations. Lyle gave me a wink and a grin. I was glad to see that his personal charm had not been altered by the strictures of education that had taken over his tongue.

"The printer said they'll be ready by noon," Miss Spark informed me. Then her eyebrows knitted to an imploring angle. "You *can* come tomorrow, can't you, Walter?"

The cork on the champagne bottle popped again.

"Wouldn't miss it," I said, and then bravely added, "Rebecca." The word came off my tongue like a mosquito barely gaining its freedom from a glob of pine sap where it had unwisely landed. "I'll try to round up a crowd for you and bring along those boys who have been visiting the library of late."

"That'd be wonderful!" she exclaimed, and I waited to see if her butterfly hands might try to fly beneath her chin again. Instead, she threaded one arm through Lyle's until the librarian and her assistant were locked at the elbows. All that was missing from the matrimonial scene was a preacher. I took their conjoined arms as a cue for my departure. I did have floors to sweep. Stopping at the door, I turned to the happy couple.

"Say, how much will it cost to become a member, by the way? In case somebody asks."

When Rebecca frowned, I could see she had not considered this detail. But it was just as clear that Lyle had. He patted her hand and shook his head, his face a mix of righteousness and resolve.

"There will be no fee," he declared. "This society will be about all those who came before us and gave us our beginning. It is *we* who owe *them*! We will not profit off their hard work."

When Lyle disengaged himself to retrieve his book from the front counter, Rebecca came to the door to see me out. "Ain't he just wonderful?" she whispered.

There was only one answer to that question, so I had no recourse but to spit it out.

"Yes, ma'am," I said. " 'Wonderful' is exactly what he is."

Looking over her shoulder, I saw that Lyle held his book one-handedly again as he assumed his sword-fighting stance and made little jabs at the air. His footwork was magnificent, and the authoritative report of his boots on the plank floor made his movements seem heroic. The more I thought about it, "wonderful" just might be too small a word for Lyle Hardiman.

"I'll come by for a stack of posters after my next job," I promised.

Rebecca smiled and threw me a familial kiss with her dainty fingers. Had she performed such a thing two days ago, I might have melted on the spot, like a snowball dropped into a hot frying pan.

The wind had died down. As I made my way across town for the lawyer's office, I noticed the towels hanging on the drying lines behind the hotel. A half hour ago they had been flapping like the tongues of politicians at a convention. Now they were as still as tombstones. In that windless quiet, the thing that had been gnawing at me became a full-fledged bite. The echo of Rebecca Spark's meek voice reverberated in my head.

Ain't he just wonderful?

My feet stopped walking, and I turned to

frown at the back of the schoolhouse. " 'Ain't he just wonderful?' " I repeated out loud. That was the moment I realized that even as Lyle's vocabulary, pronunciations, and syntax climbed to loftier heights, so did Miss Spark's use of the language seem to deteriorate. It was as if the library could contain only so much erudition, and she was sacrificing for the sake of a balance.

"Walter Wren!" someone called from the row of shops behind me. Turning, I saw Alton McGruder hurrying from his tonsorial parlor, his barber's apron wrapped around him like a second skin, his scissors attached to the thumb and finger of his right hand, a smoking cigar clamped in his left.

"Morning, Alt," I said and noted a worried look in his eyes.

Alt gestured around him, swishing his arm through the air and leaving a horizontal trail of cigar smoke hanging like an oversized halo that had slipped down around his torso. "Walter, with the wind died down like it is, the demand for haircuts fizzled out. I'm hopin' you can make it by to sweep b'fore tomorrow. We're inches deep in shorn hair inside there." He pointed back to his shop. "I'd like to have it clean for the Fourth. We're havin' an open house for the festivities, you know."

"I should be able to get to it by late afternoon, Alt. Will that be all right?"

Alt pressed his palms together under his chin like a man praying. I thought for a moment he might perform Miss Rebecca Sharp's butterfly ritual, but instead he bowed.

"You're a lifesaver, Walter." When he straightened, he relaxed considerably. "Say, are you going to the Historical Society meeting tomorrow?"

"Wouldn't miss it," I said for the second time in five minutes. I guess that was going to be my standard reply. I even felt a little patriotic about the whole thing.

By the time I finished with my broomsmanship at the law office, Historical Society posters had already been nailed up along the boardwalks. I returned to the library but found no one inside. There was, however, a box of posters sitting on the first table, so I helped myself to a few and started for the Pearl of the Prairie, my next assignment for the day . . . to be followed by another sweep through the North Star. The saloons would take in the lion's share of business tomorrow, and the owners wanted their floors spotless for the occasion. Both jobs would give me the opportunity to tack up some posters inside and to talk up the

Historical Society to the patrons. As for those old boys who had forsaken the library on account of Lyle winning the heart of Miss Spark, I planned to shame them into attending, explaining to them that they should not think less of Rebecca Spark but more of Lyle Hardiman for being the object of her affections.

And so it went. Eventually, they all came around to my way of thinking and admitted that if there were a man in the valley worthy of the new librarian, it would have to be Lyle. Each one of those former book lovers promised he would show up for the program — lecture, field trip, and all.

As twilight began to settle over town, I made my way to the tonsorial parlor. From two blocks away I could see Alt sitting outside on his bench. Stooped forward, he remained as still as a sculpture, his elbows propped on his knees, his head sagging below his shoulders. The only movement around him was a string of gray cigar smoke snaking its way up to the sidewalk awning. When Alt heard my approach, his head came up like a bird dog on point.

"I thought maybe you'd forgotten," he began. Standing, he shook my hand, cranking it up and down like a pitcher pump with a loose seal. "Thank you for comin', Walter."

"I would have come sooner, but I've been helping out with advertising the library event tomorrow."

"I'm just glad you came at all," Alt gushed. Digging into his trouser pocket, he produced a key and pressed it into my hand. "Look, I have to get home. We're having relatives over for the holiday, and I promised my wife I'd clip her hair before it got too dark to see what I'm doing. Just lock up when you finish, Walter. I have another key for opening in the morning." He pointed the cigar at the key in my hand. "I'll get that one from you later," he called out, already backing away. Within seconds he was running down the street like a racehorse.

The barber had not exaggerated. His shearing room looked like the shedding grounds of the summer buffalo. The room was six inches deep in rejected hair. Every color you could imagine for a man's pate-crop was represented: ink black, midnight blue-black, steel gray, salt and pepper, summer-wheat blond, ash blond, strawberry blond, silver, walnut brown, coffee-with-cream brown, tawny buckskin brown, auburn, rust red, and fire red. It was comfortable to walk on. I wondered if someday some enterprising businessman would find a way to link it all together to produce a fine rug that could be rolled out in homes and offices.

Starting in the front of the cutting room, I started sweeping the mass of hair toward the storage area that had a rear door that opened to the alley and the open prairie beyond. My plan was to sweep all the hair out into the alley, where I would somehow dispose of it early tomorrow morning. But I had misjudged the first part of my plan. I had amassed such a mountain of hair that it jammed at the threshold of the open back door. Using my shoulder I put my weight into it but made progress only by quarter-inch increments.

You wouldn't think that hair could weigh so much, but collectively it can add up. This giant hairball I had forced into the back room had become my nemesis. I felt like Hercules embroiled in one of his assigned labors. Pushing all that hair was like trying to move a dead mastodon out the doorway. It reminded me of a story I had read at the library in one of the rancher magazines. A foreman over in the Walla Walla Valley had attempted to pack a spare horse into his saddlebags, in case of a breakdown with his primary mount, so he said. I determined I was going to need some help in ejecting this hair-monster from the building, so I decided to wait until morning when I could call on help from someone. From the alley I might be able to haul it away with a team of draft animals and a special harness. I was betting Lyle could help me with that.

I did not sleep well that night. Rising early and dressing for the day of celebration, I left my boardinghouse to find that the wind had kicked up again. All down the street I could hear doors slamming, windowglass rattling, and curtains flapping in open windows. I thought of all the dust accumulating in the many buildings I had made spotless for the holiday. It was a vicious cycle that had always haunted my work. Nature and I kept taking turns dumping dust on each other. It seemed so pointless.

This is what had started me thinking about moving out of Montana, picking up a new trade, and just starting over. I'd been considering it for months now, but all that had changed when the new library opened and Miss Rebecca Spark had come to town.

Now that I had gotten the ball rolling on connecting Miss Spark and Lyle in the glorious entanglement of romance, maybe I would decamp after all. As much as I admired both parties, I might find it difficult to be a daily witness to their marital bliss, should it come to that. From the frisky gleam in their eyes, I had no reason to believe otherwise.

As I walked the street, I kept experiencing troublesome flashbacks of the bizarre dreams I had suffered through the night — all of them apparently inspired by the hairy conundrum awaiting me at the barber's back room. One involved wrestling a giant, pregnant she-bear from a one-seater outhouse. The privy door had been too small, and so the dream was an exercise in pure frustration. It made no sense, of course. How could the bloated creature have gotten into the structure in the first place? But that's the way dreams often work. Logic has no place in them.

In another dream I was Sisyphus, trying my dangedest to roll a gigantic ball of hair to the top of the highest peak in the Bitterroots. No matter how many times I tried, that shaggy sphere always figured a way to slip out of my grip at the last moment and roll back down the slope to the floor of the valley. More frustration! And on top of that, I was feeling close to worn out.

The worst dream involved a saber-toothed tiger. I had dodged that pair of hefty fangs by scooting down into a ki-yote burrow headfirst — a tight fit for me but, thankfully, too small for that hungry cat. After pacing back and forth in front of the hole, the frustrated animal glared at me with baleful eyes. Finally, after showing me what appeared to be a feline smirk, it coughed up a fearsome-looking hairball and stuffed it down the hole on top of me. With repetitive jabs of its paws, that tiger tamped the hair down so tightly I could hardly breathe. When I woke up in a panic, I found myself in such a tangle of sheets that the pillow had somehow gotten wrapped up and pressed right into my face.

There were other nightmares, all with a similar hair-blockade theme. I was more than ready to evict that orb of haircut debris from Alt McGruder's shop and send it on its way out of town. I resolved right then and there I would never take a permanent job of any kind at a tonsorial parlor. I know it sounds like "sour grapes" for a bald-headed man, but I was developing a strong aversion to hair.

After an early breakfast I braved the brisk wind and checked the hotel desk for Lyle's room number, for I knew if anyone could remedy my hair-jam at the tonsorial parlor, it would be Lyle Hardiman. I imagined his solution would involve a couple of lariats, a special knot or two, a pulley, and his horse. Knowing Lyle as I did, I wouldn't put it past him to use the wind to his advantage for the task. He might jury-rig a giant sail out of barber aprons and let nature pull the blob of hair out the door.

"Mr. Hardiman left early this morning," the concierge informed me. "The librarian lady called on him, and off they went. That was about six o'clock. They were talking about walking down to the creek to plan their field trip to the old Franch potato farm."

The clerk was middle-aged, overweight, and pretty pale looking, his pudgy hands as soft as biscuit dough. I knew he was no candidate for the job I had in mind. I folded my arms and cocked my head slightly.

"Well, can you think of anybody who could lend me a hand wrestling a big hair-ball out of the barber's back room?"

He studied me for about five seconds, all the while looking at me as if I had just invited him to join me in a waltz right there in the lobby . . . just him and me . . . and no music.

"You payin'?" he asked dryly.

I shook my head. "I just need a little favor. I'm not a rich man. I'm a broomsman."

"Try over to the North Star," he suggested. "A bunch of cowboys came in late last night. They wanted to get a jump on festivities, so they started liquorin' up early. Maybe you can talk one o' them into helpin' you. Those boys are always wantin' to come to the rescue of somethin'. It's part of bein' a cowboy."

"Unless they're passed out drunk on the floor," I amended. "Cowboy or not, a drunk man is not going to be much of an asset in this project." Turning to leave, I waved to the clerk. "Have a good day."

Before I had reached the door, he called out to my back, "Say, are you going to the Historical Society meeting?"

I stopped and closed my eyes. Dredging up a countenance of patience, I turned to him and managed a smile.

"Wouldn't miss it," I said — now by rote — and stepped outside into the bracing wind.

At the North Star the situation looked grim. Most of the cowboys were asleep on the benches that stretched along the back and side walls. The only man not horizontal sat at a table playing solitaire. I sidled to the bar and watched him for a while. When he placed a jack of hearts on a king of spades and called out "Bingo!" I felt my hopes plummet.

Arthur, the bartender, strolled down the length of the bar to where I stood. Standing before me, he smiled and placed his fingers on the countertop like a piano player about to break into a nocturne.

"Well dang, Walter, you look like you've got the kind o' troubles that only whiskey can drown out. What'll you have?"

Glancing back at the solitaire player, I saw that he had keeled forward, his nose pressed into the columns of cards on the table. With one hand still gripping a bottle of snake-head whiskey, he began to snore with a steady rhythm.

"What I'd like to have," I replied to Arthur, "is somebody sober enough to help me move a ton of hair out of the tonsorial parlor before Alt McGruder opens up at nine o'clock."

Arthur dug into his vest pocket and extracted a silver watch, which he thumbed open and studied. His lips moved silently as he sorted through the calibration of reading the time.

"Well," he finally said, "you've got about twelve minutes." His eyebrows lifted and his smile turned sympathetic. "I'd help you myself, but I can't leave the premises long as I got customers." Turning to the shelf behind him, he selected a bottle and placed it before me. A shot glass materialized from his hand like a magic trick. "How about one on the house, Walter?"

I took a deep breath and let the exhalation flutter my lips in a long, bubbly sigh. I sounded like a horse. Arthur's last words kept echoing through my head.

"How about *under* the house," I said, feeling a kernel of hope begin to glow inside me.

Confused, Arthur frowned at the whiskey bottle. "Never served one thataway. How do I go about it?"

"Do you have a crowbar, Arthur?"

He swept a hand through the air, indicating the full length of the countertop. "Nope . . . just this'n here for people like yourself."

"A pry bar," I corrected. "Do you have a pry bar?"

"You mean a prisin' lever. Sure, I got one for takin' apart the barrels that leak, so I can use the staves for fuel in the woodstove yonder." He nodded toward the cold heater sitting idly at the center of the room. In winter, it was the heart of the saloon.

"Can I borrow it?" I asked.

Arthur frowned. "The stove?"

"No, the pry bar," I said.

Arthur shrugged. "Sure thing, son. Sounds like you've got a plan."

"Just get it for me, would you?"

By the time I got to the tonsorial parlor and started unlocking the door, who should walk up behind me but Alt McGruder. The wind was whipping up so that I hadn't heard his approach until he stepped up on the boardwalk. In one arm he clutched a stack of freshly laundered aprons. In the other hand was his ever-lighted cigar. I'd never seen Alt without one of these sausage-sized smokes wedged between two nimble fingers. He gave the pry bar a serious look before fixing his eyes on mine.

"Did you not finish?" Alt said, a touch of panic in his voice.

I managed a professional smile. "Your front room looks like a newborn baby, Alt. Not a hair to be found." That smile was getting hard to hold on to. "You're here early," I said, trying to sound curious in a friendly way.

Taking a fierce draw on his cigar, he blew enough smoke to cure a ham. "Of course I am. I want to go to the Historical Society meeting. Don't you?"

Wouldn't miss it was on the tip of my

tongue, but I couldn't bring myself to say it. When I hesitated, he nodded toward the tool in my hand.

"So, why the crowbar?" he asked.

I looked down at the toes of my boots long enough to compose my plea. "Alt, what would you say to us temporarily storing all my sweepings underneath your floorboards for the day?"

Alt looked like he'd swallowed a pine cone. "You wanna tear out my floor!?"

"Just the back room," I assured him.

Pushing through the door, I motioned for him to follow. When I slid aside the curtain to the storage area, the mass of hair looked like it had grown overnight. It stood well over six feet and seemed denser than I had remembered. I could barely see any floorboards, much less get near enough to pry one up.

"I couldn't get it out the door, Alt. I'm sorry. It's just that I've never done a barber's floor before."

Alt stared at the mountain of hair, leaned in and sniffed the air in the storage room, and shook his head. "Pacific scalp fungus," he diagnosed. "This big hairball is growing, isn't it?"

I swallowed. As an answer, I could only nod.

"This is all on account of Buster Johnson, dang his dirty pelt. He was in here yesterday talking about his prospecting trip to the Sierras, while he was scratching up a storm." Alt clamped the cigar in his mouth, propped his fists on his hips, and glared at a particular reddish tress of hair that must have belonged to Buster. "The fungus increases the size and weight and causes the hairs to bond together by some kind of magnetic charge. I read about it in the *Tonsorial Digest*. It's like bread rising in an oven." He shook his head again. "We've got to get this out o' here fast, Walter."

We were both more than a little panicked at this point, and we reacted with typical male bravado and started pushing together on the mound of hair. We must have toiled over it for a half hour, but we were determined. My hopes surged when we made enough progress to bulge about a third of the hairball out of the door. Tasting success, we redoubled our efforts, both of us gritting our teeth and grunting like a pair of herniated hogs. The hairball gave again and slipped several more inches toward freedom, but Alt had bitten down so hard on his cigar that he cut clean through it, and the front end dropped into the hairball, its bright red brick of a coal quickly igniting the thin hairs

214

around it.

"Alt!" I yelled. "Get some water!"

But the flames were spreading so fast, we both knew that going for a pail of water was pointless. The cruel, acrid stink of burning hair assaulted my senses. Alt almost fainted. The smell was so bad I wanted to retreat to fresher air, but we both knew this was no time to surrender. The whole town depended on us.

Crouching together under the flames, Alt and I gave it all we had, and the burning hairball rolled free of the building, where the wind caught it, fanning the flames and starting the giant mass rolling downhill toward the creek. The more it traveled across the prairie, the more the burning tangle of hairs evened out toward being a perfect sphere, which, of course, helped it to roll better and pick up speed. Within seconds it was moving so fast that it barely scorched the plants in its path. It looked like the tumbleweed from hell.

"At least it's headed for the creek!" Alt yelled over the wind.

That was when I saw the crowd of people gathered together inside the bend of the creek. Lyle was addressing the crowd, speaking through his cupped hands to be heard over the constant wind. I could make out Rebecca Spark at the front of the audience, her hands pressed together prayerfully beneath her chin. None of them had seen the burning hairball. Not even Lyle, who seemed completely absorbed in his lecturing.

Not knowing what else to do, I took off running for my friends. Even as I sprinted down the hill like a crazed man in a panic, the oddest notion came to mind: I was betting that no town had ever seen such fireworks on a Fourth of July.

I ran toward the crowd, intending to warn them, but I was soundly outraced by the hairball inferno. To my great relief the wind made a serendipitous shift and pushed the burning specter further upstream toward the beginning of the bend. When I reached the Historical Society gathering, I was plum out of breath. Bending forward I propped my hands on my knees and sucked in air, trying to recoup. As my intake began to settle, I heard Lyle delivering his presentation like a seasoned orator.

"And that is when the deep-fry vat toppled and hot grease poured out on the ground, catching fire immediately from the flames of the firepit." Lyle pointed to a spot on the beach. "I was standing right there and saw it all. That burning grease channeled into

Sweetwater Creek, where it floated right on top of the water and started downstream. The flames were tall as a man. It was surreal, like a scene from a mythological story. I can still see it in my mind. It was —"

"I can see it, too!" someone yelled and pointed. All eyes turned upstream where the great burning hairball navigated its way down the creek. The spectacle was almost too much to fathom. The crowd gasped as one, and then all went quiet but for the roar of the wind, the babbling of water, and the crackling of burning hair. Thank God the wind was in our favor concerning the stench.

When the burning hairball passed us on its voyage, little utterances of awe and whispers of wonder began to escape the lips of the spectators. The vocal praise soon became a chorus of *oohing* and *aahing,* and it kept building until finally everyone applauded. Even Rebecca Spark's hands smacked together like a string of firecrackers. The people around me were excited, talking to anyone who would listen.

"Ooh, there it goes!"

"Look at that, would you?"

"I've never seen such a sight!"

"It's like a holy vision!"

"What a reenactment! We've gotta do this

every Fourth of July!"

When I stepped to the front of the crowd, Lyle fixed his studious gaze on me and raised an eyebrow. The others kept their eyes on the fire, catching its final moments of glory before disappearing around the bend. Lyle turned to walk upstream, and I angled that way to meet him.

"Well, this was a hit," he said simply. "Your idea?"

"So to speak," I said. "You can consider it my contribution to the Historical Society."

Lyle placed a hand on my shoulder and squeezed. We both looked downstream and saw the flames float away out of sight. The people who had come were now talking excitedly to one another like chickens in a coop right before feeding time.

"What was it?" Lyle asked. "A big roll of baling twine? You must have been collecting it for years."

"Hair," I said.

His eyes glazed over like ice, waiting to see if I was joking. " 'Hair,' " he said.

I nodded. "It's a long story."

Lyle snorted a quiet laugh. "Ironic, don't you think?" He fixed his gaze on my bald head.

Miss Spark joined us and hugged one of Lyle's arms as she leaned into him. Lyle lowered his head to get eye to eye with her, and when the wind whipped smartly he gently brushed a stray lock of golden hair from her eyes with his fingertips.

"Darling," Lyle said, "I believe we have Walter to thank for a new Fourth of July tradition here at Burnt Creek. We're going to repeat this every year. When the word gets around, we're going to have tourists visiting here from every corner of the world."

The look Rebecca Spark gave me would have set my blood to boiling just a week ago. On this day, however, I simply felt proud to have been a part of the Historical Society's inaugural meeting.

"It was spectacular, Walter," she said. "Thank you for this surprise." Then she turned to Lyle. "But, sweetheart, we've got much more on our agenda. Let's move these people down to the old prospectors' shacks and begin the portion we planned on the minin' industry."

When the individuals in the audience began to meander aimlessly around the beach, Rebecca gave us a little wave and hurried off to shepherd the group toward the edge of the water, where she urged all to taste of the creek. It was, she insisted, the truest way to understand the history of

Burnt Creek.

Like a big brother, Lyle patted my upper arm. "Come join us, Walter. It should be a lot of fun. We're going to let everyone pan for gold down at the shoals and see what it was like to scratch a living out of the creek bed."

"I'm leaving," I said as earnestly as I knew how.

"Well, okay," Lyle said. "Maybe you can catch up with us later at the library. I plan to read a little Emerson and apply his philosophies to life here at Burnt Creek."

"No," I replied. "I mean I'm leaving Burnt Creek."

His face slowly compressed with a question. "Now?"

"Now," I said. "I've cleaned up this town, Lyle . . . so to speak. I reckon there are other towns that need me now."

Lyle's smile turned sly as he closed one eye, squinted at me with the other, and pointed at my chest with his forefinger. "I get it. You're riding out of this little episode like the hero in a novel." He turned and looked off in the distance at the Bitterroots. Then his body shook once with a quiet laugh. "I like it, Walter. It's got class." Facing me with what I would describe only as a look of admiration, he offered his hand.

"Good luck, partner. May the wind blow at your back. May the path ahead open for you with good fortune. And always know that there's an old ex-cowboy in Burnt Creek who owes you more than a man can pay." His smile widened to a bright crescent of handsome teeth. "Rebecca and I are to be married come October."

"I figured that was in the works," I responded. "Congratulations, old friend."

Lyle kept a steady gaze on me. "But do you know what else I'm looking forward to?"

I looked around at the floodplain. "Are you going to resurrect the potato farm?"

Lyle shook his head. "I'm anxious to read that Blackfeet medicine woman's words."

Knowing this moment was inevitable, I had hurriedly scribbled a few lines on a piece of paper last night. I had carried it folded in my pocket all morning, knowing that these words would be my farewell to the man I most admired. Slipping the paper from my pocket, I handed it to Lyle with great decorum, as if he and I were the sole participants in this day's most prestigious event.

"Would you do me the favor of reading it after I walk away?" I asked.

Lyle appeared surprised, but he recovered quickly and gave me a wink. "Sure thing."

It would have been nice to walk off into the sunset. I'd always wanted to do that. But it was way too early. The sun had not yet climbed to high noon. Still, for the sake of the poetry in our parting, I did walk west for a while before veering off toward my boardinghouse.

Before I entered the town proper, I stopped and turned for a last look at Lyle across all that distance. His head was down as he read from the paper. He was as still as one of the mannequins in the mercantile window. Then he lowered the paper beside his leg as he gazed off toward the Bitterroots again. He remained in that pose for almost a minute, until he turned to look at me. Raising the written page above his head, he held it high like a man hoisting a flag to a universal truth that had descended upon him like a celestial answer to an earthly prayer.

I smiled and felt a warm glow course through my body. It was the perfect way for me to leave this town. I started down the main street and felt the wind wash over me like a holy ablution. *Let the dust blow wherever it wants to go,* I thought. *Let someone else shuffle it around for a while.* Closing my eyes, I kept walking and, without knowing that I would do it, I began reciting

from memory the lines I had written in lieu
of a Blackfeet incantation.

"Some men accumulate cattle and tally
  their wealth by the head,
Others live by the gun and reap a
  reputation in lead,
Miners dig at the earth, chipping their
  treasures from caves,
Doctors count their blessings by all the
  lives they have saved,
But no one can best Lyle Hardiman, as
  he lies in his bed in the dark
Listening to his pulse beat in step with
  the heart of Miss Rebecca Spark."

ABOUT THE AUTHOR

Mark Warren is the author of *Secrets of the Forest,* a four-volume series on primitive survival skills; *Two Winters in a Tipi,* a memoir; *Indigo Heaven,* a novel of Wyoming; and a trilogy of historical fiction titled *Wyatt Earp, an American Odyssey,* which includes *Adobe Moon, Born to the Badge,* and *Promised Land.* He lives in the Appalachian Mountains of north Georgia.

■ ■ ■ ■

THE BOOK MAMA

CHARLOTTE HINGER

■ ■ ■ ■

CHAPTER ONE

Her breath came in harsh gasps and she stumbled for the third time. She was nearly seven miles from their house when she lost all sense of time and direction. The sun had turned the land into a fiery cauldron. Images wavered on the horizon. She was dangerously hot.

There was no shade, no roads. Only the naked Western Kansas prairie and clumps of bluestem competing with buffalo grass. The sun was no longer straight over her head. Her shadow was ahead of her and slightly to her right. She knew it was much too far to go on, and too far to turn back.

She had fled senselessly without planning. Fled from the ruined laundry that had spilled out of the washtub when she tried to brace one arm against the side to wring out Roy's work pants. Fled from the ruined stew she had forgotten to salt. Fled in her riding boots that were rubbing blisters on her heels. Fled with only a dab of money she had squirreled away in a teapot.

Her boot caught in a prairie dog hole. She cried out at the jolt, the pain. There was no one to hear. Legs bent, she braced herself and looked around for a stick. Anything to support her. Realizing her boot had prevented the ankle from twisting, she managed to rise to her feet. Hobbling, with one foot bearing her weight, she turned back toward home.

But she knew she was done for. The next time she ran away, it would not be on an impulse. She would think things through.

Her husband found her wandering like a mad woman. Heat crazed and crippled.

Red with fury, Roy scooped her up and plopped her down on the hard seat of their buggy. She lay there sobbing. He made no effort to comfort her. He smoldered for the first three miles.

When he finally spoke, he didn't try to temper his rage. "Are you crazy, Jane?"

Was she? She wasn't sure. In fact, some days she could swear Roy was the one who had lost touch with reality.

"Do I have to remind you of the stakes involved? I have promised, swore, by God, that newcomers will find only Britons from the upper classes here in Herrington Park.

Swore that they will be welcomed into a refined community. Not peopled by Australian squatters, or shanty Irish, or God forbid, ignorant people of color who are drawn to the prairie like a swarm of locust. And now my very own wife is wandering around like an escapee from an institution. Dressed like a servant. Lady Jane Woodruff, indeed."

She could not speak. Would not speak, even though she knew it drove him wild. She winced at the "shanty Irish," which was a veiled dig at her, even though her father was now landed gentry with substantial holdings in Northumberland. Nevertheless, Roy's father was an Earl.

Wearily, she tried to remember when she first realized she had married a fool.

Was it when he decided to build a two-story house when there was not a plentiful supply of labor? Or was it when he imported his first flock of Leicester ewes that could not withstand the hot Western Kansas summers instead of the Merinos she had read about. He didn't need to point out that she didn't know a thing about farming. She already knew that. But he didn't either, and the way he scoffed at her book learning wounded her.

He pulled up in front of their unfinished

stone house that he intended to be the grandest structure in the settlement. But instead of the magnificent two-story house that existed in his imagination, there was a simple box without even a porch to provide a shaded place to sit.

"Get out," he ordered.

She could barely stand and stumbled into the house and sank into the nearest chair.

He stormed inside after he had put up his horse. "I don't have time for this. There's no food either. Nothing cooked. I can't do everything around here."

Wearily, she watched him pace. Pace and swear. Coming up with a solution would be up to her.

"It's not too far to Tom's house. Perhaps Betsy would loan out one of her girls." They had to have food. Someone needed to finish the laundry.

"No, by God. Not over my dead body will I let my sister-in-law or any of her servants see the house like this."

"Then you have no choice but to fetch one of the Russian women."

"No. I don't trust them."

"Roy, I'm sick. I got too hot. I need some water. And I hurt my foot. It's starting to swell." She began to weep.

He stared at her for an instant, then

whirled around and went to a pitcher setting next to a dishpan. He returned with a tin cup filled with water and then slammed out the door.

Toward evening he returned with a stoic German Russian woman. "She didn't speak a word all the way over here," he announced with disgust. "I don't know how we can tell her what we need done."

The woman had a kerchief that went around her hair and was tied at the nape of the neck. "Berta," she said, pointing toward her ample bosom.

"Jane."

"Lady Jane," Roy snapped. He gestured toward the stove. "Food first." Then he waved toward the deplorable mess in the room. "Then fix this." He mouthed the words slowly, contemptuously.

Jane winced. It was his lack of feel for people that hampered his ability to keep help.

"Jesus Christ," he blurted. "Look at that stupid face. Like a goddamned cow. She hasn't understood a word I've said." He walked to the nearest pile of clothes and made an exaggerated show of folding them. Then he went to the stove and picked up a spoon and mimicked eating.

Jane caught the measured flash of anger

in the woman's eyes. Berta nodded and after Roy left, she quietly walked over to the stew Jane had started and finished peeling potatoes. Before she tackled the abandoned laundry, she wrung out a cool cloth and laid it on Jane's forehead. When everything was neat, she examined a pile of socks, found a needle and thread, and sat in a rocking chair while Jane dozed.

Later, when Roy came in for the night, Berta silently ladled soup and sliced off a hunk of the good bread she had brought with her. After she washed up, she fetched her needles and work basket, the remainder of the bread, and headed for the door.

"Goodbye."

"Goddamn piker," Roy raged as he stared after her. "Useless foreigners. She was supposed to stay for a week."

But Jane looked gratefully around the tidy room. Perhaps tomorrow would be a better day. She hobbled off to bed. Beyond the curtain, Roy's shadow loomed in flickering candlelight as he poured over accounts. His accounts. His candle.

From the time she was a tiny girl she had read in bed until she fell asleep. The ritual was as deeply ingrained as breathing. They had not been married a week before Roy put a stop to it. He swore candles were too costly and he couldn't sleep with a light shining in his face. She smoldered when she recalled her mother's stern instructions to obey her husband in all things. She could surrender her body, but not her books. They lay in a sorry pile next to their bed, beckoning to her in the darkness. They would comfort her after this humiliating day if Roy would only let her light one little candle.

Before she fell asleep, she mused over all the ways Roy had changed since they came to America. Changed for the worse.

The Earl of Sedgwick had been all too eager to send this restless third son to America to seek his fortune. Roy could not inherit the title or the land — that would go to his brother, Marmaduke, the first born. But upper-class Britons were delighted when the Homestead Act provided an opportunity to get extra male children out of their hair. These sons were gleefully shipped off to America with a remittance and told to make something of themselves. The Earl was no exception. He had two sons who spent too much time whoring and gambling. Let them get rich in America!

Jane's father had been all too eager to marry her off. There was all that money and Roy Woodruff ran a courtship campaign worthy of a general. Roy looked like an aristocrat and thought like an aristocrat. As for his reasons for marrying her, Jane realized too late he had looked her over like he would a horse and assessed her qualities for breeding. She was a fine specimen of womanhood with bright auburn hair and large blue eyes. She had a strong straight back and perfect proportions. She would undoubtedly bear splendid children.

He had not counted on her fiery temper.

Before coming to America, she had not been aware of his strange ways, which were becoming more worrisome all the time. He was exuberant one day and despondent the next. He kept track of things that didn't make sense. He counted the number of nails he had purchased and the mice he caught. When he did his accounts if there was the slightest smudge on a page he would start afresh. One evening he redid his addition five times.

As the days grew cooler, Roy became easier to get along with. Nevertheless, they had quarreled again. No blows, no raised voices. But they stormed out of the house separately, he to the sheep barn with its special shearing pens, and she to the small stable where they sheltered their two thoroughbred riding horses.

This was her first time out since her aborted escape. She saddled her gelding, then looked around helplessly. That disastrous evening Roy had savagely chopped her mounting block in half. "Just in case. Can't risk you ruining a good horse the next time you go crazy."

She needed help to spring into the English sidesaddle. Her cheeks flamed. Humiliated, she led Royal to the shed where Roy was repairing harness. He helped her mount. He no longer worried about her running away after he pointed out that the trip back to England would require a lot of money. Money she would never have access to.

If she was formally attired, he was proud of her appearance when she rode. He looked them over, proud that these two beauties were his property. Jane's hair was the same color as Royal's coat and her top hat drew attention to her beautiful features. The gleaming white stock above her closely fitted jacket matched the patch on Royal's nose.

"Don't do anything foolish with this horse. He's quite valuable, you know."

She shot him a look, then trotted away from their homestead.

Jane slowed her horse as she approached a

gentle draw. She had ridden miles from the little stone house she had come to despise. It was early autumn. The native blue grass swayed in the breeze and the Kansas prairie was alive with flowers and the hum of insects. When she first arrived in Kansas, she was blind to the flowers. Now she thrilled to the subtle palette of pink iron-weed next to cheery goldenrod. She loved the scattered patches of sunflowers and even the whitish pink bindweed that clung to slopes of bare earth. She dreaded another winter holed up with Roy.

She wanted to stop, dismount, and rest awhile. Contrary to that desire, she yearned to kick Royal in his withers and ride as hard and fast as she could. Away. Far, far away. But she had learned her lesson.

She yearned to dismount and rest. But she wasn't sure she could mount by herself and it would be dark by the time she walked back. Heedless of the consequences she slid off anyway and rubbed her aching back. Instead of lowering his head to the lush blue grass, Royal pushed on up the little ridge. Delighted, she heard the murmur of a little creek.

Royal snorted and eagerly began drinking the water. Grateful for the break, she eased onto the bank and arranged her skirt. She flipped her veil away from her face and removed her top hat. Her thoughts buzzed around like the blue relentless bottle flies.

Every muscle in her body stiffened at the sharp snick of a rifle being cocked. Frozen in place, her throat closed. She could not speak.

"What are you doing on my property?" A woman's voice. Low and oddly musical.

"I beg your pardon. I was just watering my horse. I didn't know this was your land." Jane scrambled to her feet. A Negro woman wearing a turban had a rifle trained on her. She did not lower it.

"After your horse drinks its fill, be on your way. And don't come back."

She grabbed Royal's reins and pulled him away from the water. She looked around but could not see a house. The woman was tall and gaunt. Her blue-black hands were strong and corded. They were so large they looked like they could snap Jane's neck. She didn't know what to say. She had never been around Negroes. Her parents' servants were Irish, not African. Frightened she looked around for a high stump so she could get back in the saddle. There wasn't one, so she simply coaxed Royal back up the bank.

Her head swirled. The muggy air pressed

against her throat and the ground rushed up to meet her.

CHAPTER TWO

When Jane awoke, she was in a bed. Her stays had been loosened. Her riding habit was neatly folded and placed on a small table. Her body was encased in a snow-white gown. Her riding gloves had also been removed and replaced with coarse cotton mittens. She wiggled her fingers and knew they were swathed in some sort of ointment. The black woman sat in a chair beside her, calmly darning a pair of socks as though she had every confidence in the world that her patient would come to.

Jane jolted upright. "What? What happened?"

"You passed out. I 'spect it's because you ain't got no more sense than to go riding off all laced up in a damn fool outfit and hooked over a saddle that ain't good for nothing except to get folks killed."

"My hands. What have you done to my hands?"

"They is hurt. Little cuts. Blisters. They can go bad. It is hard to heal hands once they go bad. You need to take care of them. Work up gradual. You doing for yourself?"

Jane did not reply. Partly from the shame of having to do her own work, but more from the shame of not knowing how to do a damned thing. She couldn't cook a meal. Couldn't keep her house clean. Couldn't turn out a decent wash. But she didn't owe this woman any explanation. Her hands were her own business. Then she realized her hands betrayed her. Anyone could see she did her own work. It was obvious to this sharp-eyed old woman.

"My husband. He'll be worried sick. I've got to get home."

"You is in no shape to ride home."

She sank back on her pillow. "I'm sorry. I simply must get on my way. If I don't, Roy will have the whole colony out looking for me."

"And what might that be?"

"We're the English people living over at Herrington Park."

"You is a long ways from where you belong. You is pert near to Nicodemus."

"Nicodemus?"

"Yes, we mostly come from Kentucky."

"My name is Jane Woodruff. And you are?"

"I is Queen Bess. This is my house."

Curious, Jane studied the woman's harsh face. Surely she meant her master's house.

She recalled the words that had accompanied the shotgun reception. "Get off my property." What had she meant by that? In England, all property belonged to the men. Any property a woman held belonged to her husband the moment they were married. Only single women could own property.

"I've got to get home. Right away, before it gets dark. Or my husband will come looking for me."

Bess was quiet for a moment and then laid down the sock. "I don't want no bunch of white folks tromping around here. Imagining things."

"There's no danger of that."

"There's plenty of danger where white folk around. But it's clear, I can't keep you here and you is no shape to ride. There's a family about a mile away that has a good horse and wagon. I'll go ask the man to take you home. You just lie here nice and quiet and don't cause no more fuss."

Jane gasped at the thought of a black man taking her back to her house. Roy would have a fit. She started to protest that it had not been her intention to cause trouble to begin with, but the old woman was already out the door. She sat up on the edge of the bed and slowly began to change back into her riding habit minus the top hat. She could not properly lace up her stays, but she rotated her corset to the front and manipulated the ties.

When she was completely dressed, she cautiously stood and then walked around the single room. It was spotlessly clean. The floor was obviously dirt, but it had been pounded and packed into a shiny single layer. There was a colorful rag rug and three shelves with little glass bottles neatly labeled.

Another wall contained a shelf of books arranged alphabetically. She scanned the titles. There was a copy of *McGuffey's Primer* and Jane wondered if the old woman was trying to learn to read. Next to that was *Alice in Wonderland.* A personal favorite of hers, but it was back in her bedroom in Northumberland. Stunned, Jane realized the book lying on its side was *Washington Square,* a book she had been yearning to read. It was hard to get a copy in England. There was even Shakespeare's *Macbeth.* She was so disoriented that she felt like she had fallen down the rabbit hole, just like Alice. There were several other titles she didn't recognize.

A basket containing Bess's darning was on the table next to a large book of *Das-*

sler's Compiled Laws. She immediately dismissed the idea that the old woman could have been reading it. She spied a newspaper — *The Colored Citizen* — folded to focus on a certain column. It read:

Wise legislation has provided schools the length and breadth of the land, where neither race or nationality is held as a barrier to admission. And I hold it be the duty of parents, next to serving their God, to see that their children attend them. (Jed Talbot)

Who were these people? Who was this woman that bossed her around like she really *was* a queen? And who was this Jed Talbot?

Jane was overcome with nausea again and went back to the safety of the bed. She sat there with her eyes closed until Bess returned.

"You is in luck. Silas is home and ain't got nothing better to do. He's gone to fetch your horse and tie him to the back of the wagon. You'll be home before dark." She walked over to her shelf and fetched a small tin. She reached for a larger container and filled it with a smelly ointment. "Here. For your hands. To take with you."

Jane kept her face impassive as she imagined Roy's reaction when she came riding up to the homestead with an African American.

"He's white," Bess said reading her thoughts. "You'll be plenty safe enough."

"I wasn't worried."

Bess scoffed.

"You've been so very kind. Thank you. What do I owe you?"

"Don't owe me nothing. I was just being neighborly."

"Thank you. And before I go, I have to ask. That book, *Dassler's Compiled Laws*?"

"Yes?"

She wanted to ask if she was able to read that book. Or any of the rest of them for that matter. "That's such hard reading and I thought . . ."

"You thought my people can't read?"

"Yes."

"Just because we were beaten within a inch of our lives for doing it, didn't mean that we didn't."

"Those books . . ." Jane gestured toward the shelf.

"Oh land, no. I can't read them. I can read the primer. The others belong to my daughter and her husband, Jed. You a reading woman?"

245

"Yes. It's what I like to do best."

"You got plenty of books?"

Jane shook her head. "I've read everything I brought with me. They are starting a library in Herrington, but I don't get there very often."

Bess gestured toward the shelf. "Take your pick. Just three. Not for keeps, mind you. When you bring them back, bring three of yours to us."

"Three?" She scanned the titles and pulled *Washington Square* off the shelf, plus two other novels. "I don't know when I can get them back to you."

"That's the bargain. You bring these back and three from your pile. You do gots three for us, don't you?"

"Heaven's yes." She bit her lip. The problem was returning the books. Roy would never let her associate with people of color.

Chapter Three

There were no roads leading back to their farm. No trails. She was dependent on the instincts of Silas Werther, a grizzled little man with a battered hat and stained clothes who seemed to know where he was going. He had bright shrewd eyes and Jane caught the amused glance he exchanged with Bess when he helped her into the wagon. No doubt it was the top hat and veil that did it. Royal was tethered to the back.

Jane plied him with questions about the mysterious black woman.

"Well, ma'am, to understand Queen Bess you have to know a little about Nicodemus. That's the most special black settlement you're ever going to find." Silas happily gave Jane a brief history lesson about this community that had the first black state officer, and the first black census taker. "And one of them folks was the first to persuade a United States senator to talk to the folks back in Washington about giving them money for all the time they was slaves. Course they run him off," he added thoughtfully. "Nobody really liked him."

"This Bess. Why do they call her Queen Bess?"

"Don't know. They just do."

"There's something about her. She scared me to death."

"You're just lucky you caught her on a good day. That old woman would just as soon blow your head off for trespassing as not. For that matter, just a couple of years ago she didn't have nothing to do with white folks period."

"But I didn't do anything. I just let my

horse get a drink of water."

"Doesn't matter. You were on her land."

"Her land? How can that be?"

"She's proved up. These people came out here about five years ago and a lot of them have lived on the land for five years now. They own their one hundred and sixty acres."

"Own? A black woman can own land?"

He chuckled. "Says so in plain English. Part of the Homestead Act. You can own one hundred and sixty acres. Man, woman, black, white. Myself, I've got a year to go."

"But why would a lone black woman want to live out her in the middle of nowhere? I didn't see any animals except for a few chickens so she doesn't work the land. How does she make a living?"

"Well now, she damn sure makes out a lot better than most of us. That's a fact. She's a healing woman and people call her out at all times of night."

"How does she get around?"

"Shank's mare. Or folks come and fetch her." He smiled at the blank look on her face. "Shank's mare means she walks. Says she can't have a bunch of animals at home that need tending to when she needs to stay with sick folks."

"Those books. Surely there's no one

around who can read those books."

"They probably belong to her daughter, Bethany. She got married and moved to Topeka with her husband, Jed Talbot. He was one right smart son-of-a-bitch. A real lawyer. Those books might belong to him. I don't mind telling you those folks have had one hell of a hard time, and Bethany's husband was right in the thick of it. But things have settled down a lot since I first moved here."

He fell silent for a couple of minutes.

"She loaned me some books."

"Good. You need to get along with those people. 'Specially Queen Bess." He glanced at her riding attire. "Another thing. We don't take to people putting on airs."

She settled back against the weathered board that served as a seat and mulled over everything he had just told her. A black woman owned property. Everyone could own property. Not just a first son through primogeniture.

She caught sight of their little stone cottage on the horizon. In the distance she could see their flock of sheep. It was sundown and a gentle breeze rippled the long bluestem grass. Richly nutritious grass that was ideal for their flocks. Roy kept meticulous records of everything that occurred on the farm and on evenings when they were not quarreling, he gloated about the increase of weight and quality of fleece the sheep would produce come shearing time.

He was in the yard standing by their other riding horse. Preparing to look for her, no doubt. She was just in time. They pulled up in front.

"Looks like you got yourself into a bit of trouble," he said as he helped her down.

"Yes. Royal shied at a snake and dumped me off." She lied easily by now.

Silas shot her a quick look, but didn't contradict her. "Mr. Werther here came along just in time."

"That's very kind of you, Werther." Roy stood stiffly by his horse and did not offer his hand.

"Glad to help."

"Do I owe you anything for your trouble?"

"Just being neighborly."

"Would you care for tea?"

Jane winced. Lord of the manor no matter how ridiculous it sounded. Sheer madness. What did he think he could serve? He was typical of their colony of remittance men in that they all seemed to believe they could make this godforsaken prairie into a little England. And even if they had crumpets and iced cakes waiting, Roy could not have

250

sounded more condescending. She was doubly mortified because Silas had just forewarned her about putting on airs.

"I'm very tired," she said, immediately stepping into the chasm of awkwardness Roy had created.

"I imagine you are." She blanched at the mocking expression on his face.

"I thank you, Mr. Werther," she said to Silas, who just stood there looking steadily at Roy. Waiting. Waiting for something.

"Oh, my horse. How stupid of me. Royal." She went to the back of the wagon and untied her gelding.

"The horse belongs in the stable," Roy said, his eyes never swerving from Silas Werther's face.

"I'll put him up," Jane said. Her cheeks flamed. Silas Werther was not Roy's servant and treating him like one wasn't going to make him into one either.

"Ain't no job for a lady," Silas said. He took the reins from Jane and headed for the stable. Roy looked on approvingly as though he had emerged victorious from a contest. He hooked his thumbs in his vest pockets.

"I'll be off now," Silas said to Jane when he returned. "Your saddlebags are draped over the stall."

"Thank you so very much. I certainly do

appreciate it."

"Ma'am." He lifted his old hat and nodded. Then he wheeled his wagon around and headed back toward his house.

"Eat some supper," Roy commanded after she stumbled inside. "We've a long day tomorrow. We'll leave for the hunt."

"I want to go straight to bed."

"Eat."

Silently she went to the stove and ladled out a small helping of stew. She had finally figured out how to keep a vegetable garden alive. The secret was endless buckets of water. This evening the mixture of potatoes, carrots, and cabbage with a little hunk of lamb tasted good.

Later, Roy was immersed in his accounts and didn't pay any attention when she slipped outside, walked to the stable, dragged a box inside to use as a mounting block, then retrieved her books from the saddlebags.

CHAPTER FOUR

The next day, when they arrived at Roy's brother's house, which was between theirs and the village of Herrington Park, Jane looked enviously at a new shed built since their previous visit. Every time they came here there was some small improvement.

Tom Woodruff was shorter than Roy — not as handsome — and had a great deal more sense. His homestead was smaller, his herds more manageable, and he had help. From the beginning he realized the merits of a system where young Englishmen came out as pupils, "pups," and were trained on host farms before they bought their own land. Her sister-in-law, Betsy, had told her sometimes these young Englishmen even paid in advance for a year's room and board.

Tom got a commission when he located and purchased land for his pups. Other newcomers worked out a "rent and purchase" or sharecrop system from land he owned. But Roy wasn't about to give up a single acre of land he possessed, and he damn sure wasn't going to take the time to locate land for potential rivals. If anything was available, he intended to buy it.

This past year, however, he had to rein in his hunger for land as his father had begun to question the amount of acreage Roy was accumulating. The Earl had not thought it would be so expensive to set up his third son.

Betsy waved from the front porch the moment she saw them. When they pulled up in front of the house, one of the pups raced up to help Jane dismount. Betsy flew to her side.

"Everyone is here. You two are the only ones staying the night with us. The others will go on to the Windsor Hotel before it gets dark. The hunt will start from Herrington. Oh, do come in. I'm dying to catch up." Betsy grabbed her arm. "It's time for tea. We are so excited. The vicar and his wife are here today."

"Church of England? Out here?"

"Yes. Clear from Salina. They will just come quarterly. But Mrs. Twell said they didn't want us to substitute the Episcopal church for the real thing." Betsy chattered nonstop. "It's so good of them to come. Won't it be wonderful to have services in our own church?"

When Jane stepped inside the house, she felt like she was in a different world. There were three other women present and they were all dressed for tea.

"Mrs. Twell, may I introduce Lady Jane Woodruff." The smile froze on Jane's face. She *was* "Lady Jane" of course, because her father was an Earl, but out here she was uncomfortable hearing herself referred to as "Lady Jane." Roy was not "Lord" because only the oldest son was privy to that title. He was usually introduced as "Honorable," which didn't seem respectful at all considering that in this country, "honorable" seemed to apply to all manner of politicians and minor officials. It drove Roy wild that there was so little respect for social position in America.

"Mrs. Twell, it is a pleasure to meet you. I'm delighted that you and your husband came all this distance." The vicar's wife was dressed in a brown brocade tea dress with an elongated bodice. She was a plump little wren of a woman with kind brown eyes and Jane liked her at once.

Mrs. Twell beamed. "My husband says Herrington Park is quite remarkable. He's eager to give a good report to his friends."

"And this is Clarissa Tapper." Jane extended her hand and nodded to a tall blond woman rapidly fanning herself with stiffly pleated cardboard. A light array of freckles covered her plain pale face. "I think you've met Mary Stelter."

"Of course. Hello, Mary."

"You'll want to change out of your riding attire." Betsy nodded to her servant and Jane followed her. Betsy had two bedrooms and although Jane knew it wasn't Christian to covet, she couldn't help it. Tom and Betsy's house was nearly finished. It wasn't grand. Not the most elegant structure on the prairie, but it was a real home.

Still laced in her stays she emerged in a lovely two-piece tea gown and gratefully accepted a cup of Earl Grey and some delicious iced cakes. She knew Mary, but not well. She didn't participate in the conversation but listened to the other women chatter. Most of it centered on the new buildings and attractions springing up in Herrington Park.

She didn't know it was possible to be this bitter. She was among women whose husbands were doing better. She could feel it.

"Will you join us next Sunday, Lady Jane?"

The question came from Mary. "We want to officially welcome our new priest. It will be our first service and we are so very pleased that we can keep up traditions here. We are so glad that Father Twell is kind enough to look after our spiritual needs."

"Lovely, I'm looking forward to it." She wasn't at all sure Roy would want to come. She fell silent. She had not known about this new church, let alone the date of the first service.

She was miserably aware that she was the only one present who did not know what was happening in the Herrington community. The only one who seemed to be merely surviving. The only one who struggled to manage basic hygiene.

She was on the verge of tears. She pressed a hand to her forehead. "Oh, do forgive me Betsy, Mrs. Twell. I am unwell. I would like to lie down for a moment." She rose awkwardly and her sister-in-law walked her into the bedroom.

"I'm sure I will be fine by morning. I fell yesterday and have not yet recovered."

"Oh, you poor dear. After we see the men off tomorrow, let's come back here and have a good visit. I believe the other ladies plan to stay at the hotel and watch all the men's antics at their leisure. We'll come back and visit. There's something I need to tell you."

Jane and Betsy — properly attired in riding habits — watched the men prepare to ride to the hounds. There were no foxes available in Western Kansas, so they substituted jackrabbits. A splendid pack of baying dogs strained at their leashes. The bugle sounded and the men were off, wildly cantering over the prairie.

Herrington Park had grown since Jane had last been here. There was a general store that also housed the post office, an opera house, the framework for the Anglican church, and other buildings that had not existed at her last visit.

Jane looked wistfully at the start of a real village. None of them lived in the town proper because they had all opted for large acreage. The buildings were all calculated to attract British upper-class settlers who were as land hungry as her husband. All of them clung to their English customs. Hunting and horses came before anything else. There was even talk of creating a polo field.

As she watched the horses and riders thunder off across the prairie, Jane could not dispel the notion that she was living a surreal existence. This was not England and all their wishing could not make it so. Nevertheless, Roy and the men in the community clung to the illusion that having high tea, playing polo, and riding to the hounds would entice other like-minded aristocrats to settle here.

When she had first objected that the time spent clearing out the grass to prepare a polo field would have been better spent clearing the land for planting, Roy scoffed at her objections.

Now Betsy was tugging her to the walkway in front of the hotel. "Come on. I want to show you around town. If you are up to it."

"I'm fine. All over yesterday's vapors. A brisk walk will do me good."

They paused at each building. Jane had been to the general store because it was also where they picked up their mail. Betsy was full of information about the planning of each structure and happily gossiped about the cost of the furnishings.

"And this is our library."

Jane stood stock still. "A library?"

"Donations of books are coming in from all over," Betsy said happily. "Everyone has been very generous. I'm so sorry you can't go through it today. I know you like to read. But it's not open on Sunday, of course."

"A real library?"

"Yes. But we have a problem. Our librarian and her husband are leaving. They are going back to England. They hate it out here." Betsy sighed. "Just when she was getting everything organized."

Back to England. Jane's heart raced. *Back to England.* So there were other people who felt as she did.

They finished their tour of the town, then visited a moment with the ladies sitting on the hotel's porch before they rode back to the ranch. When they arrived, Betsy led her to a chair. A proper padded chair with cushions and a tufted back. There was a little footstool for her feet, and once again tea served in a delicate cup by a proper Irish maid.

Did she dare talk to Betsy? Share her unhappiness with this smiling woman who had a talent for endurance?

Betsy didn't speak for several minutes. She looked at her feet, then when she raised her gaze and could look Jane fully in the eyes, the color rose in her cheeks. "Jane, there is something I think you need to know. Something I don't understand. I'm reluctant to discuss this with you." Her voice faltered and she placed her cup on the table. She continued grimly like a child determined to see this through.

"Tom was in Hays last week at the train station. He said there was a poster offering a reward to anyone who would return a red-haired blue-eyed woman to her distraught husband, Roy Woodruff, if she should attempt to buy a ticket. Jane, it has to be you. What in the world is going on?"

Jane's cup tumbled off the saucer before she burst into tears. "How could he do such a thing? How could he possibly do such a thing?" Then before she could stop herself it all came pouring out. All of it. Her fatigue, her despair, her rage at her husband's ineptness. "You don't know what it's

260

like. You don't. Your husband has some brains."

Betsy was at her side in an instant.

"I've got to get back to England. I'll die out here. Or worse, I'll be as good as dead, because if I protest about anything at all, he'll have me in one of those new mental institutions that are springing up. He thinks I'm crazy, but I'm not. I simply can't take it."

"No. I won't let that happen." Betsy began to pace. "You have no hired help at all? How do you eat. How do you live?"

"How do you think?" Jane pulled off her gloves and showed Betsy her ruined hands. "They are healing. But see! That's where I burned my hands on the stove. The blisters on my hands, that's where I've tried to hoe the weeds out of my garden."

"Oh, Jane. This is disgraceful. Terrible. We had no idea."

"Of course, you didn't. Roy won't let Tom on the place because he's too ashamed to let his brother bear witness to his failure. He's mocked Tom as being without ambition. Pretended that he is the superior son. What he writes back to his father is lies. Pure lies. He's thinks I'm going crazy, but I swear Betsy, it's Roy who is doing things that are not normal."

261

"Two days. Give me two days, and I'll have Tom send a couple of his pups over to help with the shearing."

"No. You don't understand. He'll hate him for it. No, no, no. Don't come."

"That's why Roy is afraid you will run away, isn't it? You're being treated like some old mule."

Jane was too ashamed to let her sister-in-law know she had already tried it. That was the reason for the poster.

"It's disgraceful that he would do this and put you in that kind of light."

"How many people do you suppose have seen it?"

"Not many. Tom took it down immediately, of course. You don't have to worry about it now."

"I can't believe my own husband would do such a thing to me."

CHAPTER FIVE

Jane was hanging the small amount of clothing she had washed when she saw a woman coming across the prairie. She left her basket under the line and ran back into the house. She quickly recombed her hair and twisted it into a bun. She removed her apron and smoothed the front of her dress.

It would not do to be seen doing ordinary chores like a commoner.

Although their house was poorly furnished on the inside, after their day at the Herrington hunt Roy made sure it boasted some exterior flourishes that passersby would notice. There was now a small porch with a swing. Jane headed for it as though taking her leisure like a woman of substance. When the speck on the horizon grew close, she could see it was the black woman with the arrogant title of Queen Bess.

Nervously, she hoped Roy was busy with the sheep as he would be against any contact with someone from the black community.

Queen Bess marched right up on the porch and made her way to a chair. The woman did not smile. "Mrs. . . ." Jane hesitated because she didn't know her last name. She didn't have the slightest idea what she should say. She suspected that it was not appropriate to offer refreshments to a Negress. But it seemed awkward to keep her sitting outside on the porch on this hot day without offering her a drink of water. *Yes, water,* she decided. That should be just fine. Humane, but not as formal as tea.

Queen Bess wasted no time in getting to the reason for her visit.

"I'm here to offer you a job."

Jane could not have been more astonished if this fierce gaunt woman had announced she intended to turn her into a mermaid.

"A job?"

"Yes. We is looking for a teacher. Nicodemus had the first school district out here. There's plenty more schools that have sprung up since, but our children don't have no one to teach them enough to go on past the early grades. We did for a while. My own daughter was the best, but she and her husband moved on. The teacher we been counting on got married and moved away."

"I'm not a teacher."

"Is you a reading woman?"

"Yes, of course. You know that." At least she had her books to comfort her when the life out here was nearly unbearable.

"We don't need no certificates. We just need someone that will help us."

It was impossible. Roy would never consent. One of the plums he dangled before people who were considering settling out here was that they would not have to associate with the lower classes. What would their friends think?

"I'm so very sorry. I really can't do that."

"You is not happy out here. You might as well be doing some good."

Jane's temper rose at the accusation that

she was not happy. This woman had no reason or authority to analyze her.

"My husband would never allow this. I really don't think you understand. I'm Lady Jane Woodruff. And back in England, ladies don't work at menial jobs. My husband's father is an Earl. A peer of the realm."

"Well, I is Queen Bess and I think that make me higher up the totem pole than some old Earl."

Taken back, Jane peered at her. Surely, she was joking. The woman didn't even have the right to be sitting here like she was her equal.

"We ain't got no money to pay you, 'cause I'm sure you know how bad that drought was last summer." The old woman was calm. Her hands were folded on her faded blue dress that had been through so many washings and patched so often it gave a new meaning to threadbare.

"Do you have books?" the old woman asked.

Jane was so astonished by Queen Bess's boldness that she could only nod. "You know I do."

"You'll need to bring some of those. We've got some right clever people who can make copies for the children."

Surely this woman wasn't serious. But

Bess still had not cracked a smile.

"And for no money," Jane said with amusement. "Really!"

"No money. But we will take turns helping out around here. I 'spect you could use some help."

Outraged, Jane knew at once this shrewd old woman had deduced this from the looks of her hands during the time she had spent in her soddy. Her heart caught in her throat. Servants. She would have servants. Not the good reliable Irish she and her husband were used to, but strong people to do the laundry, iron the clothes, sweep the floors, chase the infernal dust. And cook. She was sure they were better cooks.

Queen Bess saw the spark in her eyes and knew she was on the right track. "And I 'speck you need someone to help you get a garden started. If we have another hot summer it takes a lot of walking back and forth with heavy buckets to keep plants alive until they can do you some good."

Jane lowered her head into her hands and shut her eyes for an instant, imagining the wires supporting the buckets digging into her palms. Her aching shoulders. The days she tried to work outside, she was so weary she saw sunspots. "My husband," she said weakly.

266

"What you husband have to do with it?"

"He's the one who will have to decide to give me permission." All thoughts of getting relief from the backbreaking work fled. It was unheard of for someone of her class to teach school. Any school. Let alone to black children.

"Huh. Looks to me if you is a fine lady you should have some say-so over your life. Our women do. Ain't no man tell us what to do."

Jane could not think of a reply.

"Now, could I trouble you for a drink of water before I start back?"

Jane sprang to her feet and went inside and fetched a glass from the cupboard. As she carried it outside, she knew Roy would be appalled at the thought of drinking from the same glass.

"I thank you, kindly."

"You are welcome," Jane murmured. Queen Bess's comment that no man should be telling her what to do stung. Back home, before she was married, nothing would have stopped her from making her own decisions. The irony was that Roy was beating down the high-spirited impulses that had attracted him to her in the first place.

Everyone knew the best breeders had a little fire. It's what made winners.

She rose suddenly and stood facing the sun. She simply could not go on like she was. "I'll consider it. How can I get word to you?"

"It be best if you decide now. It's a long walk over here. I don't want to come back except to do some work."

"Yes. Then, yes." Jane said. She didn't know what she would tell Roy. How would she find the words? Already she was testing phrases, imagining Roy's reaction. The hardest hurdle would be explaining how this community knew she needed help.

"Thank you, kindly." Bess got up to leave. "And 'bout that wash I see baking in the basket out in your yard. I'll take care of it on my way back."

Jane watched her leave. And watched her stoop to finish putting the wash on the clothesline. A poor clothesline that Roy had put up in a fit of anger as though giving in to the demands of a spoiled child. It drooped and the left post was not upright.

"Ma'am," Jane called.

The old woman turned and smiled for the first time. "Yes?" She came over to the porch, balancing the empty basket on her hip.

"I was wondering if you would consider sending some men over, too. My husband really needs the help. He's overburdened."

"We could do that. And come slaughter time, we would welcome a hog and maybe one of his sheep and some of the fleece at shearing time."

Jane nodded, then watched until her figure disappeared over the horizon. She had a feeling that including some relief for Roy was all it would take to make his objections disappear.

At supper she told him about Queen Bess's visit and the offer that had come out of a clear blue sky.

"Absolutely not. I don't want you associating with black people. By God, I don't understand why none of the Irish out here won't stick around. It's like they forget their place the minute someone dangles land in front of them."

Jane lowered her eyes. It wasn't them. It was her husband's arrogance.

"No. It's out of the question. It's a sign of her ignorance that she would come here with such a proposition. But at least we know one thing now. They are looking for work. All of them. They don't have the backbone to survive out here. We are the superior race."

Please, oh, please, Jane pleaded silently. *Please let me have some help.*

"How the hell did that woman know where to find you and that we needed help?"

"I suppose Silas Werther told her that you were working alone," she said cautiously. "There were no extra horses in the stable so it would have been obvious."

He grunted. "Werther is just the kind of lowlife who would hobnob with a bunch of degenerates."

She cleared the table and he went out on the porch and brooded for another hour before he came inside. "I'll go over there the first thing tomorrow morning. And talk to the men and see what it would take to hire some help. That old woman can't make deals on their behalf. They'll work cheap. No doubt I'll have so tell them how to do every last thing, but it will be worth it to have another man on the end of a board."

He returned early afternoon and raged for an hour. "I've met that hateful damned old woman. I don't know what kind of hold she has over those people, but to a man they refused to work for me if you don't start teaching the upper grades. It's like she cast some kind of a spell over them. Plus, the men demanded more money than I was ready to pay for help with building."

She let him rant.

"Here's what I've decided. No one must know you are doing this. No one. You can't talk about it and no one must know where you are going. I don't think it will last long. How much can they learn, anyway? By the time they decide that higher education is not for them, I'll get some of them used to working for me. I'll figure out what it takes to sweeten the pot."

"You're very wise," she murmured. She didn't tell him that she had already given her consent.

CHAPTER SIX

Three days later, Bess was back with two other women. An hour later five men from Nicodemus joined them. Jane watched in amazement as the women took over her house. One immediately gathered up laundry and set water to boil. Another who had brought her own rags filled a pail and set to work cleaning.

She and Roy used a sheet to divide their bed from the rest of the room. Her clothes hung from pegs that had been pounded into the mortar. Bess looked through her dresses. She hung the riding habit on a separate peg along with two good silks that Jane wore when she and Roy went to events in Herrington Park.

"None of these will do you a bit of good," Bess muttered. "Ain't you got something simple? Never mind. I can see that you don't." She answered her own question. "LuAnn, do we still have some of that grey linsey-woolsey left? Enough to make this child some dresses?"

A stocky woman walked over and stood next to her. "Two maybe."

"Two is fine. And how about one of them split skirts for her to ride in."

Jane was at her side immediately. "No. There will be none of that. I won't want to wear my habit, but I intend to ride with the saddle I always use." Roy had already said he didn't want their neighbors to know she was doing this. She had no idea how he intended to prevent word from getting out, but nothing made her more visible than riding out in a top hat and fitted coat with a blazing white stock. She liked the idea of subdued colors. Besides if she used her habit every day, she would soon wear it out.

"I will not ride astride, and that's that. It's not ladylike." She absolutely refused to give up her wonderful posture on a horse for the hideous slump she had seen some Western women use. They swayed back and forth in the saddle like they were part of the horse.

They looked quite vulgar in their broad saddles that jarred and jolted. Having one leg firmly anchored over the upright pommel and the other hooked over her thigh was so much more secure than bouncing along.

"There has to be more material in the skirt right in front if she's going to ride that way," LuAnn said. She quickly sketched a two-piece design

"No stays," said Bess.

"I've always . . ."

"Never mind what you always done," Bess snapped. "No stays." She turned to LuAnn. "No stays. Fit it without stays." She turned to Jane again. "Can't have you passing out in front of the children."

The women moved through her home like visiting angels. The laundry was dry by sundown. "We'll bring sad irons next time," said LuAnn. "For your fancy clothes. When you go to meeting."

The aroma of good bread wafted through the house. Everything was neat. Her spirits rose. When Roy came in that evening, he smiled for the first time in a month.

In the following weeks, the men made short work of building a new shearing shed. They straightened the posts supporting the open shed that would protect the sheep during the winter. They finished building up the sides and put on a roof of corrugated tin.

Jane beamed when she walked into the schoolroom for the first time. This large stone structure had been built of the same easily quarried limestone used to build their own house. The building doubled for storing seeds and supplies and was used as a community center when there were special occasions. It had a dirt floor, but it had been patiently sprinkled and pounded by the same method used in Queen Bess's soddy until it was hard and shone like quartz.

Benches made from boards spread across logs had no backs. There was a stove in one corner. In the other was a wooden pail with a dipper and a tin cup hooked over the rim. She had not seen a pump or a windmill outside and realized it would be necessary to send one of the older children to the creek when she ran out of drinking water.

There was a crude desk and back of it a shelf that contained one copy of *Monteith's* and *McNally's* geography and two old editions of *Clark's Grammar*. There were three *McGuffey's Readers* and a Bible. Next to three quill pens on her desk was a bottle of ink and five slate tablets. Beneath the shelf was a much larger slate and a piece of easily erased soapstone.

School would not begin until nine o'clock or just until everyone got there as she doubted that any of the families had a watch.

When the first children came in Jane was astonished that several were accompanied by their parents. But when others came trickling in with their whole family, she was aware of the importance these people placed on education. Some families came in and handed her precious books with a warning they had to be returned in perfect shape.

A man she guessed to be about six foot two stepped forward. He had closely cropped nappy hair and was thickly muscled. "I'm Sam Barnett. Don't you forget this here book belongs to me. I brought it from Kentucky. I want it back when you done teaching my boy."

She glanced at the title: *Oliver Twist.* How had he gotten hold of it?

"Can't read none myself." He touched a brand on his cheek. "That was done for thinking I had a right to try."

"You were branded for wanting to learn to read?"

"Yes, ma'am. Want my boy treated right. He special. Come here, Little John."

Jane smiled at the unlikely nickname as his son was nearly six feet tall. He came forward but looked at his feet. He mumbled, "pleased," then stepped back.

The parents gathered at the back of the room and studied Jane solemnly. The weight of their expectations humbled her. She had never seen people who cared so much about seeing their children learn. She smiled, remembering Roy's words that this would be over in no time. After he was able to pay the men wages and they could put the bizarre demand that she teach school behind them.

Daunted, she realized she did not have the slightest idea how to begin. She had been schooled at home. Her tutor began with a reading from the *Book of Common Prayer,* followed by singing "God Save the Queen." She surveyed all the black faces and fought the urge to flee. She turned her back to the room and murmured one of the classic prayers she knew. "Oh, God make speed to save me. Oh, Lord make haste to help me."

Inspired she turned back around and asked them to bow their heads. She repeated those lines.

"I see our sister know the psalms." She looked gratefully at the large black man in the back of the room who had spoken. Before the session began, one of the parents had referred to him as Reverend Myers. "Our children will be in good hands."

She knew she had passed a subtle test when he stepped forward. "Let's all join our voices in praise and prayer. Praise to the Lord for sending us this fine lady." Grateful, she was the first to bow her head. Reverend Myers's prayer was powerful and simple and could not be found in any book she was familiar with. It went on longer than she thought necessary.

"Sir, as you know I am a stranger to this country," she said, when he finished. Her voice trembled, thankful for his intervention. "I would ask you to lead us in a song."

His strong bass rang out in a chorus the children all knew. Jane retrieved her handkerchief from her sleeve and dabbed at her tears. Their songs were not her songs, but her gratitude for their acceptance flowed through her body like the praise they were invoking in the music. And when the Reverend led the chorus the third time, she joined in. Her clear strong soprano vibrated with "peace like a river."

CHAPTER SEVEN

In two weeks' time she had sorted out the children who were just beginning from those who were already reading and had made some progress in basic arithmetic. She quickly understood just how special Little John Barnett was. He had remarkable math skills. Far beyond her abilities. She had to find someone who could guide his next steps. It certainly would not be any of the men she had met so far in Herrington Park. Their days were focused on horses and hounds and having a jolly good time. And her days were now focused on thinking of ways to make the school better.

Although she was steeped in knowledge about the history of Britain, the children needed to know about the history of their own people. So they would be aware of what made them "us." But there were no books on the shelf or in her home about these people's heritage.

Surely the new library would have something. Roy would not give her permission to ride off to Herrington. She would have to make the trip behind his back. One morning she made arrangements for her oldest student, Faith Chaney, to monitor the class. She rode off in the direction of the school as usual, then abruptly turned east when she was out of sight of their homestead.

Eliza Markley was a small woman with a sour expression on her narrow face. She followed Jane around the library and complained constantly. "They just pay me a pittance for keeping track of these books and not many people come here anyway. God knows how we ended up in this godforsaken place."

Jane wanted to tell the librarian to leave her alone, but the books were helter-skelter on the shelves and she didn't have much time.

"Are you looking for anything in particular?"

"No."

When Eliza pointed toward novels Jane promptly came up with a credible strategy. She had to get home before sundown. "As a matter of fact, I have a cousin who is very interested in America's civil war. Do you have any books written by black people?"

"Yes. But they have no credibility. In fact, there is general agreement that they were written by white people." She went to a shelf and plucked out two books and handed them to Jane. They were a slender volume of poetry by Phillis Wheatley and an autobi-

279

ography by Frederick Douglass.

"Are there any people-of-color books written for children?"

"No, of course not." Eliza looked at her sharply. "And besides, I doubt they would be of any use to you interpreting history. Rumor has it that quite a number of books are being written about that war, but we don't have any here."

Jane thanked her and headed back to the schoolhouse.

Giddy with purpose, she flew across the prairie every morning. Her face was lightly tanned and her complexion glowed. Her eyes sparkled again, and the vigorous ride brought a natural blush back to her cheek. At first, she had missed the splendid autumns in Northumberland and the glorious display of color when the leaves on the oaks and alders turned. Then she yielded to the prairie's exquisite preparation for winter. The prelude to fall was subtle. There was a quickness in the air. The blue of the sky intensified and some days she sensed a vibration emanating from the earth itself. Even the scattered patches of buffalo grass defiantly brightened before it was forced to settle into a tired bluish green.

With growing wonder, she realized that

for at least part of the day she was very close to being happy. Like the woman she was before she was married.

She was falling in love with her pupils. Sylvia, with her constant chatter. Mary Lou, who insisted on mothering the littler ones. She was moved by their innocent trust that she knew everything. Their belief that she was the smartest person alive. Until she found juvenile books with Negro heroes or heroines, she settled for reading fairy tales to the students. She cast a magic net over these overworked children who needed to believe in happy endings.

One morning reading instruction was disrupted by the youngest pupil who said something that set the other children on the bench giggling. "Estes," she said sternly, "Alice was reading to us. You've spoiled it for her. And she was doing such a good job. Stand up at once and tell us what was so funny."

He rose promptly but kept his head down and mumbled something she couldn't hear. She could not bring herself to be too sharp with this little boy. "Well, what was it? Speak up. We would like to laugh, too."

"I just say Queen Bess is our Healing Mama, she know all about sick people. Lu-Ann is our Fixing Mama. She know how to do everything. And you is our Book Mama. You've read every book in the world."

"I see." No one laughed. There were a few anxious glances as the children waited for her reaction. Inwardly she smiled, but simply said, "You may sit down. It's now Jeffrey's turn to read. We were on page thirteen." Her heart leaped with pleasure despite the severe expression on her face.

Nevertheless, when the day was done her happiness faded. She rode back to her husband's farm — she could never think of it as theirs, just his. She slowed Royal to a walk and was strangely reluctant to top the hill. Beyond that rise lay the rank evidence of Roy's delusions of grandeur. He had gotten worse now that he had men to carry out his orders. Her heart sickened every evening when she came over the rise and surveyed the piles of stones and lumbers and slabs of tins and scattered tools. A sense of hopelessness crept over her. After the first round of finishing shelters for the sheep, Roy dreamed up other projects.

At least her house was in order now. One of the women of Nicodemus came over every day. She came home to a clean house with a delicious supper waiting. She spent her evenings planning lessons and reading. Roy no longer cataloged her imperfections.

He was totally focused on building.

One evening when she returned, there was a huge pile of rocks outside the house.

"What is going on?"

"We are caught up," Roy said. "I want to finish building our house. The finest structure on the prairie. A showplace, worthy of our status."

She chose her words carefully. "I think, for now, we would be better off just putting on a couple real bedrooms. And a little mud porch where I could do laundry. A summer kitchen would be nice, too." She honestly thought he had put the grand plans aside. Recently, he had focused on increasing the herd and hadn't mentioned the house.

"We'll do the wings you want first. That won't take long. Then I'll start on the second story."

"Oh, Roy, surely you're not going ahead with it. The two extra rooms will be all we need. Have you thought about the money this will take? Your father has been so generous. I don't want you to do anything that will strain your relationship."

"Father will be all too proud to know that we are doing so well."

"We don't need a second story."

He ignored her protests. Didn't even bother to address them. It was as though he hadn't heard her and was talking to himself. "Yes, there will be stone on the bottom, and then a basic Tudor structure with timbers and cupolas."

"Oh, Roy. Please don't do this."

"Building is a man's territory," he snapped. "You don't have the mind for it. I'll thank you not to interfere."

"But Roy, you will need so much more money."

"I said hold your tongue woman. Father will be happy to support this project."

Two weeks later the men began constructing rooms on either side of the one-room house she and Roy had occupied since coming to America. They did not cut the doorways until the very last so other than the noise, the building was not bothersome. Jane was delighted when the openings were finished, real doors hung, and she had two real bedrooms with small closets extending into the room for her clothes. Roy ordered a fine bed and a dresser. At last their little house started to resemble a real home.

Then he began work on the upper story.

One week later, she found LuAnn waiting on the porch when she returned from school. The woman did not smile, even when Jane took a seat opposite her.

"Is something wrong, LuAnn?" Their

work was usually finished by noon with supper either waiting or left for her to finish when she returned from school.

"We is not coming back. None of us."

Shocked, Jane's heart sank. "Why? Have I done something wrong?"

"Not you, Miss Jane. It's Mr. Roy and his confounded building and stomping around on the roof. This just ain't right. It's a waste of our time. There's dust drifting down from the ceiling every time the men work on something. It even get in the food."

"He will be done in a very short time," Jane said. "Truly. It won't take long."

"Ma'am, he ain't never going to be done. And this ain't right. All of us done talked it over. We through." She rose then and headed toward Nicodemus.

Jane went inside and sank into the nearest chair. She looked around at the rock silt that covered everything. There was no food waiting and she was starved. There was a basket of folded laundry next to the stove, but it, too, was accumulating the fine coating of limestone particles that filtered through the air like dust motes. There was a plate of biscuits next to the sink. Those, and a bunch of late bitter radishes and a few potatoes, would have to do for supper.

As she began fixing their meager meal she

veered between rage at her husband and a growing sense of desperation. Most worrisome of all, was Roy's changeability. He would mull over the progress the men made every evening, then just as likely as not propose an alteration the next morning to what had been accomplished the day before.

Two weeks after the last woman departed, Sam Barnett was waiting for her to return from school. "I would like a word with you, ma'am."

"Yes?"

He held his hat over his chest. "This is kind of hard to say, but I'm going to get right to it. We afraid the mister don't know nothing about building. I kind of thought so and some of the other men did, too. Then when my boy, Little John, took a look at this place he like to have a fit. Little John good at figuring in his head."

"I'm aware of your son's abilities."

"He say what Mr. Roy wants can't be done without tearing up what you got down here. Some of us men have been talking and we was wondering if one of your white friends — a man he might listen to — would talk some sense to him. Do you have an architect over at Herrington? Someone he might respect?"

She was speechless. It wasn't proper to

listen to someone criticizing her husband, let alone a black man. And leaning on the perceptions of one of her students at that. How did Sam Barnett even know the word "architect"? Or what they did for that matter?

"I'll look into it," she said stiffly.

Tom and Betsy came over for a visit one fall evening just before the days started to cool off in earnest. Roy immediately took Tom behind the house to show him the fine new outbuildings. His brother had not seen the shearing shed and the splendid winter protection he had built for his sheep. There was the beginning of a real barn.

Jane led Betsy up to the porch. "We're finishing our house. I'll let you inside for a little peek, then I'll bring our tea out here. When the men come back, we can all sit and visit for a spell."

"Lovely. I have so much to tell you. Mostly about the church. Our next service will be this Sunday. I hope you can come."

"Well . . ." Jane hesitated. The truth was that Roy had lost all interest in religion. Still smarting from the humiliating poster Betsy had shown her, she didn't want the evening to focus on her marriage. "Come see what Roy has done so far. I'm so pleased."

"Jane, I had no idea," Betsy exclaimed when she peered through the door. She stepped inside and gingerly worked her way around a pile of boards. "You have two new rooms now. That is simply wonderful."

"Roy is working on something else. But I can't show it to you right now. Go on. Shoo. Get back out on the porch and I'll bring tea in a minute."

Betsy left and waited outside on the porch. Jane returned shortly with a clay pot and two cups. "Sorry. It's not as hot as we like it."

Betsy bubbled with questions. "Roy couldn't have done this by himself. Where did you find the help?"

"From the black community." She hesitated, then decided she had said enough. Roy would be terribly upset if she told Betsy about their strange arrangement.

After a tour of the outbuildings, the two brothers ambled toward the porch. Tom was obviously impressed with the improvements. "And that's not all," Roy said. "I've arranged to buy a tract of land that's adjacent to my claim. I might try my hand at cattle, too, after I get my flock of Leicesters built up."

Tom stopped in his tracks. "What the hell, Roy? How can you manage all of that?

Besides, people are starting to grumble about the number of acres we Brits are buying. Calling us 'land-grabbing son-a-bitches.' There's even talk of limiting the amount of land someone can buy if they are not an American citizen."

"Yeah? Well it's not yet the law. The land is there for the taking. Might as well be me."

Then Tom caught sight of the enormous pile of stones and lumber next to the house. He stopped and tried to make sense of what he was seeing. "What is all this? What do you have in mind?"

"It's material for the second story. This will be the grandest home in our settlement. With a central hall and music room. And a grand bedroom upstairs."

"You can't add those rooms on top of what you have now," Tom protested. "They have to be planned for at the very beginning. The weight must be managed just right. There must be bearing walls. Poles."

"I know what I'm doing."

The very air seemed to turn to ice. Tom slowly shook his head.

"This won't work, Roy. And even if it would, I can't believe Father has agreed to give you money for this. Have you told him what you are doing?" His voice rose.

"You get money from him, too."

"Yes, but what I ask for is an investment for him. Everything I'm doing will make him more money. I don't understand this. Besides, if we are going to live out here, it's a mistake to build something so far above what anyone else is doing."

"You're jealous. Shortsighted. You always have been."

"Admit it. You haven't told Father what you are doing. He thinks his money is going to increase your herd. Not for new land and a house that's a showplace."

"Get off my property."

"Roy, let's not quarrel. What I'm trying to tell you is that money is tightening back home. The banks are scrutinizing every loan. You need to take care not to put Father under unnecessary pressure."

"I said get off my property."

It was hard to say if Jane or Betsy was more miserable when the men began to quarrel. Jane's stomach clenched when Tom voiced his doubts about tacking a structure on top of the lower level.

"Roy, I'm not trying to start a fight. I'm trying to tell you for your own good." Tom looked at him wearily, with the resignation of a man who knew further argument was useless.

"Leave. Don't come back."

Sorrowfully, Tom unhitched his horse and buggy from the rail in front of the house. Betsy rose, then went to Jane and squeezed her hand before she walked away. Jane's heart was like a stone in her breast when she saw her best friend head back for Herrington Park.

Chapter Eight

By Sunday Roy's mood had lifted. He woke in a good humor as though he had received divine guidance in a dream. Jane watched in wonder as he dressed in his finest clothes.

"Are we going to church?" She asked cautiously, as often the slightest inoffensive comment would strike him the wrong way.

"No, I'm going to Clarksville to direct the delivery of a load of supplies. I ordered some good oak to build the stairs."

"When will you be back?"

"Tomorrow or Tuesday." He frowned at her like she had no business asking.

The moment he disappeared over the horizon she flew to their new bedroom and grasped her silk dress from the hook. She could not lace her stays properly. Although Roy wanted her to look her best, he had only helped once, and then he had been so impatient and rough — like he was handling a heifer — that she never asked him to help again. But she had learned that by wedging a stick where the latticed ribbons crossed and giving them a twist, she could manage to work her way down. The effect was quite presentable.

It was two days since the row between Roy and his brother and she could think of nothing else but Sam Barnett's warning, and then Tom's, that Roy knew nothing about building. What if they were right?

The new buildings in Herrington Park were well-designed. The layout was pleasing and symmetrical. Someone with brains had to be behind it. That someone had to be an Englishman as the good people of Herrington did not cotton to having outsiders play much of a role in their lives. And every proper Englishman would be in church. She would be there, too, this Sunday and talk to this miracle worker.

She checked her appearance in the mirror and was pleased that she still could look elegant when she chose to. The blue silk accented her large blue eyes and set off her auburn hair. No one would guess the strain she was under. She was sorry her husband would not be beside her, but there were other women who attended services by themselves. Widows mostly, but surely she would not be too conspicuous. She grabbed her *Book of Common Prayer* and headed to the stable.

When she arrived, she took a seat at the back. She spied Tom and Betsy immediately and envied the normalcy of the couple. They seemed to function as one. They went to church together, to meetings together, and rode out in their buggy together. Her heart ached with longing for such a marriage.

After the final hymn Jane marched right up to them. Tom looked at her warily, but Betsy's eyes were full of compassion.

Jane launched right into what she was going to say. "I'm so sorry you had words with Roy the other night. I'm sure you know his views are not my views."

Tom and Betsy exchanged glances. "We figured that."

"Roy went to Clarksville to get some lumber. He's wearing himself out. I think that's why he won't listen to anyone."

Tom lowered his eyes.

He didn't believe her? Fine, no matter. She plunged right ahead. "I want someone who knows something about building to talk some sense into him. You can't be that man, Tom. And heaven knows I don't have a bit of influence. Is the man here today who is in charge of the construction in this town?"

"Of course. That's a good idea. I'll introduce you."

Tom led her over to a tall man with blond hair. He turned to meet her.

"Lady Jane Woodruff, I would like you to meet Avery Gentry. Mrs. Woodruff is a great admirer of the buildings you have constructed here in Herrington Park."

Gentry had soft brown eyes and a generous wide smile. "I can assure you, madam, that this was only accomplished through the willing workers of this fine community."

As a married woman she had no business noticing if a man was plain or handsome. Certainly she should not be puffed up with vanity over her own appearance. Grateful that she had chosen the blue silk, dismayed by the sudden blush in her cheeks and the unfamiliar warmth that stole over her body, she reconsidered what she had planned to say.

She was suffused with a surge of Irish pride.

She could not, would not let this fine elegant gentleman see her at a disadvantage. She wanted him to think well of her. She checked herself before she took the fatal step of discrediting her husband.

Only Tom and Betsy knew about the

poster. Only Tom and Betsy knew about their troubles. Knowing Tom and his pride of family she could count on him to protect Roy's reputation. She drew herself up to her full height and responded to Gentry like the proper lady she was trained to be. "I'm sure you have remarkable ability, sir. My sister-in-law gave me a tour of the new buildings the last time I was here. I see there are a few more now."

"You are very kind."

"I'm an avid reader. I had occasion to visit your wonderful library."

He frowned. "I'm afraid it's closed now. The Markleys have deserted us and left for England."

Shocked, Jane chatted a few minutes longer. All those books and no one to care for them! She excused herself and joined a group of women who were talking about the latest fashions. The town needed a librarian. How she would love to do that, but she had to keep working at the school or Roy would lose the men who were helping him build.

All the while she listened to the women, she gave thanks for being able to control the wild impulse that had sent her here today. At least she had not recklessly presented Roy as a fool to Avery Gentry. Roy was her husband and she did not have the right to dishonor him. She could not do it.

They were quality folk.

But on the trip back to their house she kept carrying on imaginary conversations with the elegant handsome stranger. Explaining that she had thought Roy would turn out to be like Jane Austen's difficult hero, Mr. Darcy. She had read *Pride and Prejudice* before they were married. She had assumed she could make his moods banish with a dose of female tenderness. She wanted this Mr. Gentry to know that Roy was basically . . . basically, what?

Then she wept.

She was exhausted the next morning. She could only remember fragments of troubling dreams during which she kept defending Roy to Tom and Betsy, then to Avery Gentry, and then to herself.

Tuesday, when Roy returned from Clarksville his buoyant mood had left him. When she asked if the oak was the quality he had expected, he said it was "satisfactory." The wood arrived and the men from Nicodemus laid the precious lumber on a large tarp.

"I'll show him," he muttered after the wood was covered with more tarps. "The narrow-minded son-of-a-bitch. My brother has always been envious." He simply would not settle down.

The next evening when she returned from school and tried to cobble together a meal, she imagined what it would be like to just stop with the extra bedrooms. They were perfect. The way the house was now was all that she needed. Inspired, she walked outside and imagined grafting a two-story structure onto the front of the house. It could be as grand as Roy desired, but the construction would be sound to begin with. The existing core would house the working rooms: a kitchen, a laundry area complete with a spinning wheel and a loom, a dry storage area for firewood.

She daydreamed all the time now and walked on eggs around Roy.

She had lost the women who helped her cope with the endless work of managing a homestead, but the men still came every day. Sometimes they would bring a meal that Queen Bess had prepared. But most of the time in the morning she peeled the vegetables for a dreary little stew and hoped she would have enough time to finish it when she returned from school.

Then one evening a rider appeared in the distance. As he drew closer, Jane could see that it was Avery Gentry. She smiled when he doffed his hat because his blond hair had a touch of red. Not bright, more like the sun had kissed in reddish highlights. Although hers matched the coat of her roan gelding and his gleamed in the light, she suspected he either had a touch of Tudor in his ancestry or a hint of the Irish like herself.

He wore simple corduroy pants and a broad Western hat. His rugged boots anchored well in his stirrups. His shirt was intended to be white but was stained with dust. Jane was aware of features she had not noticed the past Sunday. He had fine even teeth and a clipped mustache. His broad firm chin had a slight cleft. He sat firmly in the saddle like a proper Englishman. There was none of the Western slouch she so disapproved of.

"Ma'am." He lifted his hat but did not fully remove it. "It is a pleasure to see you again. I would like to speak with your husband."

Roy had seen him ride up and walked up from the barn as soon as he could get there.

"Avery Gentry, sir. Your brother said you might welcome my help in planning your buildings. I am in charge of the new construction in Herrington. I also planned a village very close to where your father, the Earl of Sedgwick, lives in England. He can vouch for my work."

"Get off my property. And tell Tom I don't need any help."

Jane gasped at his rudeness. Gentry did not reply but just sat on his horse coldly looking him over. Then his mouth quirked into a little half-smile. "As you wish, sir."

He lifted his hat again to Jane. "Ma'am," and whirled around and galloped back across the prairie.

Roy went to bed before Jane and she did not join him until she was sure he was asleep. She sat in the living room, rocking and rocking, without touching her needlework. She picked up a book but could not concentrate. Finally, she went into her bedroom and changed into a nightgown and eased under the covers, taking care not to wake Roy.

But she could not dispel a sense of doom. If it weren't for her teaching, her life would be unbearable.

CHAPTER NINE

Roy's behavior became more erratic and Jane dawdled on her way home from school. There were days when she wished she could simply stay the night there on a little pallet. But it was out of the question. She needed food and so did her husband.

Two nights after the visit from Gentry she could hear Roy yelling at one of the men. As her horse came closer to the house her heart sank. The man was Sam Barnett.

"You lazy bastard. All of you. This should have been finished a week ago. Monkeys have more brains than you do. And they are a hell of a lot more ambitious."

She plunged forward, heedless of the consequences, and slid to the ground in front of them. "Roy. I won't have this."

Her husband looked at her like she had lost her senses. Sam was packing up his tools. Jane rushed over to him. "Mr. Barnett. My husband is not himself today. I want to apologize for his harsh words. They were uncalled for. He is a gentleman at heart. He's simply not himself today."

"Ma'am, your man most surely *is* himself today." Sam picked up his satchel of tools and flung them over his shoulder. The look he gave Jane was not that of a chastised man but rather one of a man full of righteous anger.

The school was her sanctuary. Her oasis. She could not keep herself together without having the children to look forward to. She had started going there earlier and earlier to escape. A week after the men quit, as usual she eagerly trotted over the last rise before the school came into view. She stopped short. There was a double buggy parked in front. It could carry four people and had a folding top. She didn't know of anyone in Nicodemus who could afford such a luxurious conveyance.

Curious, she rode on in, dismounted, and tied Royal to the hitching post in front. She wished she had worn a better dress. This one fit well enough, but she had a blue calico that complemented her eyes. She smoothed her hair and removed four textbooks and some supplies from her saddlebag.

She pushed through the door. Queen Bess and three smiling strangers faced her. The gentleman was the most handsome Negro she had ever seen. He was tall with luminous grey eyes. His skin was the color of her saddle and he had military bearing.

Next to him was a small woman dressed in dark green velvet. She had not seen this quality of clothing since she left England. The bodice was long and fitted perfectly over her bust and hips. The skirt was swept back over a bustle. Jane was mortified to be caught without stays, because this adorable woman was obviously cinched in. Although

301

her skin was the color of cinnamon, her almond-shaped heavily lashed eyes and straight slim nose spoke of more than a few white ancestors.

The other woman was darker than these two and wore a simple indigo high-necked dress with a gathered skirt.

Queen Bess stepped forward. "Miss Jane. This here is my daughter, Bethany Talbot, and this is her husband, Jed. He's a lawyer."

"I'm so very happy to meet you both. I've heard so many good things about you." She smiled at Bethany. "I'm sure your mother has told you how much I've enjoyed your books. They have been a godsend."

Queen Bess gestured to the other woman. "And this here is Lavina Collins. She the woman who is going to be taking your place."

Jane's smile froze. She shook the offered hand, but her stomach tightened and she could not move a muscle on her face. She focused on thwarting the tears threatening to well up. Her heart beat wildly, then slowed. The color drained from her cheeks and she was dizzy. Confused, she could only reply on the training instilled by her stoic English ancestors. She managed to be courteous. "How do you do?"

Queen Bess looked at her sharply and

intervened. "These folks is going to my place for the day. You and me will have a good talk after they get on their way. I wanted Miss Lavina to see the school. We proud of what you done."

Jane did not go with them out to the yard. When Queen Bess returned, Jane slowly lifted her head from her hands. "Have I done something wrong?"

"No, darlin', you've been just about perfect. You've kept everything humming around here. But fact is, this isn't your right place and this ain't where you belong. You belong back with your own people. And these colored children need someone of their own kind to look up to."

Jane looked at her with puppy-trust blue eyes trying to take in the extent of her betrayal. As though at any moment she would be assured it was all a joke.

"We made a bargain, Miss Jane. You was supposed to teach this school and we was supposed to help you. Help you in the house and Mr. Roy with his doings. Well that all changed. Ain't your fault. Mr. Roy done run everybody off."

Jane still could not find her voice. Could not form a coherent thought. She would no longer be their Book Mama.

"I has got the children to think of." Queen

303

Bess's voice was relentless, stern. "We can't have white folks treating us like that no more. 'Bout everyone know how Mr. Roy talk to Sam Barnett."

"But the children weren't exposed to it," Jane said. "They were never around Roy."

"The menfolks talk about it when they get home at night. The children know. Children always know."

"This Lavina . . . This Lavina."

"She plenty good. Jed see to that."

"Today? Will I have today to say goodbye to the children?"

The old woman shook her head. "Ain't good for them, ain't good for you. Not today."

Jane clenched her teeth together to control a quiet tremble.

"You all right, girl?" Queen Bess was at her side in an instant and pressed her fingers on Jane's pulse.

Jane nodded her head. "I'm fine."

"No, you ain't." Queen Bess helped her to her feet and led her over to one of the benches. "Want you to lay down for a little while before you leave."

"The children!"

"I'll take care of them when they get here and tell them there's no meeting today. You'll be gone by then." She went over to the corner and ladled out a cup of water and brought it over to Jane. Then she moved one of the chairs in the room over to her side.

"There's something I gots to say to you, girl. No pretty way to do it." She reached for Jane's hand. "They's something wrong with your man. He's not right. It's not just that he be mean to the bone. It's more than that. I've seen this before when someone is down in the dumps one day and high-flying the next. Don't do too much harm if he ain't mean."

At these words, anger jolted through Jane and gave her the energy to push off the bench and then struggle to her feet. "How dare you criticize my husband. You do not have the right."

Queen Bess remained sitting while Jane went over to her shelf and plucked out the books she had contributed to the school. She whirled around and walked outside. Queen Bess followed. She placed the books in her saddlebag, then led Royal to the mounting block. She swung into the saddle and anchored her right leg over the top pummel and her thigh under the bottom one. She looked down at the sad old woman and her English manners came to fore after all. "I wish you all the best of luck."

Queen Bess grabbed Royal by the bridle to delay her departure. Her gaze was so intense that Jane was forced to look her fully in the face.

"Miss Jane, I is trying to tell you. Your man is going to hurt you. Hurt you real bad."

CHAPTER TEN

When she was a half mile from the house, she caught sight of a man riding away from their homestead. She recognized him from the general store where they collected their mail when they were in Herrington. The community paid him extra to personally carry to the residents anything marked special delivery.

Inside, Roy sat motionless at the table staring straight ahead. In front of him was a half-empty bottle of whiskey.

"Roy? What is it? What did that man want?"

Dazed, he turned toward her. "He delivered a letter. It's Father. He died. Two weeks ago. They have just now been able to get word to us."

"I'm so very sorry. So sorry, Roy."

An old man's death was never unexpected, and his father had been in the late seventies. There was no great love between her husband and his father. The loss of a parent would be a blow no matter what the relationship, but the death didn't account for Roy's shaking hands and the despair in his voice.

"What else?"

His hands were over his face and he didn't reply.

"What else, Roy?" She removed the letter from the table but before she could read it through, Roy exploded and snatched it back.

"Marmaduke is now the Earl of Sedgwick. He inherited everything, of course. But now the little bastard informs me he is cutting off all my funds. He expects me to make a living right here in America. That stingy little bastard. That miserly little son-of-a-bitch. How can he do this to me?"

Shocked, Jane stood stone-still. Nothing Roy had undertaken had turned a profit. His fine plans would come to nothing. Dazzled by the other English settlements at Studley, Runnymede, and Victoria, Roy intended to make their homestead the most glorious of all. Surrounding their incomplete stone house were half-starts of the buildings and projects he believed would impress other Englishmen. The only buildings that were finished were a combination stable and barn, a shelter for the sheep, and a shearing shed.

She knew better than to ask what he was going to do. It would be like waving a red flag in front of a bull. She knew her judgment was better than his. But even though he had never hit her, now she was afraid he would. She dreaded the times when he belittled her in public. Even more, when they were alone, she dreaded his cutting remarks that somehow branded her as inferior to other women. That her own husband would post a reward for her return if she ran away was still nearly unthinkable.

She couldn't erase Queen Bess's dire warnings from her mind.

Stunned, she sank into the nearest chair. There would be no more money coming. How could they exist? It would be a financial disaster to sell their land because they had paid too high a price to begin, though acreage here in America was so much cheaper than in England. Even if they got a good price for it, where would they go?

Roy would only live in a place like Herrington settled by English quality folks. He would never mix with commoners.

She knew how important status was to him. In the beginning when she had timidly suggested that they would be better off with a smaller house, less land, and sturdier sheep he left no doubt that he intended to return to England as the owner of massive tracts of land and a magnificent showplace of a house. Everything he wanted required money. Lots of it.

She let him rant. If she tried to comfort him, he would turn on her. The fact was, she didn't feel like offering any words of comfort. Perhaps he would get this madness out of his head and they could go back to England.

"Not a word of this. No one must know that I have run out of money."

"Of course," she said. Her voice was cool but inside she was rejoicing that even he would surely see there was no good way out of this. Since she had lost her beloved school, she no longer had any desire to make a go of it in America.

Outside the sheep bleated softly. "Make them stop," Roy mumbled. Then he jumped up from the table, stumbled onto the porch, and grabbed a piece of wood. Alarmed, Jane followed.

He wove unsteadily toward the shed where the dogs had herded the flock. Frightened by his approach, the sheep ran to the opposite side.

"Shut up," he yelled. "Shut up." He grasped the stick with both hands and raised it over his head and charged toward one of the ewes. She easily eluded him. Then his favorite dog turned on him and growled menacingly, protecting the flock from its shepherd. Roy faltered, then fell onto the ground weeping. In a few minutes he began to snore.

Jane stared at the sodden lump of flesh at her feet. She couldn't leave him out here in the cold night air. But she certainly could not move him by herself. There were no close neighbors to call on, and even if there were, when the liquor wore off, he would be furious when he realized someone had seen him in this state. She turned back to the house. Her stomach clenched. She had not eaten any supper. She went to the stove and ladled up a half cup of stew, then only ate about half of it.

She did not know what to do. Roy was not a drinker. She had never seen him like this before. He was not a drinker, nor a gambler, nor a womanizer. So, what exactly was wrong with him? Something was and it was far more insidious than the usual flaws. She was afraid of this man. Always on guard.

Unbidden, Queen Bess's face swam before her eyes.

She rose from the table and walked out to the farmyard again and stared down at her husband. One arm was outstretched. He lay on his side, breathing easily.

She went back to the house and went to bed and drifted off into a fitful sleep. A couple of hours later, Roy came into the bedroom, sat down heavily on his side of the bed, and removed his boots. She feigned sleep but by the dim light filtering through the window she watched him unbutton his pants and shirt. He slipped into bed and quickly fell asleep again.

It was a long time before she did. And then her dreams were filled with memories of England and waking to a sideboard laden with eggs and ham and tasty bread and popovers. England with green pastures and sheep that weren't tortured with heat and insects. England with people playing crochet on green lawns.

England where she always knew what to do.

She awoke before sunrise and dressed quickly. She tiptoed through the house. Once outside, she ran to the stable. Her hands trembled as she slipped the bridle on Royal. Her fingers fumbled with the saddle. She led him to the mounting block and swung astride. She trotted out of the farmyard and over the rise. When she was safely out of view of their house she slowed to a walk and let the horse wander aimlessly.

Now that she was no longer lying next to Roy, she could think more clearly. She couldn't just ride off half-cocked.

Her body ached and she trembled in the morning air. A meadowlark called but the cheery sound did not lift her heart as it did most mornings. She was hungry and haunted by the memory of a good English breakfast.

She had to think. Had to think.

Her husband would assume she was on her way to the school until she told him differently. That was an advantage. But she couldn't keep up that ruse for long. When she left Roy, she had to have Tom and Betsy's help to get back to England. But she wasn't sure she could count on them. It wasn't likely Tom would help her run away from his own brother.

To get back to the safety of her father's house, she needed money. She needed clothes. She had to have a plan.

Royal began to trot along the path she rode every day. The school came into view. She yanked on the reins and brought him to an abrupt stop. Soon the children would go outside for fresh air. Tears welled in her eyes. Would this Miss Lavina follow her schedule? Would they be reading right now? With the older students helping the younger? Or would there be a new routine?

Would Miss Lavina become the new Book Mama in the eyes of the children or was that title reserved for her? The adored teacher who had read every book in the world.

She did not want anyone to see her looking like a child Santa had overlooked at Christmas. The goodwill she had built with the black community was all used up.

Overwhelmed with grief at what she had lost she turned around and raced back home, no longer concerned with what excuse she would offer Roy for being home midmorning. She would bide her time and work at being her very best self. Perhaps things would be better if she helped her husband instead of ruminating over his faults.

Roy was gone and did not return until evening. He came through the door silently, then he went to the cupboard and removed the bottle he had been drinking from the night before. He took it to the table and sat there without saying a word. The bottle was nearly empty. Jane doubted there would be a repeat of the previous night's horrors.

Suddenly he rose and went outside, and she followed him. He walked some distance and mounted the slight rise leading to their house where he could survey their homestead. Hesitantly, she walked over to stand beside him and wondered if they were seeing the same thing at all. She glanced at his sorrowful face and wanted to hold his hand, not because he was her husband, but because he was another human being who was in pain.

There would be no more money. She saw an enormous shearing shed with a half-finished roof. A house that should have been adequate that now had scaffolding up to a half-started second story that looked at odds with the rest of the structure. The money he had already received so far should have been enough. Plenty enough for Kansas.

But not enough money to make this godforsaken prairie into another England.

CHAPTER ELEVEN

Dust drifted down from the ceiling the next morning. A little crack started at the corner where the second story was located and stopped midway to her stove.

Two days after Roy received the letter

from Marmaduke he still had not settled down. He muttered to himself and added various sums over and over. He was acting so strangely she worried that he would harm himself.

They had no warning. It started on the second story. The story that was damned to begin with. One block of dressed stone had been placed precariously on the block below. When the tub holding the supplies caught in the wind and slammed against the column, it was just enough to topple the stone and send it crashing onto the poorly anchored roof. That in turn pressured the crack and the whole upstairs construction cascaded down into the original room.

Roy sank to his knees and howled. Jane had never heard a sound quite like it.

"Those black bastards. They did this to me on purpose. I knew I couldn't trust them."

Shocked, Jane was too angry to check her words. "Do not ever, ever say anything again about people who are my friends and have done everything they can to help us. How dare you? Several people, including your own brother, tried to tell you that what you were doing wouldn't work, but you wouldn't listen. You never listen. Not to any of us."

"This is my brother's fault." Roy immediately switched the blame from the blacks to Tom Woodruff.

Everything was ruined. Both the upper story and now the lower, too. They were without a functional home. Only the two wings now stood, and without the center portion that had contained the stove, they could not exist. Jane knew people could and did make a cooking trench outside, but she did not know how to live that way. The pump by her sink was destroyed. She would have to go to the creek for water, and she didn't have the strength to do it. The marks on her hands that Queen Bess had treated had disappeared, and she didn't have the heart to deal with them again.

"My brother. This is his fault. If Tom hadn't poisoned Marmaduke against me, I would have had the money to hire decent men instead of black trash."

"Don't, Roy. I mean it. They are not trash."

He rushed toward the shelf where she kept her books and pulled them off one by one. He tore pages from each volume and then ripped them to pieces. Frightened by the wildness in his eyes she was paralyzed.

When he reached for Sam Barnett's precious volume that he had brought from

Kentucky — the book she had promised to keep safe for Little John — she gave a little cry and leaped toward him. Triumphantly, he raised the book over his head, holding it in his hands like a club. She stopped. Her heartbeat was erratic, and she pressed two fingers into the hollow of her throat as though she could slow the beats. Her breath came in shallow little puffs.

"Does this belong to one of your nigger pets? Well, does it?" Then he slowly shredded the pages.

She whimpered and closed her eyes for an instant. Knowledge flooded her with icy certainty. He was insane. Dangerous.

Sheep bleated and there were no walls now to block the sound. He lurched outside and stumbled toward the pens.

Jane picked her way across the rubble, and quickly decided she could make it to the stable before he could notice her. There was no time to grab clothing or any of her possessions. She darted inside, quickly saddled Royal, and led him to the mounting block.

Roy appeared in the doorway before she could hoist herself into the saddle. "Where do you think you are going?"

"Nowhere."

"Nowhere," he mocked. "Going nowhere. You've got that right."

"Tom and Betsy's." Terrified, she struggled to keep her voice steady.

"You're in it with them. You're the one who got us in this arrangement in the first place. Something no decent white woman would have done. You with this bizarre teaching arrangement. You brought this down on our heads."

She sorrowfully pressed her forehead against Royal's belly and winked away tears. Then she put one foot on the block and sprang up, hooking one leg over the standing pommel and her thigh under the lower one.

"You're not going anywhere. I forbid it."

Fully mounted now, she moved toward the opening. "Stand aside, Roy. You can't stop me."

"The hell I can't." He lunged for Royal's bridle, but the horse twisted its head violently upward and Roy lost his balance and fell onto his rear. Jane cantered past him onto the open prairie. Roy struggled to his feet and yelled after her. "Bastards. All of you. This is just a trick to get back to England. Well, I won't give up."

Hungry, thirsty, and bedraggled, Jane reached Tom and Betsy's place in an hour. She slid to the ground. Alarmed by the

318

panicked expression on Jane's face and the sweat covering her horse, Tom took charge immediately and led Royal to the stable. He called to his newest hand to rub the horse down and see to water and grain. Betsy put her arm around Jane's shoulder and guided her toward the house.

"What happened? Is it Roy? Has he been hurt?" Jane shook her head and pressed the palm of her hand against her forehead as Betsy settled her into a chair.

"No, not that. One minute, Betsy. Wait until Tom gets here. I don't want to tell this twice."

"I'm already here." Tom removed his hat and set it on one of the shelves in the living room. "Ted is seeing to your horse."

Jane blurted out the whole bizarre episode.

Tom threw up his hands as if to block any further information. "I swear to God, I've never written a single critical word to Marmaduke. In fact, sometimes I've envied Roy's vision. His guts. But I can't do some of the things he does. I'm a plodder."

"Oh, not so," Jane said bitterly. "You're the one who knows how to get things done. If you think your being a plodder makes him a dreamer, and that dreamers are somehow superior to men who have their feet on the ground, I've got news for you."

She launched into a bitter litany of the ways Roy had mismanaged his animals and his property. She made sure they understood the vast scale of abandoned projects.

"Is he all right?" Tom asked cautiously. He tapped his temple. "You know, in his head? Not everyone can live out here, you know. We talk about the women going crazy, but it's hard on the men, too."

"No, that's not it. It's not the hardship." Her voice broke off. "He's just . . ." She did not know how to describe his erratic moods. His far-fetched plans. "He's up one day and down the next." She was too ashamed to tell them how mean he was to her on the days when he was down. Yet, they had had a glimpse of this when Tom saw the humiliating poster offering a reward for her return.

A shot rang out from the yard. Tom jumped to his feet and peered out the window. "Stay back," he yelled to the women. "Stay low. Get down on the floor."

Roy hollered from behind a wagon where he had crouched.

"Come out and face me like a man, you lying hypocrite."

"Roy, what the hell?"

"You know why I'm here. You told Marmaduke a bunch of lies about me. Admit it."

"Swear to God. I've never said a single bad word about you. Nothing that would make him think anything but that you are doing just fine."

"Liar. Damned liar."

Betsy reached for Jane's trembling hand and the two women huddled on the floor. Then Jane broke away, and ignoring Tom's orders she crawled to his side. She inched up the wall until she was standing on her feet.

"Roy. I'm here," she called. "What do you want?"

"Come out of that house right now. You're my wife. Get your ass home."

"Roy, you're not yourself."

"I said *now*. Or someone will get hurt. You leave me no choice."

"Betsy," Tom called, "fetch my rifle."

Jane's face paled and her throat was as dry as a ball of cotton. "No, Tom. No."

"I can't just let Roy kill us all."

"He won't," Jane sobbed. "He's not that kind of a person."

Tom did not reply and snatched the rifle from Betsy's hands. "Roy, I've got a gun. It will be a hell of a lot easier for me to shoot you than for you to shoot me. You're a sitting duck. If you try to shoot through this window, you're shooting blind. You could hit one of the women."

Jane peered out at the wavering figure of her husband. Then slowly he steadied himself and braced the stock of the gun against his shoulder. Terrified she drew back and hugged the wall. "Keep talking," she whispered to Tom. "If he's talking, he won't be shooting."

"Roy, goddamn it, don't do this."

"Let me talk to that worthless goddamned woman I married."

Jane edged over to the window again before Tom could stop her. She drew back quickly when she realized this man, her own husband, had the rifle aimed right at her.

He would shoot his own wife. His brother. His sister-in-law. Willfully, deliberately, without a twinge of conscience.

Then she spotted three of Tom's hands moving steadily up behind Roy. One of them was twirling a rope over his head. Quicker than a snake could strike, the loop soared through the air and in a moment, Roy was encircled with rope, and knocked off his feet. He fell hard. The gun lay next to him.

Tom flew out the door. There was a knot on Roy's head from where he hit the ground. Tom knelt and pressed a couple of fingers against his brother's temple. His pulse was strong but irregular.

"Carry him inside. Put him on the bed in the back room." Two of the men picked up the unconscious man.

"He can't threaten anyone, anymore," Tom said.

Jane sank into a chair and buried her head in her hands. She could not stop trembling. "I can't go back to living with this man. I just can't."

"I know that," Betsy said softly. "I know that. But you're his wife. You might as well think of yourself as his property. All the laws are on the side of men."

"I'll file for divorce."

"It won't work. I know Roy. He'll say 'no,' and you'll end up in an insane asylum." Tom stood in the doorway, keeping an eye on his brother.

CHAPTER TWELVE

They talked for two hours. "This isn't the sheriff's business," Tom said. "None of it. Roy didn't shoot anyone. What he did is no worse than some of the boys do that get liquored up and shoot up the towns around here. This is a family quarrel. I'll make sure it stays in the family."

"You're just going to let this go?" Jane

cried. "I mean it. I can't go back."

"Of course, I won't just let it go. I'm trying to figure out what would be best for everyone. Damned if I see a really good way forward for anyone, let alone everyone."

"What would be best is if we never came here in the first place."

"But we did. And I don't think I've done so poorly. Betsy and I have come to like this country."

"You can live here, and Roy can't. He just can't."

"So what do you propose?"

"Help us get back to England."

"He'll be the same kind of person back there. The very same. Is this the kind of man you want to live with for the rest of your life?"

Stunned, Jane realized the implications of what Tom was saying. In her quest to get back to England, she had never considered what it would be like to live there with Roy. She would still be his wife. Still must defer to his wishes. Anything that she eventually inherited from her parents would be his property, not hers.

She rose from her chair. "Excuse me. I need a little fresh air."

They exchanged worried glances as she pushed through the screen door and made her way to the porch.

Jane hugged one of the pillars. She stared into the distance. If she went back to England with Roy, she would be giving up so many of the rights she had come cherish here in America.

She could not go on living with Roy here in America, but she had not given any thought to what it would be like to live with him in England. It would be living in hell.

Tom was asking her to choose between England and America.

She could not give up England where everyone knew their place! England with its green pastures and gentle rains. England with its sensible monarchy instead of America's wild political system where everything went topsy-turvy every four years. England with its lovely miraculous roses. England with proper teas and delicious breakfasts. Tears streamed down her cheeks.

Then that image of England gave way to imagining life with Roy. Taking orders from an arrogant man who had no respect for women. Living in a velvet-lined prison doing needlework all day long. Taking to her sick bed when she felt the slightest pain. Thrilling to the gossip of idle women. Living an utterly useless life.

Thanks to Roy, she had been deprived of

the dearest life of all. She was no longer the Book Mama to little children who thought she was the smartest person in the world.

She had to choose. England or America.

Slowly she looked around at all Tom and Betsy had done. She knew then she wanted what they had. She went back inside.

"I want to stay here." Her words were soft and tentative as though they were a surprise even to herself. "I want Roy to go back to England, but I want to stay here."

"That's not possible."

"It has to be. I won't go with him. Here in America I am no man's property and I can own property myself. In England everything a wife owns belongs to her husband but that's not true here."

"Even if that could be arranged, what would you do, Jane?" Betsy frowned in disbelief. "You can't live by yourself."

"Yes, I can." Queen Bess came to mind. There were other women who lived by themselves. She would certainly be in less danger than trying to live with an insane husband with a vicious temper. "It's the law. I can file for a homestead. I can own land."

"That's nonsense. You can't work the land. You don't know how, and you don't have the strength." Tom rose and glanced out the window at the setting sun. "We'll send you some of our men, of course, to start rebuilding the place where you already live, but you will still need to support yourself."

"That's Roy's property. I don't want to rebuild that abomination. Not now, not ever. I want nothing to do with it. That place belongs to Roy. He can do whatever he likes with it."

"How will you live?" Betsy persisted.

"There's one thing that will make or break you, Jane." Tom turned and looked at her solemnly. "Do you really *want* to do this? Do you want to stay here in America?"

"Yes," she said. "If I go back to England as his wife, I might as well be living in bondage. I'll be subject to all his whims again. I want to stay here."

"I can't see the slightest indication that Roy wants to return to England," Betsy said. "These are fine ideas, but he might have some of his own. He hates Marmaduke. He won't just step onto the boat."

"That's easy enough to arrange." Tom grinned. "Some of the men I have working for me know a little bit about rounding up working hands for a ship's crew. Reckon the same methods would work on a fine English gentleman."

"You would do that to your own brother?"

Betsy looked at him like he was a rank stranger.

"You bet. This will involve a train ride, a river trip, and men to keep everything on course until we get him on a ship headed to England. There will be an abundance of volunteers to help Roy on his way. We've been a little short of adventure lately."

"I think you should keep him sedated when you load him on the ship," Betsy said. "Until he's well at sea. I happen to have a couple of friends who made sure they had a good supply of medication before they left England."

"All hell will break loose when he comes to. We must send someone with him on the ship. There's a man living right here on this ranch who wants to return to England. I'm sure Cedric will be delighted to accompany Roy and see that he gets to the right place after he lands."

"Won't Marmaduke be surprised," Betsy said.

"I need some money right away," Jane said. "To file for my claim. To pay the men at Nicodemus to build a soddy for me, to buy a stove. To start my household."

"We'll loan you some, of course. Happily." Betsy patted her hand.

"Thank you."

"You'll always have us. We love it here."

"We will take you to the land office this week so you can file your claim."

"Good. I must own property. It's my protection." Jane shut her eyes for an instant. But when she thought about the isolation, the physical drain, the insects, the heat, she burst into tears. "You're right, Tom. I don't have the strength. I just don't. I want to stay here. I don't care if I ever see Roy again, but I'm not up to living in a sod house in the middle of nowhere."

"How have you managed so far?"

She told them about the arrangement with Nicodemus and how she lost the job. "For a while, I was happy."

"I've just thought of a way out of this," Tom said. "Buy a lot here in town. There are still plenty for sale. She still has to make a living though."

"I know. Teach school here." Betsy beamed at Jane. "Do you remember meeting Clarissa Tapper? Well she and Mary Stelter were in the general store just last week and Clarissa said she wished they had a proper school because there were no tutors to be found and she was ill-suited to teach her own children. Do it here!"

"Yes, oh yes." Jane didn't even have to think before she seized the opportunity.

"Yes. Oh, Betsy, that's perfect."

"But we don't have money to build a school and more people are leaving to go back home."

"The library. Let me be the librarian, too. I'll hold my classes in the library."

"Wonderful. No one has bought the Markleys' property," Tom said. "Their lot is behind the library."

"Perfect. That's just perfect." Jane's heart soared.

"Betsy, round up some of my clothes for my brother."

"They'll be too short."

"Right. Ask Avery for a couple of changes. Pack them in that small case. Enough to see him through a sea voyage. Cedric can escort Roy back to England. Avery will take them to the train tonight. As for keeping him sedated, we'll have to do it the old-fashioned way. Liquor. We need to start things rolling at once." Tom grabbed his jacket and went into the bedroom and uneasily looked at his brother. "I want him on the way before he regains consciousness." He left and headed toward the barn.

After the men loaded Roy in the wagon and got under way, all three were too keyed up to sleep. They talked for a couple more hours before they headed to bed.

"How will I pay for my property?" Jane asked. "Eliza Marley told me the librarian's job just paid a pittance. I doubt if there will be much money available for a school-teacher."

"That won't be a problem," Tom said. "From the sale of your sheep. Remember that young man I sent over to help Roy with his building? Avery Gentry? I'm certain he will buy them. He has talked about Roy's sheep ever since he went to your place."

"They really are wonderful," Jane said. "Top of the line Leicesters. But I just supposed they were the wrong breed to have out here."

"Not according to Gentry. He claimed Roy's methods were all wrong. Avery is very close to proving up on his claim. I suspect he would pay a pretty good price for those sheep. He's got a real knack for making things work."

"I can't believe my luck. So many things are falling into place."

"Gentry took Roy and Cedric to the train and will bring the wagon back by morning. Then he'll take you to your place and you can gather up anything you want to bring to town."

"What's my next step?"

"The land office to transfer the deed after you get the money for your sheep and pay the Markleys. The house is in pretty good shape. It's cheap enough, but there aren't any buyers. Folks want acreage. You'll own everything free and clear."

Jane's heart skipped a beat. She could organize her own library. And get paid for teaching a handful of students. She would spend her days surrounded by books. And read at night for as long as she wished.

It was possible to do all manner of things out here. All manner of things.

If she stayed here in America it would not take long for Roy to deliver what he would view as the ultimate humiliation.

To her it would be the ultimate liberation.

He would divorce her on the grounds of desertion so he could marry again and make some other woman's life miserable.

"Gentry's a generous man. A real gentleman. You can count on him to help you fix up your house to suit you."

She nodded. Even as her yearning for England faded, a new vision was creeping into her consciousness. She would be no man's wife. Her property and her life would be her own. And in time, she would see to it that African American children could check out books.

She could not permit herself to dream beyond that.

For now, it was enough.

ABOUT THE AUTHOR

Charlotte Hinger is a multi-award-winning novelist and Kansas historian. Her historical novel, *The Healer's Daughter,* won the Kansas Notable Book Award, the Will Rogers Silver Medallion, and was a finalist for the High Plains Book Award. She still calls herself a Kansan, although she now lives in Fort Collins, Colorado.

■ ■ ■ ■

Terrible and Wonderful

CANDACE SIMAR

■ ■ ■ ■

Chapter 1

1902

Pearl Ellingson eyed the canned goods as she waited for Mr. Rorvig to finish packing Mama's grocery list. Dust mites rode the light streaming in through the only window. The dim building smelled faintly of sour milk.

Pearl ran her hand over a bolt of blue calico next to the jars of peppermints and horehound candies, bending closer to sniff the new fabric. She sighed. No new dresses this year. Papa said they must tighten their belts. Everything had depended on Papa's wheat.

If Pearl were rich, she would buy new dresses for Mama and her little sisters. She didn't care about new dresses for herself. If she were rich, she would buy books. She would buy all the books in the world. No books for sale at Rorvig's Store. No books for sale anywhere in Nickelbo, North Dakota.

Charlene Dahl reached in front of Pearl for the bolt of cloth. "My mother is making me a new dress," she said. Charlene looked Pearl up and down with a distinct look of pity, pausing at her worn shoes. "Sorry to hear you were hailed out."

Charlene was everything Pearl was not. Dark curls framed her plump and pretty face. Charlene's dad owned the feed store, and Charlene got everything she wanted. Billy Hanson named Charlene as dumb as a block of salt. He said that Charlene only passed eighth grade by copying Pearl's answers on the proficiency test. Pearl pushed a loose strand of mousy hair behind her ear.

"Anything else, Miss Ellingson?" Mr. Rorvig interrupted.

The storekeeper was middle-aged, kindly, and absentminded in his round spectacles. Everyone said his wife was the brains of the business. Pearl glimpsed Mrs. Rorvig through the open curtain that separated their living quarters from the store. She pumped her feet on a treadle sewing machine in a feverish manner. Pins bristled from her mouth. Mr. Rorvig called his wife to help Charlene. Mrs. Rorvig stopped sewing and came out to measure the fabric at the other end of the counter.

"Your father's peanuts, I suppose," Mr. Rorvig said as he spread a sheet of old newspaper on the counter. Papa loved his peanuts, and belt tightening was targeted mostly at female expenses.

"The usual," Pearl said as she craned her neck to read the newspaper headline. A Carnegie library coming to Grafton. Just the thought of a library made Pearl's heart race. Books free for the reading. But Grafton was over a hundred miles away from Nickelbo.

"Have you noticed how flimsy the papers are these days?" Mr. Rorvig said with a wink. "Best to double up." He reached for another sheet of newspaper from the stack, and then another. "Have you read this one yet?" He held up the woman's page, which included poetry, recipes, and a pattern for a crocheted fascinator.

Pearl grinned. Three pages of newsprint. A windfall. Mr. Rorvig scooped peanuts and tied the newspaper package with a piece of string. Charlene left, bumping into Papa who came inside. Mr. Rorvig reached for the swatter and began the massacre of sticky flies that flew in with the opened door. The sewing machine started grinding again in the back room.

"Ready to go, Pearly-girl?" Papa was always in motion, always heading somewhere, and always in a hurry. He wore bib overalls and his best town-shirt. His straw hat showed perspiration stains and a hole where little Opal had poked her finger. "Chores waiting at home." He dipped into the peanut barrel and broke a shell with white teeth.

Papa paid the bill, grumbling about the prices, but grinning in a good-natured way. Papa often commented on Mr. Rorvig's kindness toward local farmers, and how the store carried more credit than was good business. Pearl knew that Papa hated to ask for credit, and that the dollars he used today were among his last. If only their wheat had survived.

Old Doctor Gamla entered the store looking shrunken, ancient, and dressed in black widow's weeds. She walked like a spider, leaning on a diamond-willow walking stick with her back bent and her feet spread wide apart for balance. The old woman paused by the peanut barrel, her face as white as her hair, and her lips berry-blue.

More than once rumors floated around town of Doctor Gamla's death. Billy said that she was almost one hundred years old, but sometimes Pearl's best friend exaggerated.

"Arne Ellingson," Doctor Gamla said, her voice quivery. "I was hoping to find you." She leaned against the peanut barrel.

Olava Wick wasn't a real doctor, but the townspeople named her Doctor Gamla, the old doctor woman. Doctor Gamla had helped birth babies, set bones, treated whooping cough and pneumonias, and slathered her famous salve on wounds of all descriptions. These days Doctor Gamla was too old for doctoring, but her blue eyes still carried a strange fire. Like Papa, she was always getting things done.

"I found a cure for your lost wheat," Doctor Gamla said. Her eyes sparked a challenge, as if daring Papa to contradict her.

Papa scratched his head. "Too late for the wheat, Olava."

"Clarence Scrimshaw passed yesterday, God rest his soul," Doctor Gamla said. "His nurse took the train back to Bismarck." She spoke to Papa, but eyed Pearl. "His widow is looking for a hired girl. Someone to keep house and be a companion." The old woman paused for breath. "Her eyes are bad. She needs someone to read to her, a good girl who knows her place." She pointed her walking stick at Pearl. "I thought of your girl."

Pearl's heart almost exploded. The Scrimshaws were the richest people in town and lived in a big house across from the Lutheran church. Billy said that Mrs. Scrimshaw had a front and back stairs, and an indoor water closet. They had a coal furnace in the basement and four bedrooms upstairs. Best of all, Mrs. Scrimshaw had a whole wall of books. Billy saw them himself when he tended her furnace last winter.

"Pearl?" Papa said with a snort. "We've plenty of work at home for her. Besides, she's too young to be out on her own."

"Mrs. Scrimshaw is a godly woman," Doctor Gamla said in a calm voice, still looking at Pearl. "A dollar a day cash money, room and board, and a respectable household. You need not worry about a daughter under Brunhilde Scrimshaw's care."

Pearl held her breath. The garden produce lined their cellar shelves, and last week she and Mama had finished the sausage. Hams and bacon filled the smokehouse. Even Mama declared the end of fall cleaning. Clarice and Jewel were old enough to do chores and help with Opal and the new baby.

Papa's jaw set hard. Mr. Rorvig slapped a

fly on the counter and flicked it into the spittoon on the floor. The sewing machine stopped grinding in the back room. Pearl wanted to scream. This was her chance to do something other than farm chores.

"Charlene Dahl might do it," Mrs. Rorvig said as she poked her head through the dividing curtain. She mumbled her words through the row of pins still clamped between her lips. "Her mother says they're waiting until next year to send her away to high school." The sewing machine sounded in the back room.

Doctor Gamla straightened her back. "Of course," Doctor Gamla said quietly, "it is to be expected that wages would be paid to the father until a daughter reaches majority." She picked a thread from her apron and brushed an invisible piece of lint from her sleeve. "One less mouth to feed, a steady flow of hard cash through the winter — a cure for your lost wheat."

Lately Papa and Mama had been arguing about Papa taking a logging job over the winter. Mama feared being alone out on the farm if emergency or sickness threatened. Besides, Uncle Pete had been killed by a falling tree at a logging camp in Minnesota. Mama had reason to worry.

Papa could stay home where he belonged

if Pearl earned cash money over the winter. To be paid money for reading books was better than high school.

Papa's jaw relaxed.

"And a Christian act of charity to help a widow in her hour of need," Doctor Gamla said. "Brunhilde has had a hard time since Walter's death, then Clarence's long illness and now her eyesight going."

Papa looked at Pearl. He was weakening.

"And a good chance for your daughter to learn something besides chores. Brunhilde is a stickler on manners and society."

"Please, Papa," Pearl whispered. "I want to do it."

"I cured your lumbago," Doctor Gamla said. "My cures always work."

The sewing machine quit grinding. "Arne said he needs Pearl at home, Olava. Maybe you didn't hear him," Mrs. Rorvig called from the back room. "Charlene would fit in better than a country girl."

Pearl felt her temper rise. Charlene could have a new dress, but she couldn't have this job. Pearl wouldn't allow it.

"I'll do it," Pearl said, surprising even herself.

Papa eyed her with that what-do-you-think-you-are-doing look. But something else flashed in his eyes. Something that Pearl recognized as respect. He had looked the same way when she had taken top honors at eighth-grade graduation last spring. Charlene Dahl had won an award for penmanship, but had barely passed.

Again Pearl was struck by the strange fire in Doctor Gamla's eyes. Those eyes were as blue as the morning glories that grew on Mama's garden fence, as brilliant as the flash of sun on the Mad Dog River. Bright blue in the old woman's flour-white face.

"Good." Doctor Gamla fluttered a hand to her chest as if in pain.

Mr. Rorvig hurried to bring a chair. "Are you all right, Olava? Someone fetch a glass of water."

Doctor Gamla slumped into the chair, and waved away the water brought by Mrs. Rorvig.

"She won't put up with no nonsense, Brunhilde Scrimshaw won't," Doctor Gamla said. "No sass. No mess. No fuss."

"Yes, ma'am," Pearl said. Her heart pounded and beads of sweat dripped between her shoulder blades as if she had been shoveling grain instead of talking to an old lady.

"She's particular about her water closet," Doctor Gamla said in a wheezy rasp. "My advice is to use the backhouse like at home."

"Of course," Pearl said. She wouldn't know how a water closet worked, though she was curious to find out.

"Selma won't like it," Papa said. He gathered the groceries from the counter and reached for another handful of peanuts from the barrel. He agreed to bring Pearl to the Scrimshaws the next afternoon. "In case you sold me a few rotten ones," he said to Mr. Rorvig with a grin.

Pearl would live in town away from the never-ending drudgery of farm work. Pearl had borrowed Miss Hatfield's *Little Women* last year, but returned it at eighth-grade graduation. She liked the way Miss Alcott portrayed the family of girls growing up in New England during the Civil War. Pearl had not held a book in her hands since then.

Pearl grabbed the newspaper-wrapped peanuts as soon as she climbed into the wagon. Grafton wasn't much bigger than Nickelbo. Mr. Carnegie, the second-richest man in the world, was building libraries in cities all over America. Grafton received $10,000 to build a library. It would be finished next year. If only there were a library in Nickelbo.

Old Daisy clopped along, slow as could be, swishing her tail at the flies, stomping yellowed hooves at the tormenting black cloud that drew blood on her nose and ears. The wagon squeaked forward as Pearl daydreamed about a library where she might read any book she wished. She would wear a pretty blue dress with a matching hat and choose *The Red Badge of Courage* by Stephen Crane. Pearl had clipped a book review about it the last time they bought peanuts.

She wondered how old one had to be before asking Mr. Carnegie for a library. At fourteen, she was too old for baby games and play, but too young to keep what she earned, even if she worked for Mrs. Scrimshaw. She sighed.

She turned the peanut bundle and chose a long word from an article about Yellowstone National Park. "Conservation," Pearl said. She always looked for new spelling words to stump Papa. It was a game the whole family played.

Papa spelled the word.

"Administration," she said.

Again Papa nailed it. She searched for a more difficult word in an article about a train wreck in Missouri.

"Commodities," Pearl said.

Papa reached for a handful of peanuts, sucking the salt before cracking the nuts with his teeth. He spelled the word without a mistake, hesitating a bit before he added the second m.

"If we had a library in Nickelbo, we could look up the correct spelling of any word we wanted," Pearl said.

"A library in Nickelbo? Doubt it will ever happen," Papa said with a harrumph. "Would be nice, though. Real handy."

They passed empty fields and pastures of brown grass. Pearl's eyes lingered on a haystack in Mr. Browning's field. She breathed in the scent of hay as they passed. Pearl loved the prairie. If only she had books to read, she would not mind living in Nickelbo for the rest of her life.

Mr. Browning plowed black ribbons behind his team of Belgians. It was Indian summer, that short summer between the first frost and serious winter. Her favorite time of the year.

"Papa," Pearl said, "What happened to Mrs. Scrimshaw's son?"

"Walter?" Papa said. "Killed in the Civil War. The missus never got over it, he being their only child."

"But that's been forty years ago," Pearl said, calculating the years. Mrs. Scrimshaw must be almost as old as Doctor Gamla.

"Grief has its own calendar," Papa said. He grabbed another handful of peanuts and slapped the lines. They were almost home.

"Now to tell your mother that her oldest chick is leaving the nest." A peanut cracked between his teeth and he spat the shell to the side of the trail.

CHAPTER 2

Mama's brown eyes leaked tears when Papa told her about the job at Mrs. Scrimshaw's. Little Opal hung on Mama's skirts, fussing to be nursed. Opal was having a hard time since little Ruby had been born. Clarice and Jewel were doing chores out in the barn.

"Maybe this is our answer to prayer," Mama said.

"It's Doctor Gamla's cure," Pearl said. "Papa won't have to go to the logging camp."

"But Old Lady Scrimshaw, of all people," Mama said. "And leaving tomorrow. Hardly time to get your things together."

Mama didn't exactly give her permission, but instead bustled to iron Pearl's best dress and petticoats. Opal bawled as loud as a distraught heifer. Papa hoisted her to his shoulders and trotted around the room pretending to give the fourteen-month-old a horseback ride.

"Blacken your shoes," Mama said. "Once

you start earning regular money, we'll try to get you some new ones." Mama packed her own best handkerchief and second-best apron. "Mrs. Scrimshaw won't want you looking like a *cotter,*" Mama said. "She'll take one look at your old clothes and send you packing."

"I'll be fine, Mama," Pearl said. "Besides, Mrs. Scrimshaw's eyesight is bad. She might not notice."

"She'll notice," Mama said with a groan. "You don't know Mrs. Scrimshaw. Of all times to be cash poor."

"Don't worry," Pearl said.

But Mama's words planted anxiety in Pearl's mind. That night she lay in bed between her sisters, unable to sleep, thinking about leaving home and pleasing Mrs. Scrimshaw. Doctor Gamla had warned no mess, no fuss, and no sass. She imagined the titles hidden in Mrs. Scrimshaw's bookshelf. Pearl set her will. She would do it if it killed her. She would do it for the family. She would do it for the books. She fell asleep thinking of all the books she wanted to read.

CHAPTER 3

The next day Papa brought Pearl to Mrs. Scrimshaw's home. The large room over-flowed with heavy furniture and finery. An ornate oriental rug spread across the floor. Burgundy draperies hung at the windows. A parlor organ sat in one corner. A pink chandelier hung in the middle of the ceiling with at least a dozen lamp globes. The globes sparkled as if they had never been lit. Elaborate lace doilies covered every flat space. Pearl avoided gawking at the book-case.

Mrs. Scrimshaw did not invite them to sit down, but instead motioned Pearl closer to her horsehide-covered chair where she sat like a queen, leaving Papa standing on a rug in front of the doorway. Pearl bristled. When they had guests at home, they always bade them take a chair. Mama made coffee and did her best to make the visitors feel wel-come.

Instead, Mrs. Scrimshaw sat tall and thin, stiff as a flagpole with a wrinkly face and red veins showing across her nose. Her mouth showed yellow stumps of teeth when she spoke, like Old Daisy's teeth, revealing her advanced age. From time to time the old woman held a delicate lace handkerchief to her nose, releasing a brief whiff of rose-water.

Pearl's inquisition began. Pearl's dress felt thin and faded, unsuited for such a fancy house. The blacking had done little to disguise the condition of her shoes. Drops of perspiration gathered on Pearl's neck as she answered the questions that came in rapid succession. Yes, Pearl knew how to cook and tend house. Yes, Pearl knew how to keep fires and scrub floors. Yes, Pearl could add coal to the basement furnace. Yes, Pearl attended church every Sunday, and no, she did not smoke cigarettes, frequent pool halls, or partake of spirits. No, Pearl did not have a beau. There would be no visitors of any kind inside the house and Pearl would not use the water closet. No, she was not careless with candles or fire. No, she was not prone to lung catarrh or head lice. No one in their family had scabies or consumption. Their family did not suffer bedbugs. She said her prayers every night. Pearl had no strong opinions against President Roosevelt. Pearl could empty a mousetrap and kill bats. She was not afraid of spiders.

"Show me your hands," Mrs. Scrimshaw demanded.

Pearl stepped closer and held out both

hands. Mrs. Scrimshaw bent low to inspect them.

"Not a nail biter," Mrs. Scrimshaw said. "Can't abide that filthy habit."

"No, ma'am," Pearl said with a smile, glad she had taken the time to pare and clean her nails that morning. Charlene Dahl was a hopeless nail biter. And Charlene was always googly-eyed over one boy or another.

"Doctor Gamla is usually right," Mrs. Scrimshaw said. "But you're small for your age and scrawny. I expected a sturdier girl."

"I'm stronger than I look," Pearl answered. "Being the oldest in a family of girls, I help my father with outside chores."

Papa shifted weight from one foot to another in the doorway and cleared his throat. The sweat gathering on Pearl's back caused a ferocious itch between her shoulder blades. The clock ticked on the fireplace mantel. A desperate fear almost toppled Pearl. A fear that she would not be good enough. Mrs. Scrimshaw was sending her away. Pearl remembered the dollars her family so desperately needed. She looked toward the shelf of books with such a longing that tears gathered in her eyes. She blinked them away and stiffened her spine.

"Charlene Dahl is eager for the opportunity," Mrs. Scrimshaw said. "Her father was

Clarence's associate."

"I'll work hard," Pearl said. Her words came out jumbled and too fast. Pearl took a breath to calm herself. "I graduated top of my eighth-grade class and love to read. Doctor Gamla said you need someone to read to you."

Mrs. Scrimshaw dabbed her hanky again and rosewater filtered through the air. "My eyes have been ruined by weeping in this valley of tears," she said. "Life has been most unkind to this poor, banished child of Eve."

Pearl viewed the lovely home, the thick rugs on the floor, the mantel clock, and the ornate lamps and vases. This was a mansion compared to their small dwelling out on the prairie. It didn't look to Pearl as if life had been unkind to the old woman at all.

"Name your favorite book," Mrs. Scrimshaw demanded, sharper and more intent.

"I can't say," Pearl said. "I've read so few."

Mrs. Scrimshaw snorted. "You mean to say that you want to read every book in the world before you decide your favorite?"

"Yes, ma'am," Pearl said.

Mrs. Scrimshaw pursed her lips and chuckled, holding the handkerchief to her mouth. More rosewater.

"Well, then," Mrs. Scrimshaw said. Her

face flushed and merriment glowed in her dim eyes. At least that's what Pearl thought. "We've a lot of reading ahead of us."

Mrs. Scrimshaw handed a newspaper to Pearl and commanded her to read aloud the front-page story. Pearl read an article about President Roosevelt's presidency since the assassination of President McKinley. The writer predicted Teddy Roosevelt would run unopposed in the 1904 Republican ballot. The words rolled off Pearl's tongue without a stumble.

"Do you want me to keep reading, ma'am?" Pearl said when the article ended. "There's another about Roosevelt's opinions on antitrust laws."

Mrs. Scrimshaw did not answer. The clock chimed twice. "You're rough around the edges, and your voice is young. But you're not without potential," Mrs. Scrimshaw said. "I can't abide a nail biter."

Pearl held her breath.

"We'll try it for a week," Mrs. Scrimshaw said. "I will defer to Doctor Gamla's judgment on a trial basis. By then I will know whether or not you are more suitable than Miss Dahl."

Pearl exhaled. She looked toward Papa, who gave her a wink. Pearl had the job.

"The Hanson boy does the outside

chores," Mrs. Scrimshaw said. "You will be kept busy as my companion. I cannot abide barn filth inside my home."

One cow and a dozen hens could hardly count as outside chores. Why even Jewel or Clarice could handle that.

"I hire a weekly charwoman," Mrs. Scrimshaw said. "I am not unreasonable in my expectations."

Pearl took a breath. No cleaning? What would she do with herself?

"Mrs. Dublin sends bread, butter, and baked goods twice a week. My needs are few and I prefer simple meals."

Pearl gawked. She couldn't help herself. No outside chores, no charring, no baking or butter making. Pearl would live like a princess.

"You may go," Mrs. Scrimshaw said to Papa with a wave of her hand. "You may collect your wages every Saturday at the kitchen door."

Papa turned to leave. Pearl ran to give him a hug. His whiskery cheeks scratched against her forehead.

"You'll be fine," Papa said in a husky whisper. "Be my brave girl. I'll see you on Saturday."

Tears choked her throat, but Pearl determined to do her very best. To think, a whole dollar every day. Doctor Gamla was right. This job was the cure for her father's lost wheat. And also the cure for her book hunger. A whole wall of books. She would read every one.

Mrs. Scrimshaw showed her the house, going room to room with a long list of rules that Pearl must follow. Mrs. Scrimshaw leaned on furniture or doorframes as she spoke. Pearl had once read about blind people using white canes to feel their way across rooms. Even Doctor Gamla used a walking stick. Pearl did not dare suggest a cane.

Pearl would sleep in a small room next to the master bedroom on the ground floor, separated by the water closet. It smelled of disinfectant. The porcelain gleamed whiter than winter sun on new snow. Pearl eyed the tank and chain above the porcelain stool.

"How does it work?" Pearl said.

"You will use the backhouse," Mrs. Scrimshaw said.

"I know, but I've not seen one before," Pearl said. "How does it work?"

Mrs. Scrimshaw yanked the chain and a flush of water whirled in the bowl and down the stool. Pearl dared not ask any more questions.

"I want my breakfast egg cooked five

minutes," Mrs. Scrimshaw said when they entered the kitchen. It was warmer by the cookstove, and smelled of stale smoke. "Not six minutes, not four minutes." She pointed to a timer fashioned into an hourglass. "Put the pan on the stove with the egg in it. Turn the hourglass when the water comes to a boil. That's all there is to it."

"Yes, ma'am," Pearl said. At home they boiled the eggs for a while. No clock was needed. No one complained if some days the eggs were harder or softer than others.

"Billy Hanson brings the milk to the door morning and night. Do not let him inside the house in his barn shoes."

"Yes, ma'am," Pearl said, wondering what Mrs. Scrimshaw did with all the milk from a cow.

As if reading her mind, Mrs. Scrimshaw said, "He brings only a quart of milk to the house and brings the rest to the Dublin family down the street in exchange for the baking and butter." Mrs. Scrimshaw took a deep breath. "I do not abide waste in my kitchen. Skim the cream for household use. I like custard puddings or tapioca. I take a small glass of milk with every meal and a cup of warm milk before bed. Extra eggs are sold to Rorvig's Store."

Mrs. Scrimshaw pointed out a narrow

staircase that led from the kitchen to the basement. "Our coal furnace is in the cellar along with a room for preserves and potatoes." She said that Billy shoveled the walks. He mowed the grass in the summer and kept the flower beds. Then she pointed to a narrow door that opened to a stairway leading upstairs. "That is the back stairway that you will use whenever you must go upstairs."

She led Pearl into the parlor with its grand open staircase that led upstairs. Mrs. Scrimshaw motioned for Pearl to follow as she climbed the stairs with great caution, grasping the railing. Mrs. Scrimshaw did not enter the closed bedrooms. She opened a small door that showed a narrow staircase leading to the attic. "You will hang the wash in the attic during the cold of winter. Otherwise I keep the upstairs closed off. Except, of course, when I have out-of-town company," she said. "My niece from Grafton visits every year."

Pearl's head whirled as she fixed cornmeal mush for supper. Mrs. Scrimshaw would take her meals in the dining room. Pearl would eat in the kitchen. Pearl had never eaten alone before. At home her little sisters would be washing the supper dishes. Pearl found an old newspaper in the kindling box to read as she ate. Pearl cut out an article about fly-fishing and slipped it into her apron pocket for Billy.

A rap sounded at the kitchen door. Billy stood grinning with crooked teeth. His red hair stuck out from underneath a cap. He held a quart can of milk in one hand and a filled bucket in the other. Billy had been her best friend since first grade when Charlene Dahl had pushed Pearl off the swing at recess. Billy came running to Pearl's aid and punched Charlene in the nose.

"I have a newspaper clipping for you," Pearl said.

A bell startled them. Pearl's heart thumped as she rushed into the dining room.

Mrs. Scrimshaw held up a spoonful of mush with a look of disgust on her face. "There is a lump in my porridge."

Pearl stood for a second without speaking. At home, no one noticed a few lumps in the mush. Hungry folks were thankful for anything. Pearl gathered her wits and whisked the bowl off the table. She resisted an urge to throw it at the old woman.

"My apologies, ma'am," Pearl said. "It won't happen again."

Then Pearl went into the kitchen and strained out the few lumps with a fork. She shook her head with amazement. Life had been unkind to the rich woman? As if lumpy mush was anything to be upset about. Pearl reminded herself that the woman had just buried her husband. Her son had died in the war. She was nearly blind. It was to be expected that she would be irritable.

Pearl's mood lightened when Mrs. Scrimshaw announced they would read after the dishes were done. Pearl hurried to finish in the kitchen. She didn't mind what they read, as long as they read.

Mrs. Scrimshaw waited in the parlor in her chair.

"We'll begin with a chapter of Holy Scripture," Mrs. Scrimshaw said. She directed Pearl to the ancient King James Bible on the shelf. "I believe we will read Second Timothy tonight. Chapter 2."

"Thou therefore endure hardness as a good soldier of Jesus Christ," Pearl read. It was as if the words spoke directly to Pearl. She would swallow her humiliation at being Mrs. Scrimshaw's servant, no matter what. Her family needed the money.

"I would normally spend the evening in a novel," Mrs. Scrimshaw said. Her words slurred and she dabbed a stray tear with her hanky. "But it has been a trying day, and I am weary."

Mrs. Scrimshaw looked as used up and worn out as Doctor Gamla had looked the previous day.

"We will go to bed now," Mrs. Scrimshaw said. "I'm a light sleeper and will not sleep if you are up and about in the house."

It was still light outside. Children's voices sounded from the street. The clock chimed six o'clock. Pearl wasn't tired at all.

"Oh, it's early," Mrs. Scrimshaw said as if just noticing the time. "You may read in your room. Choose a book from the book-case. Be sure your hands are clean. Use only a thread for a marker. Do not bend the pages in any way. Be careful with the light."

"Yes, ma'am," Pearl said. She could have wept from pure joy. "I'll be careful."

Pearl replaced the Bible on the shelf and hurriedly looked through the titles: *A Tale of Two Cities, Ivanhoe, The Scarlet Letter, The Deerslayer, Uncle Tom's Cabin,* and *Tom Sawyer.* What wealth, what richness. She wanted them all. Then her eyes rested on a thin brown book. Her heart quickened. *The Red Badge of Courage* by Stephen Crane. She carefully pulled it from the shelf and scurried into her room before Mrs. Scrim-shaw could change her mind.

Pearl reveled in the luxury of a room all her own, not shared with two younger sisters who sometimes wet the bed. Little sisters who kicked in their sleep, stole the covers, and refused Pearl even a wink of privacy. She lit the lamp, plumped up the pillows, and crawled into bed, careful with the fire, and even more careful with the book. She opened the cover and smelled the delicious aroma of new paper and fresh ink. It was published in 1895 but obviously had not been read. Pearl scanned the name of the publisher and a short dedication on the first page.

She opened the first chapter and the words pulled her to another time and place. Pearl read and reread the first paragraph and its description of an army at rest. She imagined herself sitting on that foggy hillside. She pictured the soldiers lolling by smoky fires. She read ten pages, and twenty more. She read fifty pages and wiped tears from her face.

The Red Badge of Courage was as captivating as *Little Women* had been. Maybe even more so. Would every new book open doors to something equally astonishing?

Pearl marked her spot with a thread and lay the book carefully on top of the bureau. She blew out the lamp and pulled up the covers. Mama's face crowded into her mind. Pearl pushed it aside and considered how the mother in the novel begged her young son not to volunteer for the Union army. Then she imagined Mrs. Scrimshaw begging Walter not to enlist.

A glimmer of understanding, at least the beginning of a beginning, stirred inside Pearl. Books had the power to bring understanding. She had expected this to happen with Scripture, of course, but never before had she known it to happen with a work of fiction.

CHAPTER 4

This understanding stayed with Pearl the next morning and made it easier to follow Mrs. Scrimshaw's stream of orders: the five-minute egg, the bread lightly toasted — neither too brown nor blackened, the scrape of butter, the spoonful of jelly. Mrs. Scrimshaw was always polite, always mannerly, but demanding.

Billy knocked on the door when she had finally served breakfast to Mrs. Scrimshaw's satisfaction. He grinned as he held out the quart of milk.

"How are you doing?" he whispered, craning his neck to see where Mrs. Scrimshaw might be. "Is she as bad as they say?"

It wouldn't be right to take Mrs. Scrimshaw's money and complain about her.

"I'm reading *The Red Badge of Courage*," Pearl whispered. She told him about the first pages. "You would love it so much, Billy. Someday we're going to have a library in town where anyone can read any book they want."

"Pearl," Mrs. Scrimshaw called.

"I have to go," Pearl said. "I'll tell you later."

"I begin every day with a psalm," Mrs. Scrimshaw said when Pearl entered the dining room. She motioned to an empty chair beside her. "Today is Psalm 116."

Pearl dutifully read the psalm. Mrs. Scrimshaw stopped her after verse 15. "Precious in the sight of the Lord is the death of his saints." The rosewater hanky dabbed her eyes and blotted her nose. "That will be enough for today."

Pearl should have skipped that verse, it being so close to Mr. Scrimshaw's passing. But, that might have brought a scolding from Mrs. Scrimshaw. If Mrs. Scrimshaw read a psalm every day, she would notice something left out.

"I'm sorry," Pearl finally said.

"Not your fault," Mrs. Scrimshaw said. She waved her hanky, and the smell of rosewater wafted out.

They sat in silence, the coffee cooling in Mrs. Scrimshaw's china cup. The parlor clock kept ticking.

"Did you sleep well last night?" Mrs. Scrimshaw said.

"Yes, ma'am, I slept well."

"And you found a book to read?"

"*The Red Badge of Courage,* ma'am," Pearl said. "I cried after only fifty pages."

The clock ticked.

"Do you recommend Mr. Crane's book?" Mrs. Scrimshaw said. "I've not had opportunity to read it."

"It's sad," Pearl said. "About the Civil War." She could not wait to delve back into *The Red Badge of Courage,* but she had a strong intuition it was not suitable for Mrs. Scrimshaw — especially since her son had died in that war. "Perhaps we need to choose one that brings a little cheer."

Mrs. Scrimshaw took a sip of her coffee. "Have you read *The Last of the Mohicans* by Mr. James Fenimore Cooper?" Mrs. Scrimshaw asked. "It was Walter's favorite, and reading it always makes me feel closer to him."

Pearl fetched the book from the shelf and began the wonderful adventures of Natty Bumppo. Mrs. Scrimshaw corrected her pronunciation of the Indian names, but

Pearl didn't mind. It was a thick book. She loved every word.

"Oh my, it's dinnertime," Mrs. Scrimshaw said when the clock chimed noon. "How do you like Mr. Bumppo?"

"He's splendid," Pearl said with a deep sigh. She'd rather read than eat any day. "I hope the book lasts forever."

Mrs. Scrimshaw laughed, then raised her handkerchief to her eyes. Tears ran down the wrinkles of her face, gathering in the crevices around her mouth, and dripped from her chin. Mrs. Scrimshaw's thin shoulders convulsed and the handkerchief did little to keep up with the rivulets of tears flowing from her eyes.

"You must miss your husband," Pearl said at last. How awkward she felt in the face of grown-up suffering. She knew how to comfort a bawling sister. She knew how to soothe a fussy baby. She had no idea how to comfort an old woman.

"I wouldn't wish Clarence back to his suffering," Mrs. Scrimshaw said. She gasped for breath and blotted more tears. "It's Walter. Always Walter who brings my tears. The book brings him back. Memories of his laughter. His urge to read no matter what time of the day or night." She sniffed and wiped her eyes. "It's a miracle he didn't

369

burn the house down with his late-night candles. We were living in Minnesota then. No North Dakota to speak of before the Civil War." She blew her nose. "His books are all that I have left of him."

Pearl marked the page with a piece of string. She closed the book and replaced it on the shelf. "I'll fix dinner," Pearl said. At home, the noon meal was the largest of the day. She expected to fry meat and peel potatoes. "What would you like?"

"Never mind," Mrs. Scrimshaw said. "I'll have tea and toast when I get up from my nap. Find something for yourself, and fetch the mail."

"Yes, ma'am," Pearl said. If she were lucky, she could sneak another chapter of *The Red Badge of Courage* before Mrs. Scrimshaw woke up.

CHAPTER 5

The first days passed and settled into sameness. Mrs. Scrimshaw made no comment about Pearl staying or leaving. Indian summer ended and Pearl began feeding the furnace twice a day. School began without her.

On Friday, Pearl hugged her shawl closer around her shoulders as she fetched the mail. She kicked at a tumbleweed rolling across the street. It snagged on the fence, fragile to the touch with barbs that scratched — like Mrs. Scrimshaw. Pearl craned her neck for a glimpse of Clarice and Jewel as she passed the school. She missed her sisters more than she had expected. She swallowed hard as she saw Miss Hatfield through the window, standing at the blackboard.

"Wait up," Billy called from his house across from the school. He came running, catching his breath when he joined her on the path. "Funny not to be going to classes this year." He walked beside her. "Even Charlene can't go to high school," Billy said. "The hail hit everyone hard. Even the businesses are feeling it."

"Are you going next year?" Pearl said.

"If I save enough money for room and board," Billy said. "Thank God for Old Lady Scrimshaw's job. My dad lets me save part of my wages for schooling."

She reached into her apron pocket and gave Billy the newspaper articles. "For you, Mr. Hanson, and one for your little brother."

Billy bowed from the waist. "Why thank you, Miss Ellingson. How can I ever repay you?" He pocketed the clippings.

"Not much time for *The Red Badge of*

Courage," Pearl said, "but we started *The Last of the Mohicans.*" She sighed. "You must read it sometime. Remember when we studied the French and Indian War? Mr. Cooper makes that history come alive on the page."

They chatted about town news. Billy said Charlene was mad as hops that she didn't get the job with Mrs. Scrimshaw.

"She told Mildred Dublin that you stole the job from her," Billy said. "She said Mrs. Scrimshaw pitied you out of Christian charity because your father lost his crop and your family is destitute."

Pearl sighed. True enough. The job was Doctor Gamla's cure for Papa's wheat. The school bell rang for recess. Billy returned to his father's woodpile. On her way back from the store, Pearl scanned the newspaper headlines. Nothing about libraries. Pearl found a recipe for Clarice who was learning to cook. She would save the poem for Miss Hatfield. It would be a good excuse to stop at the elementary school.

A slim letter addressed to Mrs. Scrimshaw was the only mail. Pearl crept into the house as quietly as possible so as not to awaken her employer. She placed the letter and newspaper on the kitchen table and tiptoed into her little room. She picked up *The Red*

Badge of Courage and sat on her bed. The springs squeaked.

"Is that you, Pearl?" Mrs. Scrimshaw called.

"Yes, ma'am," Pearl said with a sigh.

"Any mail?" Mrs. Scrimshaw said.

"Yes, ma'am," Pearl said. "A letter."

"Bring it to me," Mrs. Scrimshaw said.

Pearl glanced in the mirror and pushed a stray lock behind her ear. She straightened her dress and brushed a crumb from her shirtwaist. Then she squared her shoulders, retrieved the letter, and bravely entered Mrs. Scrimshaw's bedroom.

It was dark with the shades drawn. A heavy layer of rosewater hung in the air. Mrs. Scrimshaw lay beneath an afghan the same color as her lavender dressing gown. A wet washcloth stretched across her eyes. Her dress lay neatly over the back of the chair. She looked smaller lying in bed. Shrunken and less formidable.

"Is there a return address?" Mrs. Scrimshaw said. She pushed herself up on her elbow and removed the compress from her eyes. Her voice was swallowed by the heavy draperies and linens.

"It says Mrs. R. Taylor, Grafton, North Dakota."

"Thank God," Mrs. Scrimshaw said. "A

letter from my niece. Please read it aloud."

Pearl pulled a thin sheet of stationery from the envelope. Spidery penmanship crawled across the page and the reverse side. "Dear Auntie." Pearl read about the niece's sorrow over her Uncle Clarence's passing. She thanked Mrs. Scrimshaw for the telegram. There was mention of children's health and a family reunion planned in Fargo.

Then Pearl gasped.

"What's wrong?" Mrs. Scrimshaw said. "Is someone sick?"

"Nothing wrong," Pearl said. "Your niece mentions being on the library committee for the Carnegie library."

"You needn't be so dramatic. You scared the life out of me," Mrs. Scrimshaw said, plainly irritated. "A library is a worthy endeavor."

"I've read about the Grafton library. I wish Mr. Carnegie would build one in Nickelbo."

"Andrew Carnegie's philanthropy won't cover his sins," Mrs. Scrimshaw said with a wagging finger. "He and his cronies caused the Johnstown flood, you know. And the way he treated strikers at his steel mills was criminal."

"But he's building libraries across America," Pearl said. "There must be something good in him."

"He may be the second-richest man in the world, but even Andrew Carnegie can't afford to build libraries in every town," Mrs. Scrimshaw said with a sniff. "It costs money to keep a library going. City governments must commit to ongoing expenses. My niece wrote all about it."

"Who is on our city government?" Pearl said.

"Clarence was the mayor for years," Mrs. Scrimshaw said. She dropped her head back against the pillow and put the compress back on her eyes. "Mr. Rorvig took his place when Clarence became ill. Do you think that old skinflint would promote taxes for a library?"

Mr. Rorvig was not an old skinflint. Pearl held her tongue. The door knocker sounded on the parlor door.

"Answer the door," Mrs. Scrimshaw said. "Tell the caller that I am indisposed."

Chapter 6

Doctor Gamla stood in the doorway, grasping the frame for support. Her eyes shone like blue flames from her colorless face.

"How is Brunhilde?" she said in a quiet voice.

"Mrs. Scrimshaw is indisposed," Pearl said. She was not exactly sure what indisposed meant, and it would be a good spelling word to stump Papa. She looked back toward Mrs. Scrimshaw's closed bedroom door. "She's in bed," Pearl whispered.

"In the middle of the day?" Doctor Gamla said. She didn't wait to be invited inside, but lumbered past Pearl, veering from side to side as if she were walking on a boat. She grabbed hold of the chair and sat down. "Did she eat today?"

"A nibble of toast at breakfast and half an egg," Pearl said. "Nothing at noon. Usually tea and toast for supper."

"As I thought," Doctor Gamla said. "Please ask her if she's well enough to come out and talk to me. Otherwise tell her I'm coming into her bedroom."

Doctor Gamla muttered something about giving up the ghost before her time, as Pearl hurried to obey. Pearl expected Mrs. Scrimshaw to object, but her employer struggled out of bed and reached for her clothes.

"Keep her company until I am dressed," Mrs. Scrimshaw said. "Olava comes at the worst times." Mrs. Scrimshaw showed more color in her cheeks than earlier.

"Do you want me to offer her a cup of tea?" Pearl said.

"Of course, we will have tea," Mrs. Scrimshaw snapped. "Use your head, girl. Keep her occupied until I come out. Then set two places at the dining room table using the good dishes. Serve a plate of those gingersnap cookies Mrs. Dublin sent over, and don't forget to put out the loaf sugar and pitcher of cream."

Pearl dutifully returned to the parlor. A feeling of dread washed over her. She was bound to do something wrong. She wasn't sure which dishes were the good ones. She didn't know if she needed to place silverware at the table or not. At home they would lay only the spoons if tea and cookies were served.

She sat in a straight-backed chair near Doctor Gamla. No words came to her. Pearl had never had a conversation with the old doctor woman before. At least not alone. She was supposed to keep her company. She couldn't think of a thing to say.

"You look troubled," Doctor Gamla said. She eyed Pearl as if she were looking for battle scars. "Is Brunhilde unkind?"

"No, ma'am," Pearl hurried to say. She answered too quickly. Doctor Gamla's white eyebrows raised into question marks. "We're reading a wonderful book together. And she lets me read in my room at night — any title of my choosing."

"That's good of her," Doctor Gamla said in a sarcastic manner. The sounds of flushing came from the water closet.

Mrs. Scrimshaw came out, elegant and collected. Pearl hurried to the kitchen to put the kettle on to boil.

"You must take care of yourself, Brunhilde," Doctor Gamla said. The women, both hard of hearing, spoke loud enough for Pearl to hear the conversation in the kitchen. "You're too thin. You need three meals a day, and a short walk outside every day. Take Pearl with you. She needs fresh air, too."

Pearl opened the cupboard doors in the kitchen. The everyday dishes on one side, and fancier china on the other. Pearl carefully removed two cups and saucers. Then she found the dessert plates. How beautiful they were. Pink and blue flowers with gold etching around the rims of each plate and cup. Someday she would buy a set of fancy china for Mama.

She found the serving tray. And the matching sugar bowl with loaf sugar, along with tiny silver tongs. Pearl carried the tray, balancing lest she spill something, and placed it on the table. She took two spoons from the sideboard, and laid the table as

Mrs. Scrimshaw had asked.

The kettle shrieked. Pearl hurried to the kitchen and measured tea into the china teapot that matched the good dishes. Then she poured the boiling water over the tea. She set the pot aside to steep and fetched the gingersnaps from the pantry.

When she had everything ready, she went to the parlor and stood by Mrs. Scrimshaw. Pearl leaned down and whispered that everything was ready in the dining room.

"Come Olava," Mrs. Scrimshaw said. "Tea is ready."

Pearl stood to the side not knowing if Mrs. Scrimshaw wanted her to pour the tea or not. Mrs. Scrimshaw took her seat and directed Doctor Gamla to the other. She lifted the teapot herself, to Pearl's relief, and poured the steaming brew into the dainty cups.

"You forgot the cream," Mrs. Scrimshaw said to Pearl.

Pearl hurried to retrieve it, almost tripping over the rug in her haste. The cream pitcher wasn't on the shelf from where she had taken the dishes. On the other side of the cupboard, with the everyday dishes, was a small crockery pitcher that said *Niagara Falls.* Pearl didn't know what to do but use it.

She realized her mistake as soon as she brought it to the table.

"Foolish girl," Mrs. Scrimshaw said. She glared at Pearl. "I said the china cream pitcher."

"I'm sorry, ma'am, but I couldn't find it," Pearl said.

"It's in the cupboard," Mrs. Scrimshaw said. "You didn't look."

Pearl wished the floor would open and swallow her. Pearl hadn't felt such humiliation since wetting her pants in first grade.

"Don't be silly," Doctor Gamla said. She reached for the Niagara Falls pitcher and poured a healthy stream into her cup. Then she swirled her spoon through the tea and took a sip. "It's just us."

Pearl turned to leave the room, but Doctor Gamla reached out and motioned for Pearl to stay.

"Brunhilde, I've a cure for you," Doctor Gamla said.

Mrs. Scrimshaw cocked her head and waited.

"Pearl is here as your companion," Doctor Gamla said. "You can make her eat alone in the kitchen and treat her like a hired girl, or you can welcome her as a young friend to your table, here to improve your life."

Pearl almost swallowed her tongue.

"You're not eating," Doctor Gamla said. "Your appetite will improve if Pearl eats at the table with you."

Pearl felt the color leave her face. She didn't want to eat her meals with crabby Mrs. Scrimshaw. Eating in the kitchen was the only time she had to herself.

"Why not start by inviting young Pearl to join us for tea?" Doctor Gamla paused to catch her wind. "She's a smart girl. First in her class. No doubt she has much to offer in the way of conversation."

Mrs. Scrimshaw's eyes bulged, and she swallowed hard. Doctor Gamla was famous for revealing the root of matters. And Doctor Gamla was not afraid to declare the cure needed. Everyone in Nickelbo accepted the old woman's wisdom, but not everyone appreciated her bluntness.

Mrs. Scrimshaw bobbed her head at Pearl. Her mouth crimped hard as steel. Pearl left to fetch another cup and saucer. Her hands shook. She knew nothing about eating at a formal dining table.

Doctor Gamla pointed to the empty seat on the other side of Mrs. Scrimshaw. "Set yourself down, Pearl. No doubt you could rest your feet."

Mrs. Scrimshaw poured tea into Pearl's

cup, but her employer didn't make eye contact.

"I woke up this morning thinking about you, Brunhilde," Doctor Gamla said. "I decided that what you needed more than anything is good company and a new cause to champion."

"I'm past championing causes," Mrs. Scrimshaw said with a snort. She sipped tea, her long, graceful fingers curled around the cup to steady it. Pearl noticed a fine tremble, barely a tremor, but enough to splash tea into the saucer.

"Nonsense," Doctor Gamla said. "Once a person settles in the rocking chair, it's over. Might as well start digging the grave."

"I don't know any causes to champion," Mrs. Scrimshaw said. "A grave is to be expected at my age." She replaced the cup onto the saucer.

"My cures work if you can stand them," Doctor Gamla said. She dipped her cookie into her tea for softening.

"I'm too old," Mrs. Scrimshaw said. She motioned for Pearl to add more hot water to the pot. "Though Pearl here would have me petitioning Andrew Carnegie for a library."

"A library. Just what Nickelbo needs," Doctor Gamla said, slapping her knee with delight. She laughed a witchy laugh, showing a mouth of broken and missing teeth. "Books are the gateway to democracy, the doorway to self-improvement. Lord knows we need both on the prairie."

"Mrs. Scrimshaw's niece is on the library committee in Grafton," Pearl said as she returned with a fresh pot. She half-expected Mrs. Scrimshaw to tell her to be quiet. "They petitioned money from Andrew Carnegie."

"A library will never happen here," Mrs. Scrimshaw said. "I doubt Nickelbo farmers even know how to read."

"You may be surprised," Doctor Gamla said. "Books make the long winters bearable." She paused for breath. "Nickelbo doesn't have to depend on some rich person out East to hand us a library."

"No one has money in Nickelbo," Mrs. Scrimshaw said.

"We have enough local resources to build a library, though folks hold their money close to their chests."

"You're forgetting my eyes," Mrs. Scrimshaw said. "I couldn't manage the correspondence needed to write the grant, even if I wanted to."

"That's why you have Pearl. She should be attending high school but instead the

Good Lord sent her to you." Doctor Gamla lowered her voice. "You don't want to slip into melancholia like you did after Walter's death." She reached for Mrs. Scrimshaw's hand. "My cures work — if you can stand them."

Pearl startled. Doctor Gamla's good opinion of her made Pearl sit taller in her chair.

"A library would add ten years to your life if you are smart enough to take it on. A legacy for you to leave behind. A cause that will put spring in your step and life to your years."

Doctor Gamla stood to her feet. Pearl followed to open the door and see her out.

"Don't be scared of her, Pearl," Doctor Gamla said, pausing and grasping hold of the doorframe. "Not all wounds benefit from salve."

A cold wind blew in through the open door. It seemed the energy of the room left with the old woman. Pearl returned to the table and stood beside Mrs. Scrimshaw's chair. The clock chimed four times.

"Well, then," Mrs. Scrimshaw said. "We'll read the paper before supper." She motioned Pearl to be seated.

Pearl read while Mrs. Scrimshaw nibbled the edges of a cookie. They read until Billy knocked on the kitchen door to deliver the evening milk.

The wind scattered a few dried leaves into the kitchen through the open door. He smelled of fresh air and cow barn. His boots were caked with manure. Pearl did not invite him into the kitchen.

"Doctor Gamla told Mrs. Scrimshaw to start a Carnegie library here in town," Pearl whispered.

Billy's eyes widened. He opened his mouth to speak, but Mrs. Scrimshaw called from the parlor.

"You'd better go," Pearl said. She didn't know if she should set a place for herself in the dining room or in the kitchen. Doctor Gamla's visit had upset everything. Maybe Mrs. Scrimshaw would ask Charlene to work for her instead. Charlene would know how to eat at the table with a rich person.

"Pearl," Mrs. Scrimshaw said. "Fetch bowls of cream and bread. Then we'll read my niece's letters telling how they petitioned Mr. Carnegie for their library."

The letters told of the need to form a committee. The niece said it helped their cause by having a lending club already established in the town. "This proves that readers are serious," the niece wrote. She also said that the town council must agree in writing to provide funds to keep the library going for ten years following the building program. "Mr. Carnegie funds only the actual building. He does not donate money for books or upkeep on the buildings. He also does not hire library staff."

"It's far too complicated," Mrs. Scrimshaw said. She pushed the bowl of cream and bread, only half-eaten, to the side. "How am I to form a committee or a reading society?"

"I'd be on the committee, and Billy Hanson would," Pearl said. Her mind whirled with new possibilities. "Miss Hatfield might be the chairperson. And we could ask Pastor Olson and Mrs. Rorvig."

"Miss Hatfield and Pastor Olson, of course," Mrs. Scrimshaw said. "But Mrs. Rorvig? Is she a reader?"

"I don't know if she reads or not," Pearl said. "But she is married to the mayor. We'll need to convince the city government to fund a library."

Mrs. Scrimshaw stared at Pearl with such focus that Pearl looked to make sure she hadn't spilled cream and bread down the front of her dress.

"You should go into politics." Mrs. Scrimshaw cocked her head and chuckled. "Mrs. Rorvig indeed."

They sat in silence. Pearl was sure she had overstepped in naming names for the committee. Papa was coming tomorrow and it would serve her right if Mrs. Scrimshaw sent her back with him. A sudden longing for Mama came over Pearl.

She read a chapter in *The Red Badge of Courage* and felt as lonely as a soldier far from home.

CHAPTER 7

The next morning Pearl forgot to set the timer for Mrs. Scrimshaw's eggs. Billy delivered the milk. Pearl smelled the toast burning. Pearl set the eggs aside for herself and started over. The bell rang in the dining room. Pearl hurried to serve the food, tripping over the edge of the carpet and dropping the toast. Pearl scooped it up onto the tray.

"You are a clumsy girl," Mrs. Scrimshaw said. She reached for the teapot and poured herself a cup of tea. "Never mind. I'm not hungry anyway."

Pearl stood, not knowing if she should sit at the table or return to the kitchen. Pearl couldn't please Mrs. Scrimshaw, no matter how hard she tried. How nice it would be to go home.

Finally, Mrs. Scrimshaw motioned her to sit down and eat. It was then that Pearl saw the fat envelope addressed to her father sitting by her place.

"I've considered your committee members. Of course, it would be impossible for them to meet here," Mrs. Scrimshaw said. "Strangers in my house, sitting on my furniture. Who knows what kind of diseases they might bring with them."

Pearl had no other idea where a committee meeting could gather. Her parents lived too far out in the country, Billy's home was full of children, and the church was not heated during the week. The best place in town was Mrs. Scrimshaw's house. It only made sense.

"We could meet in your kitchen," Pearl said. "Then the committee members wouldn't dirty rugs or furniture."

"Ridiculous!" Mrs. Scrimshaw stormed into her bedroom. The clock struck nine. Pearl couldn't stop the tears.

A knock sounded on the door. Doctor Gamla entered without invitation. The old woman smelled of cheese and sour milk. Her face pruned with wrinkles. She looked even older than yesterday.

"Where's Brunhilde?" Doctor Gamla said. "Are you crying?"

"She went to her bedroom," Pearl said. She wiped her eyes with her sleeve. "I'm not crying."

"Hmmm," Doctor Gamla said. She knit her brows together and stalked into Mrs. Scrimshaw's bedroom without knocking. She closed the door behind her.

Pearl heard muffled voices but could not tell what they were saying. She added wood to the cookstove and put a fresh kettle of water on to heat for tea, keeping one ear cocked toward the bedroom in case Mrs. Scrimshaw called for her.

Doctor Gamla came out of the bedroom alone.

"Will you stay for tea?" Pearl said.

"Not today," Doctor Gamla said. "Brunhilde has a headache and will stay in bed. She asks that you bring her a tray."

"Yes, ma'am," Pearl said.

"Soup. Hearty soup with meat and vegetables. That's what is needed," Doctor Gamla said. "I'll come back and eat with you in case Brunhilde gets broody. Together we'll get her out of this melancholia."

Pearl set to work peeling and scraping carrots, rutabagas, potatoes, and onions fetched from the bins in the basement. Jars of canned goods lined a shelf. She chose stewed tomatoes to add to the mix. A ham bone sat in the icebox. Pearl placed it all in a heavy cooking pot on the back burner to simmer until supper, adding salt, pepper and a bay leaf for flavor. She read the label of the tomato can before throwing it into the refuse.

Soon Papa knocked on the kitchen door.

"Oh, Papa!" Pearl said. She hugged him around the neck and burst into tears.

"What's wrong?" Papa said. "Is she mean to you?"

"Nothing's wrong." Pearl wiped her eyes and tried to laugh. "A little homesick, that's all."

She gave him the envelope, and explained that Mrs. Scrimshaw was in bed with a headache. "I can't invite you inside," Pearl said. Tears gathered in spite of her good resolve.

"Then let's step outside," Papa said.

They stood on the back porch. A prairie wind blew steady from the west. Across the street, Pastor Olson swept the steps leading into the church. Mr. Rorvig drove by with his dray piled high with firewood. He waved to Papa and called out that there was still firewood for the taking along Mad Dog River.

Papa said that Mama and the girls were fine. School was going well. Baby Ruby had

390

a tooth. Opal was learning to use the potty chair. Everyone missed Pearl and sent greetings.

"Thank you," Papa said holding up the envelope. "I hate taking your money. You should be saving it for high school."

Pearl gulped back a sob. She had never been away from home so long. She nodded and kissed Papa goodbye.

"I'll pay you back when I harvest the wheat next year," Papa said.

Pearl watched him drive away behind old Old Daisy. Too soon he was gone.

Pearl set the dining room table for three. No sound came from the master bedroom. Pearl sneaked into her room and enjoyed *The Red Badge of Courage* until she heard a knock on the front door.

Doctor Gamla breezed in as if she owned the place. Doctor Gamla commented on the good smells coming from the kitchen. Mrs. Scrimshaw came out of her bedroom wearing her lavender dressing gown and a bewildered look. Her hair was tousled, and she looked askance at the table settings.

"I invited myself to supper," Doctor Gamla said. "I told Pearl that it was a perfect day for soup." She sat at the table. "I'm here to make sure you eat it."

Pearl filled the soup tureen in the kitchen

and brought it to the table. The delicious smell of onions floated through the air. She brought bread and a plate of crackers.

Mrs. Scrimshaw murmured something about getting dressed, but Doctor Gamla protested.

"Don't fuss on my account," Doctor Gamla said. "It's just us."

Mrs. Scrimshaw paused, acted as if she would say something, but then instead pulled out her chair at the head of the table and sat down. She slouched in her chair, and it seemed the light had gone out of her eyes.

Pearl served the soup. It tasted good. Doctor Gamla kept them laughing with stories of Norway and the unusual people she had met in her life. It was the first time since leaving home that Pearl had enjoyed a meal. Everyone had seconds.

"You need hot food," Doctor Gamla said. "How else will you get your strength back?" She drained her teacup, smacking her lips. "Meat, potatoes, and vegetables. No more of this tea and toast business."

Mrs. Scrimshaw grimaced. She sighed and blotted her mouth with a napkin.

"I will be asking Pearl about your appetite," Doctor Gamla said. "And I plan on joining you for meals to make sure you are following my advice."

"There's custard pudding," Mrs. Scrimshaw said. She didn't look at Doctor Gamla. "Pearl, please clear the table and bring dessert."

They discussed the library committee over pudding.

"You have the most practical location," Doctor Gamla said.

"I suggested we meet in the kitchen if she was afraid of people soiling her carpets," Pearl said. She glanced at Mrs. Scrimshaw out of the corner of her eye. "No one would mind meeting around the kitchen table."

"Impossible," Mrs. Scrimshaw said. "People would think me haughty and rude if I only offered my kitchen."

Doctor Gamla let out a snort. "People already name you haughty and rude. They'll add mean and selfish if you don't host the committee. They won't care whether it's in the kitchen or parlor." Doctor Gamla took in a wheezy breath. "Think of Clarence's standing in the community. Your behavior colors the way folks remember him."

Mrs. Scrimshaw sat without speaking, her shoulders slumped and a definite pout on her face. The woman wouldn't contradict the old doctor woman, but it didn't mean she agreed with her.

"That's settled. The committee meets here tomorrow afternoon," Doctor Gamla said. "It's up to you, Pearl, to invite people to the house and serve refreshments."

Pearl wondered at the special bond between Mrs. Scrimshaw and Doctor Gamla. And she didn't understand why Mrs. Scrimshaw let Doctor Gamla boss her around as she did. Of course, everyone tiptoed around Doctor Gamla.

"We'll meet around the dining room table," Mrs. Scrimshaw said with a dejected sigh. "Less chance of spillage. But Billy Hanson must remove his shoes before coming in, or anyone else with farm filth on their person. It will be your responsibility, Pearl, to protect my carpets."

The clock chimed. Doctor Gamla offered to help with the dishes, but Mrs. Scrimshaw shooed her outside. "We must write the invitations to potential committee members. We have much to do."

The invitations could not tolerate even a smidge of ink blot. Pearl's fingers cramped. Mrs. Scrimshaw insisted on inviting Mrs. Dahl and Charlene, and also to include Mr. Rorvig because of the need for a man on the committee. Pearl had a flash of inspiration.

"We'll invite my mother," Pearl said. Her

mother's face crowded her mind, the way she sighed when the baby cried. How hard Mama worked to keep the family fed and clothed. It would do her good to get away from the children for the afternoon.

"Does she read?"

"Yes," Pearl said. She chose her words with care, not wanting to tell a falsehood. "But she has little time."

In the morning, Mrs. Scrimshaw announced they would not be attending church services. "You may deliver the invitations, but I want you to come home without staying for worship." She sniffed into her lace hanky. "This wind is a terror on my sinuses and we have much to do."

Pearl's heart sank. That meant she could not sit in church with her family as she had hoped. She must be content with greeting them in the churchyard. Pearl bundled in shawls and ran across the street to deliver the envelopes. It was gray and cold, and dreary as laundry day.

"What's this?" Mrs. Dahl squinted at Pearl's note. The wind whipped Pearl's skirts and shawls into a cloth cocoon. "A library committee?"

"Who thought of that?" Charlene said with a groan. She wore a new coat with a matching fur hat and muff. "Sounds dull as school."

"Hush, Charlene," Mrs. Dahl said. She had a habit of closing her eyes when she spoke. "It's our civic duty."

Whether or not Pearl liked Charlene, she knew Mrs. Dahl to be relentless when it came to projects and causes. She had almost single-handedly built the playground at the schoolyard, paying for it with basket socials and talent shows.

Charlene lagged behind in the freezing wind. Pearl had forgotten her mittens, and her fingers tingled with the cold. Pearl tucked her hands under her armpits. How cozy a fur mitt would feel.

"How do you like working for Old Lady Scrimshaw?" Charlene said. "I would never work for her. I heard she's mean as a snake."

Pearl shrugged. She knew to keep quiet.

"Charlene, hurry up!" Mrs. Dahl called from the church door.

"See you later today," Charlene said as she hurried into church.

No sign of her family yet. Other parishioners trickled into the sanctuary, some glanced her way, no doubt wondering why she was standing outside in the cold. Perhaps her family had decided to stay home because of the weather. Maybe one of the babies was sick. She had almost given up on them when Old Daisy pulled into the churchyard, bowing her head into the wind, her mane flying around her face. Pearl ran to hug her sisters. She marveled at how Ruby had grown, and kissed Mama's wet cheek.

"*Stalkers liten,* poor little one," Mama said. "How we've missed you." She stepped back and examined Pearl. "You're thinner. I hope she's not working you too hard."

"No, Mama," Pearl said. She had no words to explain how it was to live with Mrs. Scrimshaw. So hard to be someone's slave day and night, yet amazing to read the woman's books. Opal hung on her legs. Pearl scooped Opal into her arms and handed the invitation to her mother. The church bells signaled the beginning of church.

"Please come if you can, Mama." Pearl's voice choked. "It would be a chance to see each other."

Mama nodded as Mr. and Mrs. Rorvig scurried up the walk, almost late. Pearl handed the baby to Papa, and ran to give them their invitation. Pearl turned to say goodbye to her family but the church door closed behind them. Pearl swallowed a sob. She ran across the street.

Mrs. Scrimshaw was in a near panic.

"What took you so long?"

"The Rorvigs were the last to arrive," Pearl said, trying to catch her breath. She wiped her feet on the mat and hung her shawl in the closet.

"We've much to do. Set the table and put the water on to boil," she said. "Put the vase on the table — not that one, the blue one." She barked orders until Pearl's head dizzied.

Finally, the table was set to Mrs. Scrimshaw's satisfaction.

Pearl ran outside before the guests arrived. She looked up into a rainy mist. Leaving the baby in the care of Jewel and Clarice would not be easy. It was always simpler for Mama to stay on the farm. "God, please let Mama come." Pearl swept the floor and made sure there were enough newspapers in the outhouse. She sighed. They would no doubt track mud and snow into the house if they had to take a trip out back but Mrs. Scrimshaw would never let the guests use her precious water closet. Someday when Pearl grew up and had a water closet of her own, she would be sure to be generous in letting others use it. Even Doctor Gamla trudged to the backhouse when she visited.

Doctor Gamla was the first to arrive. Pearl breathed easier. Doctor Gamla always made every situation bearable. Mr. and Mrs. Rorvig were the next to knock on the door. Then Billy, Pastor Olson, and Miss Hatfield. Pearl scrutinized shoes. There were no signs of cow manure. Pearl directed them to the dining room table. Mama came next, and finally Mrs. Dahl and Charlene. Mrs. Scrimshaw sat like a queen at the head of the table. Pearl found a seat next to Mama. Once Pearl had served the cookies and tea, she and Mama held hands under the tablecloth.

Mrs. Scrimshaw acted like the library had been her idea from the start. She asked Pearl to read the letter from her niece describing the procedure to request Carnegie money. Mrs. Scrimshaw explained how it might work, starting with a library committee and ending with a permanent library functioning in their town.

"This is exactly what this town needs," Mrs. Dahl said with a clap of her hands and tightly closed eyes. "A library will bring in the country folk to patronize other Nickelbo businesses."

"Schoolchildren will greatly benefit," Miss Hatfield said.

"We'd be better off building a library on our own rather than trusting some do-gooder millionaire to give us money," Doctor Gamla said. She paused to catch her breath.

"But since Carnegie knows how to build libraries, it is only prudent to follow his advice," Pastor Olson said. "If we get the money, all the better."

"My niece suggests a small lending club in someone's home as a way to begin," Mrs. Scrimshaw said. "We'll use donated reading material to get started, and purchase new books when we can."

"I have old magazines," Mrs. Dahl said. "Charlene has a Dickens collection." She opened her eyes and frowned at her daughter.

Miss Hatfield and the Rorvigs offered books.

"What about thieves?" Charlene said. "Country people might steal the books."

"It's up to the librarian to keep watch so that only subscribers check out books," Miss Hatfield said.

"I could be the librarian," Charlene said. "It would be easy."

"It's not easy," Billy said. "You couldn't do it."

A silence fell over the gathering.

"Where would we house the donated items?" Doctor Gamla said. "There needs to be regular hours, according to Mr. Carnegie."

Everyone looked at Mrs. Scrimshaw. Pearl's employer's cheeks flushed pink.

"I'm not well enough," Mrs. Scrimshaw said. "I couldn't possibly . . ."

"Nonsense," Doctor Gamla said. The clock chimed twice. "It wouldn't hurt you a bit, Brunhilde, to open your kitchen door for an hour or two on Sunday afternoons after church. You're just across the street. Pearl will act as librarian and handle everything in the kitchen while you take your nap."

Doctor Gamla made no mention of Charlene as librarian. Pearl and everyone looked to Mrs. Scrimshaw, who pulled out her hanky. A whiff of rosewater came with it.

Mrs. Rorvig nodded with an approving smile. "Pearl will handle it. People in and out. Books laid out on the kitchen table. Efficient and easy."

Mrs. Scrimshaw's silence showed her reluctance.

"Remember, Brunhilde," Doctor Gamla said. "My cures work if you can stand them."

Mrs. Scrimshaw looked around at the group, dabbed her nose, and nodded. Everyone clapped.

"We'll be quiet," Pearl said. "You won't even know the people are here."

"I'll help," Billy said.

"Keep it free of charge," Doctor Gamla said. "Otherwise the people who need it the most are left out."

"The Carnegie Foundation demands the library is free of charge to patrons," Mrs. Scrimshaw said. "But our lending club could do as it wishes for now."

"A small charge, maybe, in the beginning," Mama said. "It will make patrons more careful with the materials and give them pride in the library."

"It's only practical to charge a subscription fee," Mrs. Rorvig said. "Not a large amount, but I agree with Mrs. Ellingson."

Mama squeezed Pearl's hand under the table.

"Those who volunteer their time to run the lending club would receive a subscription for free," Miss Hatfield said pointing her chin toward Billy and Pearl.

They discussed how to promote the new service, possible fundraisers, and of course, the petition to Mr. Carnegie.

"We'll work together," Mrs. Rorvig said. "I'll volunteer as treasurer."

"I volunteer to plan fundraisers," Mrs. Dahl said, her eyes squinted as if already planning the ventures. "Charlene will help. A basket social and maybe a bazaar."

"Of course," Pastor Olson said. "Any event must be planned so as not to interfere with the Ladies' Aid Bazaar held every summer."

"Can't step on anyone's toes," Mr. Rorvig said. "We must consider the good of all."

"A cakewalk or pie social goes over well," Mama said.

"The schoolchildren could put on a talent show," Miss Hatfield said. "Or a community sing. Or even a spelldown. We'll charge admission. And push the chairs back for the cakewalk afterwards."

"An ice cream social," Billy said. "Admission five cents."

A murmur of approval swept across the room like prairie wind through a field of wheat.

"A library will put Nickelbo on the map," Mr. Rorvig said. "I'm sure the city council will come on board once they learn the building is donated by Carnegie. I'll have flyers printed to pass out in the store and sell subscriptions to folks that come in."

"Who will do the paperwork for Mr. Carnegie?" Pastor Olson said. "That will be the most critical role of this committee."

No one said anything. Pearl started to

volunteer but Charlene interrupted.

"I'll do it," Charlene said. "My penmanship won awards at school."

Pearl bit back an angry retort. Charlene's handwriting would be adequate, but the content of the application mattered more than the script.

"Lovely," Mrs. Scrimshaw said. "Thank you, Miss Dahl, for shouldering this important burden. Of course, the final draft of the grant must be copied in impeccable handwriting. Perhaps you could also keep minutes of our meetings."

Charlene cast a triumphant look toward Pearl. Pearl looked down at her hands and bit her lip. Charlene would ruin everything. She always did.

Miss Hatfield declared the meeting ended. They would meet again on Wednesday afternoon to bring their donated books and magazines. The first lending library would be next Sunday afternoon.

Mama hugged Pearl goodbye. "I'm proud of you," Mama whispered.

The others left until only Doctor Gamla remained.

"I'm sorry to put the squeeze on you that way," Doctor Gamla said. "Clarence would expect you to take the lead."

"I know he would," Mrs. Scrimshaw said.

"But strangers in my home." She shuddered. "Who knows the riffraff that might show up?"

"No riffraff in Nickelbo," Doctor Gamla said with a wheezy laugh. "It will be mostly church people. Pearl will corral them in the kitchen."

"You know a library will never happen here," Mrs. Scrimshaw said. "No matter how starry-eyed everyone is. Mr. Carnegie wants to build in places where there is at least a semblance of culture and education. Not Nickelbo."

Mrs. Scrimshaw changed everything positive to negative. Pearl wanted to scream. Only the memory of Mama's hug and her family's need kept Pearl from running out the door. She couldn't quit. More than ever she must endure the old woman's gloom and doom. Mrs. Scrimshaw might not like Pearl but she would never allow someone else to manage the lending library in her kitchen.

Mrs. Scrimshaw retired to her room as soon as Doctor Gamla left, leaving strict instructions not to be disturbed.

CHAPTER 8

At suppertime, Billy brought the milk to the kitchen door.

"Can you come out and talk?" Billy said while craning his neck to spot Mrs. Scrimshaw.

She was still in her room. Pearl grabbed her shawl and mittens and stepped out on the back steps. The sky had cleared and overhead glowed a milky moon over the deserted streets of Nickelbo. Stars twinkled and candlelight showed in several windows. Chimney smoke wafted over the rooflines. The town smelled of burning coal.

"I've been brainstorming ways to earn money," Billy said. He suggested selling garden seeds door to door in the spring, raffling a calf in the summer, and putting a donation jar on Mr. Rorvig's counter.

"And best of all," he said. His words puffed vapor before his mouth and his red cowlick stuck out from his stocking cap. "A writing contest. Stories about Nickelbo. Ten cents to enter with a dollar prize. The winner will read his story at the cakewalk. All proceeds go to the library fund."

"There are no stories in stodgy old Nickelbo," Pearl said. "Nothing happens here."

"Every story is set somewhere," Billy said.

"Why not Nickelbo?"

Doctor Gamla was interesting. Her life of service to the community, her acerbic wit, and her words of wisdom had to count for something. Pearl might write a story about her if she could find ten cents.

"We'll ask Miss Hatfield to be the judge and the winning entry can be printed in the newspaper," he said.

"What if no one enters?" Pearl said.

"They'll enter," Billy said. "What else is there to do over the winter? The preacher can announce it in church."

Pearl tallied the numbers in her head. Ten entries would be the break-even point. Anything over ten was pure gravy. There were good storytellers in town. Old Man Larson always told a good yarn.

The next morning Mrs. Scrimshaw took to her bed. She placed the washcloth across her eyes and asked for a tray in her room, requesting tea and toast. Even Doctor Gamla couldn't get the old woman to stir from her room when she stopped by in late morning.

"I was afraid of this," Doctor Gamla shook her head sadly. "This is exactly what happened after Walter's death."

"What do you mean?" Pearl said.

"Melancholia," Doctor Gamla said. "She

spent time in a sanatorium in Fargo. She couldn't be left alone."

"You mean she was suicidal?" Pearl said in a horrified whisper.

"It happens sometimes when folks find life too hard to handle." Doctor Gamla closed her eyes and took a deep breath. "Someday you'll learn how terrible and wonderful life can be. Sometimes it is both terrible and wonderful at the same time. Brunhilde has chosen to forget the wonder of her son and remember only the pain of his death." She stood to leave. "You'll understand when you get to be my age."

How horrible it would be to find Mrs. Scrimshaw dead. Pearl's distress must have shown on her face for Doctor Gamla hurried to reassure her.

"She's not that bad yet," Doctor Gamla said. "But she needs something to occupy her mind." Doctor Gamla pulled her shawl tighter and made ready to leave. "Add a place for me at the supper table. I'll try to think of something."

At supper, Pearl told the older women about Billy's idea for a writing contest.

"Ridiculous," Mrs. Scrimshaw said. "There's nothing to write about here."

"Not so fast," Doctor Gamla said. "There

must be many interesting stories in Nick-elbo."

"Your son would make a great story, Mrs. Scrimshaw," Pearl said. "The soldier who loved books." A sudden idea flashed into Pearl's mind. "We'll name the library after him."

Doctor Gamla hooted with glee. "The Walter Scrimshaw Memorial Library has a nice ring to it. Don't you agree, Brunhilde?"

"He was a fine boy," Mrs. Scrimshaw said, dabbing her nose with her hanky. "I suppose I could write something about him."

"It would be a way to remember him," Pearl said.

"I'm not much for writing," Doctor Gamla said. "But I could write about my famous salve and how I discovered it."

"And include your secret recipe," Mrs. Scrimshaw said. "You're in danger of taking it with you to the grave."

Chapter 9

Mrs. Scrimshaw began dictating her story in the days to follow. Burnt toast reminded her of Walter at age three when he decided he preferred the toast "extra cooked." The smell of frying onions reminded her of Walter's refusal to eat anything with onions in it. A broken dish brought memories of Walter helping with the dishes. Pearl dutifully transcribed Mrs. Scrimshaw's words, though she realized early on that Mrs. Scrimshaw was writing an entire book, not just a little story.

Doctor Gamla declared it was just what Mrs. Scrimshaw needed to plod through the grief of Walter's death. "I should have thought of it years ago," she said. "But it took Billy's idea and your encouragement."

Mrs. Scrimshaw rallied. She came out of her room for breakfast and other than an afternoon nap stayed up all day.

"This writing is the cure for what ails her," Doctor Gamla whispered when she stopped by for tea. "And you found it, not me."

Sunday morning dawned dismal and dreary. Sleet spat against the windowpanes as Pearl and Mrs. Scrimshaw ate breakfast.

"No one will come out in such weather," Mrs. Scrimshaw said. "I worried for nothing."

"You never know," Pearl said. She was eager to find out who would be interested in borrowing reading material.

Mr. Rorvig said a few shoppers had purchased subscriptions and expressed enthusiasm about the lending library.

"Hmmm," Mrs. Scrimshaw said. She

would not be going to church since the weather irritated her sinuses. "I am going back to bed."

Pearl was almost relieved. Mrs. Scrimshaw's constant negativity was as irritating as the pellets of sleet. She did her morning chores and hurried to church as the sleet turned to snow. The family did not attend. It was unwise to bring out the babies in such weather, but even so, Pearl felt disappointed.

The committee members clustered on the church steps after services.

"I'll be there," Billy said. The snow was heavier and the wind had picked up. "I'll shovel a path."

"Such weather," Mrs. Rorvig said. "I'll walk over in case someone wants to buy a subscription."

Charlene was google-eyed over Mr. Dublin's visiting nephew. Pearl doubted she even noticed the weather. Miss Hatfield squeezed Pearl's hand.

"I sent notices home with all my students," Miss Hatfield said.

Pearl arranged the stack of books and fanned out a year's worth of *Good Housekeeping* on the kitchen table. The collection of books by Charles Dickens took up most of the space. Pearl smoothed her hand over

411

the leather covers, trying to imagine how it would feel to own even one book so elegant and beautiful. Miss Hatfield had donated her much-used copy of *Little Women.* The Rorvigs donated Ulysses S. Grant's autobiography and three books by Mark Twain. Mrs. Scrimshaw had reluctantly parted with *Ivanhoe* and *The Lady of the Lake.* Mr. Rorvig had donated a water-damaged ledger that he was unable to sell. In it, Pearl would record all the library transactions. Mrs. Rorvig had another to record donations and subscriptions.

Old Man Larson was the first to arrive. He looked as old as Mrs. Scrimshaw. "It's starting to make weather out there." His whiskers glittered with melting snow. He stomped his feet on the rug and removed his hat. "I need a good book."

His melting feet dripped on the floor. Pearl spread old newspapers in front of the kitchen table. Mrs. Scrimshaw would be horrified at the puddles. Pearl laid more newspapers.

Mr. Larson rifled through the magazines, complaining about the small print. With delight he pounced on Grant's autobiography. "I served with General Grant at Appomattox." He opened the pages and smiled at the large type. "I was there when Lee laid down his arms." He grinned a large, toothless smile. "I'll take good care of it, by gum," he said. He tucked the large book inside his coat to protect it from the snow. "I've wanted to read this book for a long time."

Pearl recorded Mr. Larson's selection in the ledger as Mrs. Dublin rapped on the door. Mrs. Dublin leafed through the *Good Housekeeping* magazines looking for a new crocheting pattern. She signed out two magazines and *A Child's Garden of Verses* for her children. By three o'clock, five citizens of Nickelbo, outside of committee members, had borrowed items from the lending library. Two purchased subscriptions.

Doctor Gamla arrived as they were taking down the display. "How did it go?" she said. She looked as pale as the snow, and was cocooned in black wool that pulled all the color from her face.

"We would have had a better turnout had the weather cooperated," Pearl said.

"That's the way of things," Doctor Gamla said. "Life happens a minute at a time, and seldom as one expects." She patted Pearl's back. "Today is the first day of the Walter Scrimshaw Memorial Library. A day for celebration."

"This hardly counts as a library," Mrs. Rorvig said looking around at the crowded kitchen with the books and magazines packed into wooden crates. Billy began hauling the crates to the basement for safekeeping.

"What is a library but a collection of reading material loaned out to interested persons?" Doctor Gamla said. "This is a library, and Pearl is our first librarian. We don't need Andrew Carnegie at all."

"Did you notice how happy Mr. Larson was to find that book by President Grant?" Billy said. "His eyes teared up when he mentioned Appomattox."

"Twenty cents added to the coffers," Mrs. Rorvig said. "Added to the four subscriptions we sold earlier this week totals sixty cents."

"A long way to go," Pearl admitted.

Pearl contemplated Doctor Gamla's statement after everyone left and she was mopping the wet floor. She threw the lumpy wads of newspaper into the fire. It didn't matter that they had only a dozen books and a bunch of old magazines. Someday they would have a library all their own, and maybe, if she could keep Charlene out of the mix, Pearl would be the real librarian.

Her imagination soared. Anything was possible.

Mrs. Scrimshaw came out of her room for supper. "What did they break?" she asked.

"Nothing was broken," Pearl said. She told Mrs. Scrimshaw about the folks who checked out books and magazines.

"I'm surprised that Alvin Larson would choose Grant's biography," Mrs. Scrimshaw said. "Alvin was never the brightest man."

Pearl suppressed a desire to punch her dear employer in the nose. She pulled her sweater closer around her arms and shivered.

"Cold in here," Pearl said. A relief to get away from Mrs. Scrimshaw and her constant complaints. "I'll fire the furnace."

A blanket of snow covered the brown grass and sounds of sleigh bells were heard on the street. The week before Thanksgiving was the library's first fundraiser. The committee met to plan Miss Hatfield's spelling bee followed by Billy's ice cream social.

The committee members agreed to each donate a quart of cream. There would be a five-cents-a dish charge for ice cream with no charge for children under twelve. That would attract young families.

"I make the best ice cream," Charlene said. Lately she had been acting as if her penmanship made her the boss of everything. "I'd rather make ice cream than partake of the spelling bee."

"Wait a minute. Everyone will be in the spelling bee," Miss Hatfield said with a laugh. "No excuses. Crank the ice cream before the bee so that everyone can join the fun."

Charlene turned her nose upward in a distinct pout.

"I doubt the country folk will have success or interest in a spelling bee," Mrs. Scrimshaw said. "Why not spare them humiliation by making it optional? It is unfair to put them in competition with more learned citizens who live in town."

Doctor Gamla crimped her mouth hard and said nothing. Mrs. Scrimshaw was just plain mean. Pearl was glad when Mrs. Scrimshaw announced that she was too old to attend the event. Mrs. Rorvig offered to sell tickets at the door with Pearl. Billy would be in charge of cranking the ice cream.

"Of course," Doctor Gamla said. "Pearl must be allowed to attend."

Mrs. Scrimshaw started to contradict, but clamped her lips tight.

CHAPTER 10

The evening arrived cold and clear. The schoolhouse overflowed with people. Children ran around getting in everyone's way, playing tag and laughing. Teams of horses huddled in the shelter of the woodshed. Each family brought a kerosene lantern to light the long, narrow schoolhouse making it as bright as day.

Pearl stopped to pat Old Daisy before stepping inside. The heavy scent of kerosene and the faint odor of cow manure filtered through the air along with body odor and woodsmoke. Myron Lofoton played his accordion as Billy and his brothers cranked ice cream in the corner farthest from the woodstove.

"More salt is needed to mix with the ice," Billy said, barely greeting Pearl. "It's not freezing as it should." His face flushed red, and sweat dripped down his cheeks. "Charlene did something wrong, I swear. It's not turning out." His brother added more salt into the ice surrounding the ice cream can.

"I'll crank a while," Johnny Dublin said.

Pearl dipped her finger into the crock and took a taste. "Oh no! Too salty," she said. "Charlene mixed up the sugar and salt."

Billy opened the freezer and stuck his

finger into the soupy mixture. "Yuck," he spat it aside. "That's exactly what she did. Spoilt."

Charlene wore her blue dress with matching hair ribbons.

"You ruined the ice cream, Charlene," Billy said. "Salt instead of sugar."

Dismay showed on Charlene's chubby face. She blushed red to the roots of her hair. "No, I did it right."

"No, you ruined the ice cream," Billy said. "Don't lie about it."

Mrs. Dahl examined the crock. "You weren't paying attention. I said the yellow crock is sugar and the blue tub is salt."

Charlene's shoulders heaved and fat tears sprouted from her eyes. Charlene let out a wail.

"We'll make some more," Mrs. Dahl said to Billy. "Folks will have to wait."

"I hope she records every bit of that fiasco in her notes for Mr. Carnegie," Billy said as the Dahls hurried out of the schoolhouse. "Charlene can't do anything right."

"Dear me," Mrs. Rorvig said when she found out about the ice cream. "You'd think Edna would have kept a closer eye on Charlene."

Miss Hatfield rapped on her desk with her pointer and called out the rules of the spelling bee. Everyone school age and older would line up against the outer walls. She would pronounce the word, use it in a sentence, and verify the spelling afterward. A misspelled word meant the person must take a seat. The misspelled word would go to the next speller. A correct spelling allowed another round. The last man standing would be crowned the winner.

"Or last woman standing," Doctor Gamla called out. Everyone laughed.

"What's the prize for winning?" Papa called out.

"The glory of it," Miss Hatfield said. She held up a blue strip of ribbon with *1st Place* embroidered on it. "And the first dish of ice cream."

More laughter and jabbing of elbows into the ribs of the person standing next to them.

"Line up," Miss Hatfield said. "Let the bee begin."

The outer walls crowded with men, women, and children. Miss Hatfield chose simpler words for the children. Jewel spelled *compress* and Clarice waded through *Mississippi.* Johnny Dublin went down on *produce,* putting an s in place of the c. Billy couldn't spell it either, but Old Man Larson got it right. Mr. Rorvig correctly spelled *commercial* but Mrs. Rorvig misspelled the word *gratuitous.* She laughed good-naturedly and took a bow. Papa breezed through *scientific* and Mama spelled *conquer.* Mr. Dahl misspelled *acrimonious* but Pearl got it right. Pearl went down on *sacrilegious* in the third round. By the fourth round only Papa, Mama, Mr. Rorvig, Old Man Larson, and Pastor Olson were left standing.

Pearl kept looking toward the door and worrying about the ice cream. The preacher misspelled *precipitousness* as Charlene and her mother came in the door. Billy peeled off his sweater and started turning the freezer crank. Charlene pouted in the corner, still claiming someone else had mixed the crocks.

Mr. Rorvig correctly spelled the preacher's missed word. Old Man Larson went down on *precariousness,* adding a *k* next to the *c.* Mama and Papa both spelled their words correctly but Mr. Rorvig went down on the word *changeable.* Mama looked at Papa askance but spelled the word correctly. Papa spelled *misogynistic* and Mama spelled *acquaintance.*

"We're going to be here all night," Mr. Dublin called out.

Papa grinned. Mama looked down, embarrassed at the attention.

Miss Hatfield called out the word *anachronistic*. Papa spelled it with ease. Mama hesitated on *buoyant* but got it right. Her flushed cheeks made her look pretty and young.

Then Papa stumbled on *colleague,* forgetting the u. Pearl groaned, knowing he had misspelled the word. Mama asked Miss Hatfield to repeat the word.

"Colleague. The man was his colleague," Miss Hatfield said.

Mama took a breath. The room went silent. If Mama missed the word, Papa would be given another. The first to miss would be eliminated.

"C-o-l-l-e-a-g-u-e, colleague," Mama said. She turned to Miss Hatfield.

"Correct," Miss Hatfield said. "Mrs. Selma Ellingson is our winner."

Mama had won. All those words she had thrown at Papa through the years had improved her spelling, too. Papa looked at Mama, first with surprise, and then with a big grin. He picked Mama up and twirled her around in front of everyone. Mama's skirt swirled, showing her long underwear and stockings. She blushed and insisted he put her down. The entire room broke out into applause. Pearl wished Mrs. Scrimshaw would have been there to see the ignorant country folk up against the more educated townspeople.

"No surprise to me," Doctor Gamla said. "It takes a woman to get things done."

Miss Hatfield fetched Mama's blue ribbon and directed her to the ice cream freezer. Folks pumped Mama's hand and congratulated her on her win.

"Delicious," Mama said after her first bite of ice cream. "Exactly the right amount of vanilla, Charlene."

"A huge success," Mrs. Rorvig said later. "In spite of Charlene's misstep."

Chapter 11

The Christmas bazaar was an even bigger event with almost twenty dollars garnered, thanks to Mrs. Dahl's hand-crocheted tablecloth that brought a whopping five dollars.

They discussed the fundraising progress at the next committee meeting in January. Mrs. Dahl looked heavenward with both eyes tightly shut and pronounced her plans for a Valentine's Day basket social.

"We must begin the actual grant writing," Miss Hatfield said.

Charlene looked up from writing the meeting notes, clearly puzzled. "What?"

"The grant," Miss Hatfield said. "The written request to Mr. Carnegie."

Billy kicked Pearl under the table and rolled his eyes.

In her schoolmarm tone, Miss Hatfield recited the Carnegie Formula, the requirements that must be met to apply for funds: demonstrate the need for a public library, provide the building site, pay staff and maintain the library, draw from public funds to run the library — not only private donations, annually provide ten percent of the cost of the library construction to support its operations, and provide free service to all. "The request must be sent to the Carnegie Foundation in writing once we have met the requirements."

"We have only to find a building site," Mr. Rorvig said. "The city can't decide between the empty lot next to the town dump or the piece of property south of the feed store."

A lively discussion followed. Mrs. Scrimshaw had strong opinions against building a library next to the dump. "Vermin, you know," she said with a shudder. "Disease and vermin go hand in glove."

Mrs. Dahl pointed out that the lot next to the feed store was needed to park the horses and wagons when the farmers came into town. "A library there might be deleterious to commerce."

Charlene took feverish notes.

The meeting came to an end, and the members bundled in their furs and shawls to brace the cold. Mama had been unable to attend due to the weather. Pearl mentioned her concerns about Charlene to Miss Hatfield at the door.

"No one expects Charlene to write the grant, but merely copy it in good penmanship," Miss Hatfield said with a laugh. "We'd hardly allow a fourteen-year-old child to shoulder such a responsibility."

Pearl let out a sigh of relief. Even so, an uneasy feeling lingered.

Chapter 12

In late January the weather warmed with an unexpected, and most welcome, chinook wind from the southwest. Mrs. Scrimshaw claimed the sudden melting caused a sinus headache and took to bed. Pearl prepared for the lending library. More people were coming every Sunday and with the warmer weather she suspected an even bigger crowd.

Billy trenched around the sidewalk to drain puddles away, but with little success. The skies darkened and a rumble of thunder predicted rain coming. Pearl laid more newspapers on the floor and found an old rag rug in the basement to place outside the kitchen door.

A new family with seven children knocked on the door and gathered around the table to look at the books available. Pearl was helping them find what they were interested in when she heard the water closet flush. She didn't pay much attention, thinking it was Mrs. Scrimshaw. Then she heard a shriek.

The children looked up with wide eyes. Their older brother pushed open the door of the back stairway and ran outside. He had slipped up the back stairs while Pearl was busy with the rest of his family.

"Pearl!" Mrs. Scrimshaw called. "Come at once."

Muddy footprints stretched down the staircase runner in the parlor and headed to the water closet. Mrs. Scrimshaw's face glowed red with rage.

"You are responsible," Mrs. Scrimshaw pointed her finger at Pearl, shaking with anger. "Look at this mess." Great tears dripped down her face and she wiped them with the back of her hand. "That's it. Tell everyone to leave. I'm done acting as lending library in this town."

Pearl turned and went into the kitchen.

Her knees weakened and her voice quavered. "I'm sorry but the library is closed for today." The kitchen emptied. Pearl swallowed hard to keep back the tears burning in her eyes.

"I'm sorry," Billy said. "It's my fault. I should have watched better."

"Please pack up the books and leave," Pearl said. The dream of a library had been too good to be true, after all. "She's furious."

She filled a bucket with water from the kettle and returned to clean the mess. The heavy gumbo left black streaks down the staircase runner. Pearl dabbed a wet rag across the spots, cleaning and scrubbing the best she could. It wasn't good enough. The muddy prints showed less on the floor.

"Ruined. My beautiful carpets ruined." Mrs. Scrimshaw shook with anger. "This is your fault. Believe me, young lady, you will pay for this out of your wages."

Pearl blotted again. It made the stains worse.

"Scrub the lavatory top to bottom with carbolic acid," Mrs. Scrimshaw said. "Who knows what diseases the boy carries." She went into her bedroom, slamming the door behind her.

Pearl scrubbed the bathroom. It was not

her fault. Everyone in town was curious about Mrs. Scrimshaw's back stairs and indoor water closet. Of course, the boy had been curious. Poor kid ran out of the house as if his life depended on it. Mrs. Scrimshaw had screeched like a wild Indian on the warpath.

Doctor Gamla yoo-hooed from the front door and entered without being invited in. "Oh my," she said. "What happened?"

"A boy used the water closet while I was busy helping others. He sneaked up the back stairway without being seen," Pearl said as she came out of the water closet. "Mrs. Scrimshaw is livid. She refuses to let the library meet in her kitchen anymore."

"A little boy had to piddle and so Nick-elbo can't have a library," Doctor Gamla said. She giggled. Then she chortled. Then the old doctor woman laughed and hooted with mirth. "Where is Brunhilde now?"

Pearl pointed to the bedroom. It wasn't funny. Pearl might lose her job. The library depended on the use of Mrs. Scrimshaw's kitchen. Pearl had no money to pay for replacement carpets. Her parents needed her wages to get through the winter. Everything was ruined. No doubt, Pearl would be sent packing and Charlene would take her place. No more books. No more library.

"I have a cure," Doctor Gamla said as she came out of the bedroom. The old woman dropped to her knees by Pearl, her joints popping and clicking. The old woman picked up the rag. "Fetch soda and vinegar."

Together Pearl and Doctor Gamla rubbed the soda and vinegar solution into the stains down the stairway. The mixture bubbled.

"Now we wait for it to dry," Doctor Gamla said. The old woman tried to get up but shook her head and reached out her hands. Pearl lifted the old woman back to her feet. How thin she was, like lifting a wounded bird.

The stains looked even worse.

"My cures always work," Doctor Gamla said. "Let it dry. Then remove the dirt with a wire brush. Next use the carpet sweeper." She sank into a chair, struggling for breath. "Don't worry. It will be all right."

Pearl gathered the supplies and headed back to the kitchen. Doctor Gamla made everything easier. People sometimes called Doctor Gamla a witch because of the way she knew how to fix things. Perhaps the old woman would change Mrs. Scrimshaw's mind. It would take all the witchery Doctor Gamla could muster to do that.

"Make a cup of tea," Doctor Gamla said. She held a shaky hand to her heart and spoke in a whisper. "Brunhilde needs a little time to cool down."

CHAPTER 13

The committee meeting was scheduled for Wednesday, and Pearl expected her employer to cancel after the disastrous water closet incident on Sunday. Mrs. Scrimshaw had been distant and as frosty as the sudden drop in outside temperatures. The frozen puddles and walks made Nickelbo an icy mess.

But, to Pearl's surprise, Mrs. Scrimshaw came out of her room on Wednesday morning fully dressed in her good clothes.

"Set the table for tea immediately after breakfast," Mrs. Scrimshaw said. "They will be here before we know it."

Billy removed his shoes by the door and placed them on a doormat. "Doctor Gamla stayed home," he said. "Afraid she'll take a fall. I offered to walk with her, but she said she was feeling tired and would stay home and take a nap."

Pearl's mood dropped. Without Doctor Gamla's tempering influence on Mrs. Scrimshaw, there was no telling what might happen.

"I don't suppose my mother will come,"

Pearl said. Outside the door sun glinted off frozen puddles on roads and boardwalks. It would be foolish to risk Old Daisy.

The other members arrived, all remarking on the treacherous streets. Mr. Rorvig had to stay with the store, but Mrs. Rorvig came.

Miss Hatfield called the meeting to order. Charlene read the minutes from the last meeting with such smugness that Billy poked Pearl's ribs.

"She's up to something," Billy whispered.

Miss Hatfield called for new business.

"As you know, I have been unwell," Mrs. Scrimshaw said. "I am no longer able to host the lending club on Sundays."

Pearl was not surprised. Doctor Gamla might have dissuaded her had she been able to attend. Everyone else stared stupefied at one another, no one saying a word.

"My mind is made up. The committee may continue to meet here as before, but other arrangements must be made for the lending club," Mrs. Scrimshaw said.

The clock ticked. Outside the scrape of Mr. Dublin's shovel sounded on his ice-covered walk.

"Let us make a formal statement of thanks in the minutes for Mrs. Scrimshaw's valiant leadership in spite of ill health and personal grief," Pastor Olson said. "You've done more than enough, Mrs. Scrimshaw."

"I second the motion," Mrs. Dahl said. "Charlene, make sure to get Pastor's quote in the minutes."

Charlene scribbled in her notepad.

"I make a motion to suspend the lending library until new accommodations be found," Mrs. Rorvig said.

"I second it," Pastor Olson said.

"I suggest we concentrate our efforts on writing the grant to the Carnegie Foundation," Miss Hatfield said. "Perhaps our efforts should be for the permanent solution rather than another stop-gap measure."

"It's done," Charlene said. "I sent the grant to Mr. Carnegie on Monday."

Billy groaned.

"But we don't have all the information needed," Miss Hatfield said. Again, the stern voice she used in her classroom.

"You gave me the requirements," Charlene said. "I answered the questions in my best penmanship and sent it off. There's nothing more to worry about."

"But how did you answer the requirement for a dedicated building spot?" Mrs. Rorvig said. "It's not been determined yet."

Charlene fidgeted and looked down at her notepad. She mumbled a reply. "I said it was undecided."

431

"That's all?" Mrs. Rorvig said. The tension in the room rose. The clock struck three. "No other explanation."

Charlene shook her head.

"Well that beats all," Mrs. Rorvig said. "All our work down the drain." She pushed away from the table and rose to her feet. "You've ruined the chance for a library to come to Nickelbo." She asked for her wrap. "Put that in your minutes." She stomped out of the house.

Charlene burst into tears. The others looked at each other, straggled to their feet, and slunk out the door. Everything ruined. There was nothing to say. Charlene had ruined everything.

Chapter 14

In March a letter arrived on a day as gray as goose down. Tears dripped from the sky as icy sleet and the prairie wind drove the pellets against the windowpanes of Rorvig's Store. Other Nickelbo citizens had the good sense to stay home in such weather, but Mrs. Scrimshaw had insisted that Pearl go for the mail. She wasn't about to let a little bad weather deprive her of the newspaper.

Mrs. Rorvig handed Pearl an envelope addressed to *Librarian Pearl Ellingson, Nick-*

elbo, North Dakota. The return address read
The Andrew Carnegie Foundation. Pearl's
heart beat in her throat and her mouth
turned dry as chalk.

"Hurry and open it," Mrs. Rorvig said. "It
came this morning and I was half-tempted
on running it over to you to find out what it
says."

Pearl's hands shook so that she had trouble opening the envelope.

"Let me," Mrs. Rorvig said. She pulled a
letter opener from beside the till and carefully slit the onion-skin envelope. She nodded encouragement and handed the pages
to Pearl.

"All our work," Mrs. Rorvig said. "Our
committee meetings, our fundraisers, and
work with the city. It comes down to this
moment."

"I'm scared," Pearl said. A library depended on the words written in this letter.

"Read it aloud," Mrs. Rorvig urged.

Pearl unfolded the letter. Outside the sleet
tinkled against the windowpanes. Mrs. Rorvig lit the lamp.

"Dear Miss Ellingson," Pearl read. "It is
with deep regret that we must decline Nickelbo's petition for funds. Your community
has not met the requirements for a dedicated building site, a written statement of

ongoing support by the city government, or a promise of providing free services." The letter thanked them for applying. "If you would meet the necessary requirements in the future, you are welcome to reapply in five years."

Pearl slumped into a chair by the checker table. They had raised more than two hundred dollars for books. The city government agreed verbally to meet the financial obligations for the next ten years. Charlene Dahl's insistence on doing things her own way had ruined it for everyone.

Sobs shook Pearl's body and the tears refused to stop.

Billy Hansen crashed into the store. His breath came in huge gulps from running.

"Hurry," he said. "It's Doctor Gamla. I think she's . . . dead."

Pearl swallowed her tears. Not Doctor Gamla. She had been unwell for so long that somehow Pearl thought the dear old woman would live forever.

"I brought milk and eggs as I always do on Wednesdays," Billy said. His face looked white as Doctor Gamla's. "She didn't answer my knock. I went in. You'd better come."

Pearl and Billy ran ahead to Doctor Gamla's house, trying to avoid the icy sleet that dripped down upon them. Mr. and Mrs. Rorvig locked the store and followed. Pearl and Billy hesitated on the porch, waiting for the Rorvigs before going in.

A white fence circled the gray house. A neat woodpile, Billy's fall efforts, stacked next to the house.

"Why were you crying?" Billy said.

"I'll tell you later," Pearl said. It felt like the world was ending. Doctor Gamla held everything together in Nickelbo. It was Doctor Gamla who found the cure for Papa's wheat. It was Doctor Gamla who cured the sick and helped people in need. It was Doctor Gamla who had convinced Mrs. Scrimshaw to build a library. What would they do without her?

Mrs. Rorvig opened the door and marched inside. How brave she was. Pearl's knees wobbled. Billy took her hand and pulled her inside.

The house smelled of boiled rutabagas. A table filled one corner of the kitchen with a kerosene lamp alongside a tidy stack of papers. The room was cold enough that Pearl saw her breath. No fire at all in the cookstove. A small bedroom adjoined the kitchen.

Together they walked into the bedroom where Doctor Gamla lay tucked in her bed.

She wore a flannel nightcap and her bed piled high with quilts. Even Pearl could tell that the woman was dead. Her face carried a strange sheen and her jaw hung open at an angle.

"Died in her sleep," Mr. Rorvig said. "A good way to go,"

"Yes," Mrs. Rorvig said. "She always said she wanted to drop in the traces."

"Such a good person," Pearl said. Tears ran down her cheeks. She fished in her pocket for a handkerchief. What would Mrs. Scrimshaw do without Doctor Gamla?

Mrs. Rorvig sent Billy to fetch the undertaker and the preacher. Mr. Rorvig fired the stove. Pearl sat at the kitchen table. What a terrible day. First the library letter. Then Doctor Gamla.

Mrs. Scrimshaw needed to know about her friend. Pearl stood to leave, but noticed the stack of papers on the table. On the top was Doctor Gamla's handwritten recipe for her famous salve. Pearl noticed lanolin in the recipe but didn't take time to read the rest of the ingredients because her attention was drawn to an envelope addressed to *Pearl* that was propped against the oil lamp.

"What's this?" Pearl said.

"You're the only Pearl in Nickelbo," Mrs. Rorvig said.

"Why would she write a letter to me?" Pearl said. "It must be for someone else."

"We'll find out," Mrs. Rorvig ripped open the letter. "Dear Pearl and the library committee." Mrs. Rorvig lifted the letter to the window to catch the light. "I've never put stock in money from strangers. My time is short and I have no desire to go to God dragging worldly possessions behind me." Mrs. Rorvig paused for breath. "I'm leaving my house to Pearl Ellingson to use for a library. It's not worth much and Lord knows, my kin would never want it. Pearl can both live in the house and act as librarian."

Pearl felt her jaw drop. She was as surprised as the day when Doctor Gamla suggested she might work for Mrs. Scrimshaw.

"If the Carnegie money comes through, let Pearl decide what is to be done with the house. I hope she keeps living here and working as the librarian. The town needs her common sense and enthusiasm."

She went on to list her "cure" for the Walter Scrimshaw Memorial Library. Pearl as librarian would be paid enough to make a living. Mrs. Scrimshaw must donate all her books to the library in memory of her son. Fundraisers must continue on a regular basis to provide new books and magazines.

The people of Nickelbo must work together to keep the library going. The city government must provide operating funds and the men of the community must build shelves and donate firewood or coal to warm the building every winter. Above all, library cards must be free so that all might benefit.

"She's thought it through," Pearl said. "Even before she knew about the Carnegie refusal, Doctor Gamla had the cure."

"We will read this letter at her funeral," Mrs. Rorvig said. "Everyone needs to hear what Olava has to say."

Pearl imagined the future as she hurried to tell Mrs. Scrimshaw the news. Books would line the walls of the kitchen. Patrons, like Mama, could rest in Doctor Gamla's rocking chair kept by the window. Pearl would ask Old Man Larson to build a stand for a dictionary. Schoolchildren would study at the kitchen table using a complete set of encyclopedias. Pearl imagined the children's faces as they chose books. They and the citizens of Nickelbo would be exposed to new ideas, new stories, and new opportunities. The library, like the church and school, would become the hub of the city.

She must convince Mrs. Scrimshaw to continue as library patron and champion. They would need her strength more than ever. Clarence's reputation and Walter's legacy depended on her behavior.

Perhaps Charlene hadn't ruined everything after all. Terrible for Charlene to lose the Carnegie money, of course, and terrible to lose dear old Doctor Gamla. Yet, at the same time, the Walter Scrimshaw Memorial Library was born. Truly wonderful.

Pearl snugged her shawl around her. She had a lot of work ahead of her. She could do it. Doctor Gamla had faith in her. And Doctor Gamla's cures always worked.

ABOUT THE AUTHOR

Candace Simar likes to imagine how things might have been. Her historical novels have received awards from the Western Writers of America, Women Writing the West, the Will Rogers Medallion Awards, the Midwest Book Awards, and the Writer's Digest. For more information see www.candacesimar.com

ABOUT THE EDITOR

Hazel Rumney has lived most of her life in Maine, although she also spent a number of years in Spain and California while her husband was in the military. She has worked in the publishing business for almost thirty years. Retiring in 2011, she and her husband traveled throughout the United States visiting many famous and not-so-famous western sites before returning to Thorndike, Maine, where they now live. In 2012, Hazel reentered the publishing world as an editor for Five Star Publishing, a part of Cengage Learning. During her tenure with Five Star, she has developed and delivered titles that have won Western Fictioneers Peacemaker Awards, Will Rogers Medallion Awards, and Western Writers of America Spur Awards, including the double Spur Award–winning novel *Wild Ran the Rivers* by James D. Crownover. Western fiction is Hazel's favorite genre to enjoy. She has been reading the genre for more than five decades.